MEXICO BAY

MEXICO BAY

by Paul Horgan

NEW YORK ❧ FARRAR, STRAUS AND GIROUX

Copyright © 1982 by Paul Horgan
All rights reserved
First printing, 1982
Printed in the United States of America
Published simultaneously in Canada by McGraw-Hill Ryerson Ltd.,
Toronto
Designed by Jack Harrison

Library of Congress Cataloging in Publication Data
Horgan, Paul.   Mexico Bay.
I. Title.
PS3515.O6583M4   1982   813'.52   81-15133
AACR2

to
D. B.

The names of the characters in this story, all of whom are imaginary, are not to be taken to apply to any persons who by coincidence might bear the same names.

I am indebted to Henriette Wyeth for permission to use an eloquent phrase which she spoke in an interview.

P.H.

Contents

It is not a Baye in the guise of a shelter all compact from storme or pursuit, rather for its extent beyond the sight of manie days sayling it is a greate sea the whiche voyagers from farre landes observe onlie in its diverse parts. Thus there are given to it as manie characters as there be chroniclers, for one saith that it is peacefull as a lake and another that it hath as manie changes in temper as a woman and still another that with hardly a warnygne it bloweth into tempests so vanquyshyng that any few who survive declare how never did they see deathe so close or are so humblie gratefull to see safetie returne in such sweete suddain calme as in a morning after feaver.

PART ONE

※

IN HIS LONG SEARCH, HE ALREADY had most of his facts. What he
quested after now, he told himself, in the wilderness of sea and
shore where he hoped to be alone in that early spring, was the sense
of men in a particular place, soldiers, who had struggled and died
there a century ago. He was searching for final images of the war—
after God knew how many pages of notes and text—which had
possessed his thoughts for years.

※

Port Isabel, on the coast of the Gulf of Mexico, brought Howard
Debler to his war again. He put his car in a lot by a tourist camp
and set out to walk the edges of the Port Isabel harbor. There was
no way for him to ascend the abandoned lighthouse for an overview
of how affairs may have looked in 1846 when Zachary Taylor's
steamboats had put in with troops and supplies for his campaign
against Mexico across the Rio Grande.

Leading from the harbor to the Gulf was the channel bounded
by the narrow pass of the Brazos de Santiago—the Arms of St
James—through which General Taylor's old side-paddle or stern-
wheel ships threaded their way to anchorage or dock a hundred
years ago or more. Debler wondered how the approach looked from

[3]

the sea. In order to describe it in his pages, he rented a fishing boat whose pilot took him miles out into the Gulf, and then headed about to make a long, slow approach to land. Half closing his eyes now and then, Debler imagined the landfall of long ago. As they came at last to the watery pass, the pilot, an old South Texan, declared, "Plinny of wrecks through the years in this here little slot."

Debler nodded. He remembered what his notes said about Taylor's transport and supply steamers. In tide or gale, the slot could be dangerous. Pressing with too much steam, the *Neva* blew a hole in her boiler in 1846, and the *Monmouth* went aground. He drew a sketchy map to put among the other diagrams of place and movement in his pages which were as precious to him as master drawings.

He was exhilarated to be free on leave of absence from his classes at the university, and out in the open pursuing his vision. Tomorrow he would take to the route inland tracing the march of the army as it moved southwest to make camp and build a fort facing the Mexicans across the Rio Grande, in this same time of year, one hundred and four years ago, spring in South Texas.

※

Gulf-wide skies, the drifting air, were sweet with light and the scent of whole counties carpeted with wild flowers. By a circuitous route that forced him inland to skirt impassable inlets, he walked first westward, then to the south, amid thickets of mesquite in their brilliant fresh green, all alive with singing birds. At his footsteps, quail started up from the knife-edged sea grass along the dunes. Now and then a flight of great white birds—avocets—seemed to join the sea clouds to the earth; and again, a few heavy clambering brown pelicans took the sand color to the sky. He wished he could draw or paint to make a record of what he saw. The wish only made him look more keenly.

At last he turned his way again to find the sea, and came to the Gulf at the Laguna Madre, and saw empty beach reaching in both directions. The black of driftwood and the hardness of wet beach and the glistening softness of dry governed his pace. Nobody was in sight. Far out to sea, beyond the long sand barrier of Padre Island, a gesture of faint ship smoke was caught in the air. Howard felt that some new degree of human peace might be found and cherished here. Its elements were aged, and had proved themselves unchanging in the scale of human measurement—sea, sky, dunes, the sound of waves on the chordic wind saying *peace* and *forever*. For long moments the salt air turned dense and closed down the distance, and then slowly cleared again.

In his day-long walk he passed a few rickety piers built out over the surf for fishermen; and here and there he saw a weathered bait shack, still abandoned before the approaching season for fishermen and other beach people. The Gulf was a brilliant blue, set off by a close scheme of all the other colors of dune and grass and sandy surf. The soldiers of a century ago marched in his thoughts. He felt the joy of possessing and being possessed.

In late afternoon, he wondered why he had not seen much sooner what suddenly took form. It looked like a man, huddled before a shape hard to identify from a distance. Just beyond the man was the more clearly visible form of a small black automobile—a truck.

"There it goes!" Howard exclaimed at the loss of the free, shapeless concentration in which he had been living all day in his solitude.

Perhaps he should climb beyond the dunes and pass by the stranger unseen; but the distance was distortive. He was closer than he thought; and at a moment the man seemed to feel a presence nearby, turned, saw him, and shook both arms in the air in a gesture of resignation at any intrusion.

[5]

"Just for that," said Howard half-aloud, "I'll keep going. I have as much right."

He came steadily along until he made out every detail of a man— a young man—seated on an upturned bucket, facing a low easel and painting a picture. Bits of his kit were scattered about him on the sand.

Howard now felt he should avoid disturbing the artist. Keeping a distance as if to walk right by, he headed up toward the dunes out of the prospect which the man might be painting. He hadn't gone more than a few paces when the young man hailed him. Howard turned around in a feint at looking startled.

"Hey, there, you, have you any matches?" called the artist.

"No. I don't smoke."

"So be it. I've run out." He looked at his cold pipe and then tossed it into a large green tin tackle box where he kept his paints. "It's all right," he added with affable arrogance. "I'd just about finished for the day. You don't interrupt me."

"Thanks, pal," said Howard with sarcasm which went unnoticed.

"*De nada,*" replied the young man, and stood up to stretch like an athlete. He exhaled noisily. "By God, this air, this beach, make you feel wonderful. Are you out training for something?"

"No, just observing, making notes."

"The best thing to do here. That's really all I'm doing, too." He gestured toward his picture. "For example."

It was an invitation to look. Howard came closer. On the sixteen-by-twenty-inch panel he saw the offshore water flowing into paler combers topped with white, against the startling blue of the Gulf, all in the brilliance of tempera. Long clouds of drifting sea vapors like spun glass both contained and gave off light that made unearthly the simple facts of nature in that place. From the sandy beach in the painted foreground protruded a hand, blackened by rot, reaching with supplicating fingers into the air—into life. Howard could tell what everything was in the painting, and

[6]

thought that in some ways this was a pity. He looked up to find the artist regarding him with an amused expression and asking, "Do you think I've caught it?"—with abounding confidence.

"I suppose you want to indicate both how it looks and what it means to you."

"Sure, sure?"

"I like the color."

"An easy way out. Of course, it takes time and it takes connotations yet unframed for such a personal work to gather general meaning. You agree?"

He quizzed Howard with an intent look. He seemed to be reading Howard, who stared back. The stranger was about as tall as Howard, but more solidly fleshed and supply sprung. With every movement he seemed almost to burst out of his clothes—a tight sweat shirt and even tighter, faded blue jeans which struck Howard as vain in their definition of the man's shapely body and groin. On his feet he wore dirty tennis shoes. The front of his shirt was like an abstraction painted in pointillist technique, the result of rapid brush wipings. Howard's whole impression of him was of physical excellence and capacity, supported by a plain egotism revealed in the energy of his talk. In his blunt, weathered face, a pale scar ran on to his forehead from under his tangled cap of hair.

"At least," said the artist, letting himself down on his rump and waving Howard to a seat on the sand, "that is always the history of new prophecies in art and writing. Are you a writer?"

Howard admitted to writing works in history.

"Ah-ha. And now you're working on another, and I am planted right in the middle of your next chapter. You can give me a footnote, anyhow. All you gents are in love with footnotes."

Howard tried to find all this offensive, but in the end he could not, for it was all friendly, confident of a welcome in anybody's terms. The young man conducted himself like an established personage.

"I am looking along here for the sake of some work I'm doing about the Mexican War," said Howard. "The campaign ran all over the place around here to begin with."

"You'd never know it now. The pathos of all battlefields, in the end. I was overseas in the last one. Army. France. And you?"

"Yes—the Pacific. Navy. —Yes, that's part of my problem—a very interesting problem for my job. I want to revive the life of the soldiers here, as well as tell what they did."

They both looked at the painting on the easel, and the dead hand reaching through to the living air. Howard said, "Hundreds of soldiers were buried not far from here, across those dunes, along by the mouth of the Rio Grande."

"I can't claim to have felt that, but something made me think of brief human life and the eternal meeting of land and sea."

This was too close to Howard's own musings about the cosmic effects of the great Gulf, and he wanted no one else's philosophy.

"Goodbye," he said and abruptly walked away to the west, along the edge where the surf reached and died back. Soon he heard the old black Ford truck behind him start up and drive off in the opposite direction.

✺

It was not long until the land again claimed him in solitude. Late afternoon light was beginning to gild the edges of things. The horizon was turning gray and violet. He began to see a straggle of green growth reaching from inland toward the surf. The beach became irregular, sloping to a tufted rise. A stirring premonition made Howard climb the rise as fast as he could go through sliding sand. He topped the rise, and through the glisten of early evening mist, he saw the surf of the Gulf of Mexico coming forever inward to arch, sigh, and break away into nothingness before the opposing flow of another energy—the flow of slowly moving but prevailing brown water of the Rio Grande heavy with silt, spending the last force of its continental fall from mountains two thousand miles away and three miles high. Where the two waters met, the place was called Boca Chica, and Howard knew how a century earlier Taylor's shallow-draft steamboats would arrive there from Port Isabel and start their laborious way upstream carrying soldiers and supplies to the campaign inland.

He threw down his backpack and made ready to camp for the night on a dune overlooking the wide brown river flow and, on the opposite shore, the last sand spit of Mexico reaching into the Gulf. When night fell, and the moon rose, the tide changed and came in. Howard stayed awake as long as he could to watch the waters—the river's unceasing entry and the tide's slow spread driving against it. In the moonlight, the contending powers seem to pass, one against the other, giving and receiving, in the most ancient of earthly, and, he thought, in a rare nod to metaphor, human, exchanges. He closed his eyes at last on an image of molten silver in motion as constant as unhurried time and as cosmic as infinity. His last thought before he slept was of the marvel that as often as he had come to that scene— he had been there during earlier days of his study—his excitement was never diminished at seeing again the empty place which he peopled with teeming armies.

At daybreak, he walked where sucking sand led to the heavy brown river. He cupped up enough water to wet his face—not that it would do much as a wash, he said, but as an awakener it was a sort of baptism. He returned to his pack, where he had his thermos of coffee and his box of zwieback.

Later, sitting at the old bankside which had been overrun so many times by the river, he wrote down what he saw and felt. Where he lingered had once been an American army station which the soldiers called Sodom. It was a station where troops were sent to await shipment upriver or transport home to the States, or, on the very site, death from cholerina. Hundreds had died there, so he had read in the memoirs of a young officer who later became a Civil War general, a governor, and a novelist. The Gulf winds had time and again blown the earth off the shallow graves, exposing forlorn bones. The lieutenant had been detailed to rebury those homeless remains. The living found their pastimes as they could—drinking, gambling, whoring in their local Sodom, until the war was over, and the strand became as barren as Howard's today.

He walked along a little rise thrown up by the offshore wind. His foot slipped, dislodging a miniature avalanche of packed sand. Something glittered dimly. He bent to take it up, displacing more grainy earth, and another object rolled free to join the first. They were two brass buttons off a uniform, emblemmed in relief with the crossed sabers of the United States Cavalry. He blew on the buttons and rubbed them on his sleeve. Here was a soldier who had lain in the old sea bed for a century. A vision of a daguerreotype which changed according to the way you held it to the light came and went before his thought—a tousle-haired youth with pale, prominent eyes, a blunt nose, a mouth pressed forward by protruding teeth, a faint blur of unfinished mustache; sloping shoulders, sleeves down to his fingers; his army tunic half-buttoned with circles of brass like those in Howard's hand; the whole edged in stamped red velvet, surrounded by lacy gold tin, and snapped shut by an embossed leather case: it had stood throughout Howard's childhood in his family's parlor in Grand Plains, Texas, and then had disappeared, without much consequence, as household trifles—and many a life—disappeared. Reality was capricious, but now he remembered how, in general, men had looked where they had once fought, and he believed he had a sense of their individual lives as evidence for his book. He put the cavalry buttons in an inside pocket for special safety. He had the elation that followed worthwhile labor.

In early afternoon he began his long walk back to Port Isabel. He told himself that he should have started earlier, and brisked his pace at what he saw out to sea—a long brown roll of cloud on the horizon. It looked like incoming fog. That would mean slow going if evening came before he found a likely place to camp for the night.

He kept to the moist sand which the outgoing tide had left. The packed beach dragged at his steps. He felt a flicker of anxiety, a sudden turn of alienation from the lifting rediscovery of his subject. The in-rolling dampness, now visible all about, made his breath constrict. How fragile were certainties, he reflected, moving faster than was comfortable. If darkness fell before he got any-where—where?—he had a flashlight to show him where to put each footstep. To be enveloped alone in fog was like a definition of a mental state. He laughed loudly and alone at his notion.

There was a rolling rift in the mist ahead of him and he saw the black Ford of yesterday, and then, in another second, he saw that it stood beside one of the bait shacks he had passed yesterday with indifference. Perhaps he would be wise to halt and catch his breath for a few minutes, to talk with the affable owner of the car, and perhaps have a cup of coffee with him before starting out again.

Nearing, he could make out further aspects of the shack. It had a shallow porch fronted by an oilcloth counter, above which weathered signs proclaimed *Coca-Cola* at one end, and at the other, *Bait*. The shack, built of unpainted boards, reached narrowly back into the dunes. At its rear was a low lean-to. The roof was made of beaten gasoline cans. A few of them curled upward and probably sang when the wind blew. The floor was held up by heavy wooden piles on which storm water had left marks. Beside the shack two dory-like rowboats were pulled well away from the waterline.

Rough enough, thought Howard, but the occupant probably did not care where he lived, so long as he could have freedom to paint and enough to eat out of cans.

Howard went to the warped steps leading to the narrow stoop, edged around the end of the sales counter, and rapped on the door, which showed etched glass panes set into wood painted dark green blasted by blowing sand—clearly a door hauled from some demolition elsewhere. It showed cracks of yellow light like that cast by a Coleman lantern.

A voice answered, "Just a minute, please."

It was the voice of a woman. The door opened and Howard stepped back and snatched off his stained old felt hat.

"Diana!" he exclaimed, using her given name for the first time, and then recovering himself to say, "Mrs Wentworth!"

In her turn, "But Howard Debler," she said, "how astonishing, it is you, isn't it?—this fog. But how nice! Do come in." Her eyes lighted with good feeling.

She was so like his persistent memory of her, now that he saw her again, that it made his spirits sink a little, as in the presence of treasures that lay beyond reach. Her hair was pale brown, just as he remembered it, but was now bleached on top by the sun to a silky pale gold. She wore it tied back on her nape with a piece of magenta yarn. Her skin was a coppery Indian gold from sunlight and sea, but so smoothly even and glowing that it might have been treated with a brush. Amidst all those tones of gold and burn, her eyes were startling, their turquoise blue set off by dark lashes. The sun, the ocean, the wild beach, were all implied in her appearance. She wore a striped cotton jersey and a full Mexican skirt embroidered in bright yarns. On her feet were rawhide *guaraches*.

If hardship was indicated in her surroundings, her effect was the greater because she seemed still to be everything that was conventional and wholesome, raised to a striking degree of freshness. She wore no wedding ring. She held a lighted cigarette. Its smoke trembled ever so slightly. He looked at her face. Just then she did not look at him. He felt sure that seeing him, and, through him, reminders of when and in what estate they had last seen each other, to the extreme contrast of this moment, made her tremble. Then,

"But I'm letting you stand there," she said. "I am so glad to see you, please do come in. —I wondered when and how I'd meet someone who knew me before . . . You must tell me all about yourself," she added, as though accountings must rest only with him.

She led him into the narrow room of the shack, where the lantern hung from old two-by-four rafters. Nothing could make the place more than adequate as shelter, but she had done things to make it personal. Colored Mexican printed cloths hung at the two small-paned windows. A number of public-library books were piled on empty crates serving as tables by the one easy chair and the large bed. On top of the cold iron stove, wild flowers gathered back of the dunes stood in a blue glass Mexican vase. On the wall hung a photograph of a late-middle-aged man in his uniform as lieutenant colonel. His expression was severe except for a deep searching light caught in his eyes. He was a handsome man whose ruddy strength was emphasized by the photographer's lighting. In a corner of the room, oddly suggesting, if not a better, a more luxurious world, were a few pieces of luggage of the most expensive kind. Everything was in order, clean and arranged. If Howard disregarded the ingredients, which for the most part were cheap and ill-made, and saw only the colors and the disposals of simple comfort, he admitted that the little room had a crazy charm. When Diana sat down on the edge of the bed and waved him to the chair, offering him a cigarette, which he declined, the illusion of her having made an attractive world was complete. She saw him looking at her skirt.

"Not to be vivid," she said, "but to be thrifty. We go shopping in Matamoros, across the Rio Grande from Brownsville. Not far."

"I know. It is very becoming."

She smiled at what must be lingering in his mind.

"I'd better explain," she said. "I am here with Benjamin Ives, the painter. I think you saw him yesterday."

"That fellow. Yes. We talked briefly."

"He liked you. He says he believes you must be a genius."

[13]

"Why on earth."

"He said it was the way you suddenly walked off in the middle of a conversation. It appears that only geniuses do things without explaining them."

Howard felt it more polite to ignore than comment upon this comic view of himself. He said, "How long ago it seems."

"Since we saw each other during the war? Not really so long, but much has happened. —As you see, I am removed from my old life in Washington."

"For good?"—meaning permanently.

"For good"—meaning for better.

"But when we do meet," he said, "I feel we take up where we left off."

"That's nice to hear. I feel so, too."

"Where is Mr Ives?"

"Ben. Somewhere at work. He often gets in after dark. He didn't take the car today, so he isn't awfully far. He may have taken a nap after painting, he so often does, no matter where. He says he learned how to from a cat when he was a boy."

"But it's dark, and getting wetter by the minute. I stopped here just to say hello to him, and perhaps"—he paused out of manners. With a smile she made him continue "—perhaps to ask for a cup of coffee before going on to Port Isabel."

"You must go all that way before night?"

"Yes. There is nowhere else. My car is there. I am doing some last surveys for my Mexican War book. —You remember about my book?"

"You know?" she said with animation that made his spirits leap with pleasure, and something more which had been there unavowed for so long. "I've thought of it so many times since we came here months ago. You gave me such a strong idea of it when you talked about the book in Washington, so I've done some reading about where we are, here, and I gather that the war began really quite close by."

"Just over there"—and he waved toward the inland sites of General Taylor's first two battles. "I've scraped the places fairly well by now, but the search never ends until you say to yourself, *It's time to get on with finishing the book.*"

"And is it?"

"It is time. I'm going home from here to do just that if nothing else intervenes."

"I am sure it will work out. —Oh: the coffee. In a minute or two."

She brewed coffee in an open pan over an alcohol flame. In painted pottery cups from Tamaulipas the brew tasted bitter and good to Howard. She had lost none of her old ease in talking, and she could see that Howard was crowded with wonderings about her new life, and what had happened to the old.

"I am separated from my husband," she said. "In fact, divorced. Ben Ives was an acquaintance of ours in Washington, after the war, no, really, a close intimate. In fact, I heard that Washington was having a delicious time about it. Well, this and that took place, it's a longish story, and not always a pleasant one, but the flat fact is that matters came to such a pass that I had to leave Jack. Ben was a great part of it. I left with him. It had to be on his terms, then, and now, which I simply accepted. Look around you," she added, with a little laugh, not apologetic, but ruefully humorous. "In due course, my husband divorced me for desertion, quite accurately. By that time, Ben and I were rattling around the nation in that remarkable vehicle of his outside."

"I wrote you a letter almost a year ago. It was returned from Georgetown, *Addressee Unknown*."

She laughed. "That sounds like Jack's touch. But I do believe he was dreadfully hurt. I've been sorry for that."

"But not—"

[15]

"Not for anything else."

Howard had no experience of grand passions, and he supposed he was in the presence of one. What else would induce anyone to abandon so much: great position, grace, wealth, style: for—*for this?*

"You've no idea," she said, reading him, "how little it matters what you give up if it never rested on anything real. Oh yes. I thought it did, but how young I was. And now I'm an old lady—"

"God no!" he exclaimed.

"—an old lady in the way I can look back and smile over what I used to think important. What did your letter to me say?"

"It said I hoped to see you again when I got to Washington to do some final research on documents there. I also said I was sorry to hear of your father's death. They told me in Dorchester."

They both looked at the wall and George Macdonald's photograph.

"Yes," she said. "Thank you. I miss him dearly." She straightened up. "In any case, I'm Diana Macdonald again."

"So I won't be saying Mrs Wentworth."

"Nor Mrs Ives. We have no plans about that. If you ever know Ben, you'll simply accept that."

Howard let go a full breath. He was bemused by too many astonishments and discoveries to know what he thought or how to make light chatter. He took a sort of disconsolate joy in simply looking at her again. Something in his strong, bony face, and his puzzled brow, gave her a turn of feeling. She laughed with fondness, as a woman would laugh at and at the same time love a troubled revelation in a child, or a man, who felt a claim on her, however unanswerable.

"But what do you *do* here?" he finally asked.

"There you have it," she replied. "Even with Ben, it is lonely at times. I make up things to do. Oh, we drive into Brownsville for errands, and the mail—we use General Delivery, and when Ben's dealer sends a check it is a great holiday and we go to Matamoros for supper. He loves the Mexicans, and their music, which I applaud vigorously to be polite, though it rather deafens me. They're often quite beautiful people to look at, especially the very young women. But I always feel something just under the lovely coffee-colored skin that is purely animal: sleeping violence. Ben says I'm mad; he's probably right. But he's an elemental creature, and I am always more comfortable when we come back across the river. I get my books at the Brownsville Public Library. They have a divine parrot who hangs upside down by one claw and looks at me and says, *Hello, Pancho,* in the voice of an old female alcoholic. And I'm sometimes alone here, when Ben goes off for a few days by himself, to paint. Of course, I don't like that."

"I'm not sure that's wise, to be alone in a place so isolated."

"I have a pistol he gave me and taught me to use, not that I ever would. I put it away somewhere. But he gave me a plausible lecture about how he had to be absolutely alone and free to think about nothing but his painting from time to time, and it had nothing to do with his feeling for me, and I'm sure he is right. Anyhow, soon, the holiday people will be coming, and we'll be thronged, and I'll be starting up with my business. Did I tell you about my business?"

She had arranged for regular deliveries of Coca-Cola, cigarettes, candy, with a distributor in Brownsville. In a few weeks the beach would be full of fishermen and other seaside vacationers, who would want refreshments.

"Ben says we will be rich—also I am given something to do. Everybody is delighted. But sometimes when the seagulls seem to be laughing hysterically, I say to them, *Yes, I know.*"

Was it possible?—this is what his silence and his set face confessed to her.

She did not dwell on other times when occasionally she longed for the comforts of her birthright and the graces of her married position. Yet she did not regret them enough to wish herself back in the closed life she had left. Ben was no saint. When he would disappear for a few days, he would bring back new paintings, and also evidence in his state that he had been ugly and drunk somewhere. He was frankly purged, and never ashamed, though he knew he'd been a fool to drink anything at all. Yet in some obscure fashion such irregularities had something to do with his nature as a man of gifts who could live happily quite outside society. He must see differently and more wholly than his fellow men. Diana sometimes thought that his adventures were attempts to find community with others—anyone at all—in commoner ways than those of the alien conventions of her earlier world. She now felt obliged to justify to Howard, at least partially, the life he found her in.

"Ben loathes the kind of artist and life that try to resemble the way the others, all the others, the doctor, and the lawyer, and the *binness* man (as he says)—the way they live. He says only a hack can play at all that, and if anyone tries, it proves he is a hack, without any originality or courage of his vision, or even talent. I suppose there's nothing new in all this. But now from inside it, I understand more than I did before."

She lifted the blue vase with flowers off the cook stove and made a little fire with some driftwood taken from a stack in a corner. It was getting late and dark. The coming night was pressing inward, bringing a damp chill. Diana took from a shelf a bottle of tequila and glasses.

"We should drink to our reunion. Then I'd better make some supper."

She gave Howard a frank and charming look, a womanly look which could astonish a man with realism and capacity for seeing every worldly aspect of a problem. Howard said to himself that she must be in love with Ben Ives to be in this place, in such sweet good spirits, enduring terms of life so foreign to her past. He felt gloomy. She began to improvise a simple supper, talking lightly, about how she and Ben had wandered for months, as far as California and back, in their old black Ford, stopping where he wanted to draw or paint; ignoring the calendar; sometimes in funds, others not, until at last, as he had often promised to do in memory of his youth, they had come to the Gulf of Mexico, whose very name held his imagination.

There was a sound out front, footsteps on the rickety steps and porch, and then Ben Ives came in, carrying his metal box, his easel, and a panel which he had wrapped in his yellow oilskins to protect the tempera paint on the gesso surface. He was wet through. His hair was glistening with beads of salt moisture. He stopped stock-still when he saw Howard.

"This is Howard Debler," said Diana. "We are old friends. Isn't it amazing? I've told him all about you—and us."

"Well," said Ben, putting out his hand, "welcome. I didn't expect to be seeing you again. But welcome."

He smiled at Diana with energy, an open secret of his gladness to be home with her again, and with a piece of nonsense to tell her.

"You're soaked," she said.

"Yes. Here. Take these." He handed her some of his gear. "I worked in and out of fog. The light was mysterious. Then I wanted to watch it turn absolutely dark. I lay down on a big timber I like to visit, right by the surf. I fell asleep and the fog really came in. It is absolute zero visibility out. When I woke up I was wet with it. Then you know? Wonderful and idiotic. I was completely disoriented when I woke up. There was not only no vision, but sound itself was distorted. I don't think I was at any time more than a few hundred yards from here, but I kept going in circles, thinking I could guide myself by the sound of the breakers. But the direction was never where I thought it was. I walked like the blind, with my ear turned here, there, my face up as if I could feel objects by their projected shapes. Amazing feeling." He turned to Howard. "An extraordinary feeling. I had all sorts of visual experiences in that heavy cloud on the earth. Everything seemed to move toward me minutes before I actually reached anything—driftwood, a hillock, a clump of grass. Good God, how little our habits of observation do for us ordinarily. It was superb. Entirely by accident, I bumped my shin against the bow of one of those boats outside, and I knew I was home. —Diny, I'm cold. Have I any dry clothes?"

He moved over to the stove and pulled off his shirt and all his clothes as though he were alone. He warmed himself at the stove.

Howard felt a rise of irritation at this indifferent display of nakedness before Diana in the presence of a stranger. Alone with her, it would no doubt be Ben's right and habit; but to Howard's way of thinking, it insulted her to proclaim such intimacy before anyone else as though she were merely a chattel. Diana threw Ben a large towel and he energetically rubbed himself dry, making little noises of physical content. He was darkly suntanned all over his hard body. He dropped the towel, turned to the stove, put on the dry clothes Diana hauled out of a wooden packing case at the foot of the bed, and then feeling splendid sat down on an upended box and rocked it to its back edge.

"You'll never get out of here tonight," he said to Howard.

"Oh yes, I have to," replied Howard. His anger had cooled but he still wanted to make his way up the beach.

"No. You can never find the road inland in this fog. First thing you know, you'd be in the surf. I've known this coast for years— ever since I was a youngster when I drifted down here looking for jobs. You'd better spend the night with us."

Howard looked at Diana. What a preposterous imposition Ben put lightly upon her. But she was smiling.

Happy for company, she said, "No, you must stay. Supper is almost ready. We can make you a warm though hard bed on the floor."

"I won't mind that," said Howard. "I'm a veteran of sleeping bags. But:"

"Then that's settled," declared Ben. His gusty good will was disarming. "It's a wonderful place, isn't it," Ben continued. He meant the natural sea and landscape, but his glance took in also the primitive shack, and Howard could see that his satisfaction extended itself even to this place where he lived.

"Yes, wonderful," said Howard mildly. "How did you ever get here and find—this?"

Ben shrugged. "I wanted to be at the sea. I told her about it, and what I remembered. Substance always the same, yet always moving and restating itself in form."

Diana looked at Ben and said, "He calls it the mother of the world."

"She says the sea is my pagan god. Maybe it's true. As a boy I longed for the sea in landlocked Iowa. Sometimes I feel I retain a stage of evolution within me that was choking until it could breathe through gills, with a body that wanted to rise and fall with waves."

"Cosmic indolence," said Diana. "It may be more voluptuous than worshipful."

They talked till late.

They felt snug within the shack, by the light of the hissing lantern. Diana worked with yarns. Ben led the talk by his dominant energy. Diana would smile and nod at what he said. If she was in a sort of bondage, it was evidently a willing one. Thinking of the nature of Ben's appeal for her, Howard felt an ache in his chest. He envied what was not or ever could be his—the life of a shack, content on an empty shore, yes, and with someone like her . . .

Ben always had a block of drawing paper, an India-ink fountain pen, and a small box of watercolors. He made little drawings as he talked or listened, glancing at Diana, or at Howard, or the wild flowers in their Mexican glass. He licked his fingers and smeared the ink to make a wash effect. Often he crumpled a page and threw it under the stove. He was full of dogmatic theories, some of which sounded like rubbish to Howard, who, reflecting that artists should never think, chose not to argue, and received a gleam of complicity from Diana. Now and then Ben made quiet little demands upon her. Her compliance was prompt and graceful, at which Howard lumped his jaws. With a contented grin Ben recognized Howard's envy, and under a guise of friendly interest, decided to require that Howard give an account of himself.

"Where do you live, Debler?" asked Ben.

"Over in West Texas—the Panhandle."

"What's a writer doing there?"

"A writer can do anywhere."

"But he has to have something to write about, and he's not likely to find it there. I could paint there, a matter of the light. But there's nothing else."

"I have my subject. It travels with me."

"Oh yes. Your border war. Like a dry-land sailor writing about an adventure at sea."

"Ben:" said Diana mildly.

"It's all right, Diny. —What's your town?"

"Grand Plains. East of Amarillo."

"Oh, I remember that. We drove through it on a hot summer day. Seeing it from a distance on those endless flats, I said it looked like an egg on a sizzling frying pan."

"Well, people live there," said Howard.

"That's one for you, Ben," remarked Diana.

"My mother lives there, I am staying with her now, in the house my great-grandfather built."

"Are you married?"

"No, but not for not wishing, now and then."

"Well, good luck. But see it doesn't interfere with your work, when the time comes. It can, you know."

Unaware that he had exposed Diana to what could be read as humiliation, Ben stood, yawned, and said it was almost midnight and he was suddenly sleepy. It was time for everybody to go to bed. Pointedly, Diana, after making up Howard's bed on the floor near the stove, turned out the Coleman lantern so that he—and everyone —would undress in darkness. The little windows were propped open by sticks. The sound of the Gulf entered in, and the cool, wet breath of the fog.

By fixed resolve, Howard awoke early, before the others. Quietly putting on his outer clothes, he took his kit and left the hut, resolutely refusing to look at the sleepers in bed. He would send a note to General Delivery, Brownsville, and then try to put out of thoughts this last encounter with Diana.

The Gulf was dancing with rosy light under a robin's-egg blue sky, in a morning so clear and bracing that he had to stand still taking it in.

He lingered a moment too long.

With a shout, Ben jumped out of the shack calling, "Wait, wait!" He was as innocently friendly as last night he had been teasingly rude. Howard argued uselessly for his escape. They kept him for breakfast, and then proposed taking him along to Brownsville, where they were going for shopping and mail. Diana smiled at him as though to say, *Won't you?* He went.

When they reached town, Ben said, "Let's take a day off and all go to Mexico."

Diana had a keener sense. "Let him go, Ben."

"All right. Let's drive him to Port Isabel."

"Ben."

"No, thank you," said Howard. "Now that I'm here, though, I'll have a look by myself at places I want to see again."

"Where? Where? What places? We'll come with you."

"Ben, for heavens' sake, he's working, don't you know how you have to be alone for your work? So does he."

Howard thanked her silently.

"All right." Ben took out his small sketchbook. "Anyway, Debler, take your pick of a drawing as a souvenir of such a good evening."

He handed Howard the book with its sketches made the night before. In a strike of gleeful divination, Ben added, "Take one of *her*."

That could not be refused. Howard chose a small drawing of Diana. Her head was slightly raised, looking up from her work; her neck line strong and tender, her face and figure shadowed on one side, full of grace and light on the other. It was a true likeness even though details were scarcely suggested. Howard was confused by gratitude and denial.

To say something, he said, "Well, I wonder if we'll ever meet again."

"Quite literally," said Diana, "I don't know, we don't know, where we'll be going after the summer season." She looked at Ben with such a hold of his being in her eyes, and such dependence, that it was like a sensual hunger, and Howard felt he had no right to see it.

"So, goodbye, then," he said, "and thanks again."

"Write us how your book is going," said Diana. "It will be forwarded this time. Benjamin Ives or Diana Macdonald. General Delivery here."

"Yes, thanks."

Howard made one of his quick turnabouts and walked off in a strong, purposeful stride which made Diana watch after him until he turned a corner.

"You see what I mean," said Ben, laughing. He drove the old Ford to the post office, where General Delivery had nothing for them.

"Good!" said Ben.

"I don't know," murmured Diana.

"You're lonely. Visitors upset you."

"Yes and no."

"This visitor, anyway."

"I met him through my father."

[24]

"You're not as lucky as I am, my love. My past—and also my future—are all just today."

⚓

Howard went to see the site of the fort where the garrison established itself near the river on March 29, 1846. The fort was now a junior college, and the river had somewhat moved its course, but he could walk from the fort to the big horseshoe curve to see Matamoros on the Mexican side, and order events in his scheme while looking at their places. He had the elation which came from the belief that whatever happened, even a coincidence that changed his plans, was designed to enrich his work. He spent the day with the river and his notebook, forgetting to go anywhere for lunch.

By evening, exhilarated by his observations, he was hungry, and he decided to cross to Matamoros for a Mexican dinner and several bottles of Carta Blanca, his favorite beer. In a café called La Paloma Azul he was lost in a haze of imagination, leafing through his pocket pages, when someone said, "There he is, still being a genius," and he looked up to see Ben with Diana. He could only ask them to join him.

"Oh no, we shouldn't," said Diana.

"Why not, we came here for supper, so did he, he owes us one," said Ben like an old friend who can presume because it is expected of him.

They all sat down.

Silence.

Then Diana laughed, put her hand on Ben's arm and said, "When in doubt, call the *mariachis*. We'll have music until we can sort ourselves out."

With a wave, Ben brought a band of five Mexican musicians to the table. They stood in a semicircle, short, fat, thin, young, old, and yelled their tourist songs to the accompaniments of their violins and guitars. In the cement room, with its ceiling of ornamental pressed tin, all painted a sickly lime green, they made so much sound that talk was impossible. Before they were done with their first song, a brilliantly dressed figure appeared from a curtained doorway and joined the musicians. It was a young girl, partially wrapped in a bright fringed shawl. She was beautiful in spite of sticky makeup. With her arms in the air and snapping her fingers, she sang and clapped her heels on the tiled floor, making every signal of available allure and romance.

"Oh, that Chicha," cried Ben, snapping his fingers in time with hers. He raised his brows in sexual appraisal. "*Yee-how!*" he suddenly yelled in a strong falsetto like a Mexican announcing a good time. Chicha flirted her fringes at him.

He left the table to go and dance facing her. The *mariachis* followed them, making animal cries of their own. The bass guitar throbbed like swollen blood, the voices went joyfully insinuating. Spectators clapped their hands with the dancers. The two moved together until their thrust bellies touched, then separated. They circled behind each other, never clasping. Their eyes and mouths glistened. Challenge and defiance animated all their gestures. In every mind their flesh coupled.

Howard looked at Diana.

She nodded, smiling in self-possession.

"They seem to have done this together more than once," she shouted against the din. "They do it so well, don't they? Ben sometimes comes here alone. How lovely she would be if someone would wash her face."

Howard learned more than he wanted to know about how life went for an artist living with a bound friend in a cracked shanty on an empty beach. Diana saw that he made conclusions. As though he had no right to do so, she sat up handsomely and asked in a cool voice if he would order a tequila daiquiri for her?

When Ben returned, she said, "Very well done, darling."

Yes, thought Howard, *to keep him at all, she has to let him go, whenever.*

Music, strong liquor, feelings opposed in odd ways, scattered order during the evening. As early as possible, they said goodbye at the door of the Paloma Azul, under the alternately bilious and feverish electric light in the Matamoros street. Howard Debler knew crosscurrents of feeling. He did not like what he observed of Diana and Ben together; but he did not want to leave them. It was some time before he could look at Ben's drawing of Diana without a curious mixture of irritation and—he prudently avoided anything more ambitious—pleasure.

PART TWO

DIANA AND HOWARD had first met at her father's house in Dorchester, New York, a few days after the country began to throw its huge energies into the new job of war against Japan and Germany.

Whatever had gone before, in private lives, seemed suddenly trivial; yet some tasks had to halt, others begin, by orderly means; and Howard Debler was resolved to use his few remaining days as a civilian to carry his work to a completed stage.

He was in Dorchester to pursue early phases of his research into the 1846–48 war with Mexico. At the suggestion of John Howell, the San Francisco dealer in rare books and manuscripts of American history, he had come to consult the private collection of George Macdonald, to whom Howell had sold many important items about the early times of the Southwest and Mexico.

"Yes, use anything you find," he was told by George Macdonald. "I will read anything at all about the affairs of Mexico and the United States, but I will never write anything. I have your book *Lost Cause*, on the stillborn Republic of the Rio Grande. I'll be glad to help in any way to see your new work get done. My library is yours. You'll be alone till evening every day—I'm at my newspaper office all day."

"It's a gold mine," said Howard. "The best private library of my subject I've ever seen." He glanced around the long, high, shelf-lined room of Macdonald's library, with its several dark wooden tables gleaming under pools of lamp light, and added, "It's a wonderful room to work in, too. I don't know how to thank you. —What got you started on the collection?"

"As a youngster I enlisted in our National Guard regiment to go to the border during the troubles with Pancho Villa and the other revolutionary leaders. Though I've rarely been back, I fell in love with that amazing land of desert, mountain, rivers of sand, the heat which seemed to hold every illusion for the sight; and when I could, I started picking up this and that, and now there are these thousands of items, most of which you know, but some of which may be new to you."

"Some of which! I tell you. —Did you serve under Pershing directly?"

"Not for long, but I pulled orderly duty at his tent headquarters for a week or two, and then my troop—we were all cavalry—moved on, under a fantastic colonel who led us over salt flats and arroyos and mountain flanks in his personal Cadillac automobile, which he rode as if it were a government remount. —But I saw Pershing again in 1918 when I was a second lieutenant in France. A routine inspection, but he looked at me as though he remembered me. I think he did. A good commander." George stood up. "Well, I'll leave you to your burrowing. Good hunting."

It was good hunting, and Howard made the most of it in the few days remaining before he would have to report to his naval reserve unit in Austin, Texas, as an ensign subject to active duty. He worked long hours now, filling his briefcases with notes. In the evenings, he dined with George Macdonald, alone or with a few friends. The most responsive of these was Marjorie Scanlon, whose husband was president of Dorchester's leading bank.

She was at once interested in George's guest, for his looks, his easy responsiveness, and the differences of style between his Texan ways and those of Dorchester, which thought of itself as an inland Boston, content in its Upstate traditions. With disarming directness, freed by her mellow beauty and her air of amused worldliness, she quizzed Howard when they had a moment alone at a dinner party.

"Then you'll be in the Navy," she said.

"Yes. I've had my notice. I'm trying to finish up here in a hurry—but it's going to be hard to leave Mr Macdonald's wonderful materials."

"You must come back to them again when you can. —Tell me, how do you like him?"

"He's great. He lets you alone when you want it, and when you want to talk, there he is. He not only gave me his library, he insisted that I stay at his house. Sometimes I think he's rather lonely."

"He was, at one time, long ago. —I know something about that. It was after his wife died, a delicious creature, but giving birth to her daughter Diana cost her own life. George has never remarried, gave his whole life to Diana, until she married a few years ago. It made him unhappy."

"Is she like him?"

"More like her mother—I knew Frances, a lovely creature, but innocent as the day is long. Diana married a man almost old enough to be her father."

"And George didn't like that?"

"She was marrying Papa, in a sense. Does that ever work?"

"Who is he?"

"A famous playwright—John Wentworth. You may have heard of him."

"Yes. I've seen plays of his, but I forget them."

Marjorie laughed sumptuously. "That's exactly right, about the plays. —They're enormous successes, though. Several of them opened here, in Dorchester, and we all partied for John—Jack, as everyone says. That's how Diana met him. She was just out of college. He was at his best—silver hair, young pink face, small black mustache, high humor, every knack for being famous and rich, and Diana was our great local treasure, so lovely, so vital, ready for any and every thing. One afternoon Jack came to me for tea and asked me if I thought it was time for him to marry. I was silenced for a moment—it never occurred to me that he ever would, or should, marry. But he so wanted me to say yes that I said 'Yes,' and he kissed my cheek and said 'Guess who,' and I said I couldn't imagine. When he said Diana Macdonald, I *really* was given pause. But he was so pleased with the idea that he didn't notice my view of the matter. A few days later, before the play moved on to Philadelphia, they were engaged. They were married here seven months later. Her father was wretched."

"Her portrait hangs in his library."

"You like looking at it."

"I do."

Marjorie sighed and felt softly of her fine shoulders, on the chance that Howard might read the gesture as an inconclusive invitation. He did not do so, looking off into his imagination elsewhere. Marjorie knew when to shift control.

She said, "George has grown fond of you. I'm glad he has a new friend with common interests. He works himself too hard at his newspaper, and everybody else, so I hear. He has made it an excellent paper. They say Washington listens to his editorials. As he owns the paper, he can write whatever he likes. Of course, the President hates him for his America First views. I must say I share them, though I adore F.D.R., which drives Michael wild—my husband."

"We should have gone in long ago," said Howard.

"Texas speaks."

"Texas was ready."

She was only half thinking of what they were saying, for she was wondering what Howard thought of her. Not yet thirty, he had authority which rose through his tall spare, strong physical presence, his weathered, ruddy face in which his dark eyes held a steady shadowed look under brows fixed in a permanent frown, after a young lifetime in the light of the Southwest sky. What he thought of Marjorie was that she made him think of late summer or early autumn—in other words, of beautiful middle age, quite beyond interest. What she might think of him never entered his head.

Later in the evening, she took to a small sofa with George.

"I like your young man," she said.

"So do I, the more I see of him. I'll be sorry to see him go."

"Soon?"

"Yes. He has to report to his naval reserve unit."

"What's he doing here in the first place?"

"Looking for materials about a book he wants to write about the Mexican War."

"What Mexican War?"

"We had a war with Mexico, a century ago. He's an assistant professor of history out there. He's using my books and documents."

"I wish he could stay."

"Ah, Margie."

"Well, I do, and I can admit it to you, only, of course."

"Well, I'm lonely, too, but it's part of the package."

"The?"

"Growing older."

They regarded each other levelly, revealing certain memories only with their eyes, for their brief affair was long since past; but both being direct in their temperaments, they had clear notions about each other.

She said, "Mike thinks you ought to marry again, especially since Diny is gone."

"Tell Mike to go jump in the lake."

"You told me to tell him that some years ago, if I remember."

"Well, luckily, you didn't."

"Do you regret anything?" she asked.

He knew that she was calling up the past to rekindle it, if possible. He let the spark go out.

"No. I'm just grateful for what we had."

"You know? I think nobody knows, to this day?"

"I'm not all that sure."

"Who, then?"

"I don't think it means anything any more, but Mike gave me some uncertain looks, there, for a while."

Mrs Scanlon lifted her shoulders in a deep breath and said, "We gave it up for Diny's sake, and then she grew up and ran away. How much we do for our children's sake, before things begin to touch them. But what could we do for ourselves—you and I—after all, in the middle of families, and positions, and the rest. —Are you still grudging about her marriage to Jack?"

"Wrong fellow."

"Let it work. It seems to be working."

"I don't know. I feel like Lear."

"Four howls? —Well, if you'll let me be both worldly and maternal, let me advise you not to let Diana know how you feel."

"She knows. We never speak of it."

Marjorie sighed. Through her own marriage, she had long learned acceptance as a matter of pride in the visible values of a suitable commitment.

❧

George Macdonald and Howard Debler had an evening to themselves in the long library at home.

"My time here is running out," said Howard.

"I know. Perhaps after the war—whenever that may be, he got us into it, and God knows if he can ever get us out of it—but you might come back to use my collection."

"I'd like to hold on to that for the duration. —As for the war, I think what got us into it was bigger than the President. I was even wondering if I ought to go to Canada to enlist there. Then they told me my naval reserve commission would prevent that."

George scowled and rubbed his stubby reddish hair—a gesture of uncertainty.

"Well, now that we're in it, I'll have to do what I can to help. —Not that I ever endorsed what those squalid monsters were up to in Germany and Italy. I just thought it wasn't our province."

Howard tactfully changed the subject. "What happens to your collection eventually?"

"It goes to the university library here. It will always be available to you and other scholars. But I'm glad I was able to offer it to you personally. —How is the work getting on?"

Howard set down his brandy glass and his cigar, got up, and walked a few steps toward the great fireplace where logs were glowing, and turned back, and said, "If I may stay four more days, I'll finish copying some extracts from papers which will round out my notes on early reports about the Gulf of Mexico. Then I can resume my own surveys there after I am out of the service, when-ever, and carry on with all the rest of the material I already have. It's going to be a sustaining private possession of mine, all the while I have to be away from it. I've got to put it out of mind for the duration, or I'll go off my head trying to think about two commit-ments. But having it to come back to—that will be my light in the window."

"Are you married, Howard?"

"No. —I see. Most fellows my age would have a family to get back to."

"Have you anyone else?"

[37]

"My mother—we lost my father when I was a boy. She lives out in West Texas. I go back to see her when I can, and I keep some books there, and a room to work in. It's an ideal place for that. Small town called Grand Plains, a house my great-grandfather built beginning with two rooms out of logs, and a breezeway, or dog run, as we natives call it. Between the plains and the Gulf Coast, I've formed the need all my life to stretch my eyes."

Yes, said George to himself, he doesn't know how well he has put it: if I had a son, I'd be glad if he were able to see as far as this young man seems to. Aloud,

"Well, marriage, don't be in any hurry, but don't wait forever. I can make the best inland newspaper in America, and you can write the best histories in your time, but there's a gap between making a career and making life. They've got to come together. They did for me, though I lost my wife early; but the few years she gave me, and the child who survived her, have meant everything to me ever since, I mean, have added meaning to anything I have ever thought or tried to do. I can't define it, but it's there."

Howard had been inclined to respond to the subject with offhand humor, but George Macdonald spoke so feelingly, quite unlike his familiar abrupt self, that any echo of the eternal male comedy about taking a wife was out of place. Howard said, "I'll keep my hopes up, if I make it home from the service."

A Negro houseman in a white coat came in and said, "Sir, there is a telephone call for you from Miss Diana in New York. Shall I connect the phone in here?"

"No, thank you, Diggs, I'll come. —Excuse me, Howard. It's my daughter."

When he returned in a few minutes, George said, "Diana. She's coming up from New York tomorrow. She wants to leave some things here for the duration. She and her husband are moving to Washington. Something in the government for him. Can't imagine what he could do."

Earlier that evening—it was December 14, 1941—John Wentworth telephoned from Washington to his wife in New York.

"I've been trying all evening to reach you."

"I just came in," said Diana. "I went to the movies."

"What did you see?—it doesn't matter. I have important news. I'll give you details later, but: we are moving to Washington immediately. Everybody is right—the place *is* a madhouse, but the government, the armed forces, all the war effort scrambling to get organized, it's all really splendid. It's like electricity in the air. And rejoice: I have been appointed to a fascinating job."

"Oh, Jack, how splendid. Tell me:"—concealing a perverse sinking of the heart at his elation, and the sudden change it signaled.

"This morning, I finally saw a certain Squire at the White House. It was frightfully difficult to get to him, but by great good luck, his secretary, you know, that nice woman, happened on me in a corridor, and remembered how often I have stayed there privately reading my new plays to amuse him. He loved to suggest changes to me, and I always made them, right then, and made him initial the script. Anyway: she found me four minutes just before lunch and sent me in to see him. He's in magnificent form. Called me Jack the Wentworthy, took a pad and wrote two lines and three initials, and sent me to see someone at State, who knew who I was, and immediately took me on. We'll be here in Washington for the duration."

"How amazing."

"Exciting, really. You might get started at once on making lists. If you need ready advice, don't bother to phone me—talk to Gregory Blaine. He can find the proper people to manage vacating the apartment, or selling it, or subletting—whatever can be done.

I'll send my secretary a bonus and a thank-you dismissal. I imagine she'll want a war job, anyhow. I've taken an option to buy an historical house here in Georgetown, heard of it by a miraculous coincidence at lunch today at the Metropolitan Club. It's a nice house and you can make it charming. It sounds rather odd, but I thank God for Pearl Harbor, it brought us in where we should have been long ago, and it vacated this perfect house for me. The people are being transferred to a naval base in California. He's an admiral, up for sea duty. I asked him if I should apply for a Navy commission, but he thought I'd be more useful, because of having immediate authority, in my new job. I said, *But I like the uniform*, chaffing, of course, but he turned rather stiff, snubbed me, and said there were better reasons for a man to join the service. I imagine he has one of those flagship wives, you know, all bow waves and steel stern. No matter. The air here is absolutely exhilarating. Everyone is plunging right in."

Diana then felt a lift of hope. Change, total change, might do wonders, she thought, for both of them.

"Jack, dear, where shall I start?"

"Pack only what we'll need for a month or so in the hotel here while the Georgetown house is being readied. The Carlton is like an expensive anthill, but I've managed for a bedroom and a sitting room by paying a month in advance at double rates. Everybody in the world is in and out of the lobby all day"—and with pleasure he named a half-dozen celebrated persons. "The pace is furious. My faith in America is vindicated a hundred times over. But listen: my appointment is top secret, don't tell a soul but Gregory—"

"My father:"

"—All right, your father, but not for publication, there must be no leaks until official notice is given out. Do be careful."

"I will. —But I think I'll run up to Dorchester to see my father and sort of say goodbye, and leave some things there at home."

"Yes. Perhaps now he will take his son-in-law a trifle more seriously."

"Oh, Jack."

"Oh, I know well enough how he has always felt about me. —But aren't you proud of your old chum?"

"Oh yes, Jack. But I knew they'd want you the minute you rushed down to Washington."

"Well, they did. Thousands of others rushed here, too, with no results, so it is all the more: what: gratifying, I suppose: that my appointment went through so fast, despite bureaucracy. Of course, knowing a Certain Person had much to do with it, on top of my reputation."

"I imagine plenty of others had you on their lists, though."

"Very likely. —Do be good, and get what rest you can. We'll be fearfully busy, here, there will be quite some establishment for us to keep up. I must ring off now. I'm having a late dinner with my new chief, and then we're going round to introduce me to the Secretary. Good night, Jadi," he said, using the nickname he had invented for each to use for the other in private or public intimacy. He had made it from letters in their names, Jack and Diana, to be pronounced *Jah-dee*. He thought it sounded Persian. "Kiss," he signaled before he hung up.

"Kiss," she replied obediently, in his established formula to be used when apart.

It was like the turn of a prism, she thought, once again alone—all the objects of her life quite visible, but suddenly in a shifted relation to each other in color, vividness, and endless duplication. Her situation was a miniature of the nation's life as a whole. Where were certainties? But where had they been, in any case, since the day, so many months ago, of her marriage? Honor still required duty, but did not preclude thoughts. It remained to be seen what the war would change in her life.

[41]

She telephoned her father, glad that she could turn to him again for the old reassurance that she had missed ever since her marriage to John Wentworth, the famous author of *The Calico Cat; Patient Griselda; Day's at the Morn; Come, Madam, Come;* and other "smash hit" comedies about matrimony among the socially well-to-do, in which "whimsy and acid provide the mixture as before," as a leading drama critic put it.

※

For fullness of feeling, both George and his daughter were lightly formal with each other when they met again.

"Looking well—looking well," he said, embracing her.

"Darling Pappy."

"Now sit down and tell me all about it."

"Shall we go into the library?"

"No, fellow working there on research. If you don't mind we'll have him dine with us tonight. Never see him in the daytime, though he's staying here."

They went to the upstairs study attached to George's quarters overlooking the deep garden which was now highlighted with patches of snow.

"It's good to be home."

"Does it still feel like home? I hope so."

"Oh, but it does."

"So old Jack has gone to war."

"Yes—he sounds very happy."

"Will you like Washington?"

"Wherever."

He looked severely at her until she dropped her gaze and then he felt a pang for having called her to witness, however remotely, to the state of the marriage he had opposed from the start.

"Yes, well, all of you," he said with a testy attempt at fun, "can now crow over getting the war you wanted, while the rest of us will eat the crow."

"Nobody's gloating, Pappy. —I've brought some things to leave with you for safekeeping: your letters, mother's jewels—I'm keeping only these"—she fingered a close circlet of fine pearls at her throat—"and some papers, marriage license and the sort, for you to put in the bank. But mainly I wanted to see you before we moved."

"Oh, I may have to be in Washington now and then to look over our news bureau there. You're not going to Timbuktu, after all. —What's Jack's job?"

"It sounded like something attached to the State Department, but exactly what I don't know yet. Evidently we'll have to maintain an *establishment*."

"Ha. A society-page war."

"Pappy: be fair: we don't *know*."

"D'you really feel all right?"

"Whyever do you—I'm splendid."

But she knew he was asking about the prospect of a grandchild, and of that she could tell him nothing, as there was not now, nor would there ever be, such a prospect.

"Good." He stood up. "I must be getting off to the paper. Your old rooms are all ready here. Come here." He hugged her and said over her shoulder, "God, how empty they have been."

She kissed him and said, "How I hated to leave you."

"Why did you?" he demanded harshly.

"Not that again, Pappy. Please."

He longed for her to say that she was unhappy, but she was determined to protect the dignity of her marriage against the intuitive assumptions of others, especially those of her father.

"No, Diny, I'm sorry. Meet me for lunch, the Club, at one. I'll take these things with me now and send them over to Mike Scanlon's bank. They'll send you a duplicate key. Marjorie was asking about you the other night."

"I can imagine."

"No-no. Just interested, in her way."

"I hope I'll never—"

"Hush. She means no ill."

"Who is your guest?"

"A young history professor from Texas. Evidently struck it rich in my collection. Something he's working on. You won't mind our dining together tonight?"

"Not if you like him, and won't keep him answering questions." He laughed. "Do I do that?"

"You're an information harvester, Pappy."

"Fat lot I get out of you."

"Darling. I'll go and unpack."

"How long can you stay?"

"I'll have to go back tomorrow night. A thousand things to do, to close up everything in New York."

"Your job."

"Yes, of course."

He shrugged heavily and, slightly hunched, went downstairs. She watched after him. Her love for him tugged at her, and she made a little silent laugh at his grudging concern for her, which told her how much he loved her still, despite her grown-up distance.

❧

George Macdonald's home was large and—as he sometimes said sardonically—historically grand, for it was designed after an eighteenth-century French house. He had inherited it from his wife, whose parents built it in the château period of American taste. Except for an occasional dinner party, George rarely kept state in it, but usually had his meals at home served on trays in the library. Tonight, in honor of Diana's return, the household was served in the great dining room, with its Italian marble fireplace at each end. The long central table was dark, and instead, a small round table was set for three in front of a hearth fire, with candles making an intimate circle of light. Two old Irish housemaids in black frocks and white caps served the dinner. Howard felt that honesty obliged him to speak of a style unfamiliar to him.

"I'm a long way from Grand Plains, Texas, here. Our idea of a party is to bring in Auntie Jen to serve, she's the colored lady who lives on the edge of town and raises herbs for a living, while one of the guests brings dessert." He smiled at Diana to excuse what might sound like a clumsy diffidence, and said, "I could very easily get used to surroundings like these, though."

"You're a poor imitation of a bumpkin," said George. "I'd guess you'd be at home wherever you found it interesting to be. —I doubt if much of this sort of life will survive the war. Not that I'll mind."

"Well, pretty soon I'll have a two-by-four steel cabin—I want sea duty."

"That will probably mean the Pacific," said George.

"I hope so. But I'll probably draw convoy duty in the Atlantic."

"My father tells me you are a Navy reserve officer," said Diana.

"Yes. Ensign. I'm to report for active duty and training in six days."

"Are you glad or sorry?"

"Both. I hate to give up my book just as it's taking hold. But on the other hand I feel pretty strongly about what we all have to do, and that as soon as possible."

"It was far worse than the public knows," said George, "at Pearl Harbor, I mean."

"Is that true, sir? Have you had information?"

"Off the record, yes, from my Washington people. Can't print it, of course. But five-sixths of the Pacific fleet was sunk in an hour, and only a handful of airplanes are left in Hawaii and the Philippines."

Howard leaned back and stared at George. In a moment, he said, "I ought not to wait another day, here."

"Just stay with your orders," said George. "A maxim I learned in 1914 on the Border with Pershing." He gave Howard a quizzical look and added, "You know? I think you'll write a better book about your Mexican War for having been in a war yourself."

Howard laughed—a youthful gust of humor which delighted in the older man's wisdom. It so fully told of hardy, physical, adventurous young manhood that Diana felt a brief flush of warmth mixed with a distant sadness for what war was about in terms of flesh and blood.

After dinner they moved into the library, where coffee was brought to them. Howard's books and papers were laid out in an orderly pattern on one of the two heavy Renaissance tables which flanked the fireplace. A comfortable bay lay between, where a sofa and chairs were placed near enough to each other for easy conversation.

"So you are going to live in Washington, Mrs Wentworth," said Howard.

"Yes. My husband has been appointed to a government post. He'll do it brilliantly. He is a brilliant man."

George looked away, and Howard nodded.

"Yes," he said, "I have seen some of his plays. I always felt his mind was two leaps ahead of the point, whatever it was, every time."

Diana laughed. The young man had happened upon a trait of Jack Wentworth's with accuracy. She felt a sudden more personal respect for Howard Debler. She looked at him less indifferently than before. What struck her most plainly was the effect he gave of healthy cleanness. His flesh was clear tanned, and she reflected that he represented a type—those who always look scrubbed and glowing no matter what they'd done. His whole bearing suggested the open air, and she thought it might have to do with his height, his strong spareness, and the lingering effect of Western sunlight. There was a clear bite in how he spoke his words. He thought rapidly, and what he thought seemed to show in his eyes before he spoke it. Sometimes he allowed a little silence, in a trance of gazing, from which he seemed to jolt himself. She now felt him looking intently at her. She turned to her father and said, "As soon as we're settled, I hope you'll come to see us in Washington."

George murmured something Howard did not hear; for he was lost in looking at Diana. Her hair caught the firelight, her eyes shone, and the high curve of her cheeks showed a golden edge. She was dressed in some dull white material which fell about her in the effect of an antique sculpture, describing her slim figure in looping folds. A line of pearls showed at her throat. He had never seen a woman so elegantly simple and so beautiful. He wished she would notice him.

George stood up and said, "I am going upstairs. I have some letters to write. I'll leave you two to close down the evening."

He kissed his child and she put her palm to his heavy cheek and let him go.

"My father tells me you are gathering material for a book. You're a writer?"

"Yes—but you wouldn't have much occasion to know my work. Pieces of history, mostly Southwestern."

"What is the present one?"

Now he was on firm ground. He gestured toward his worktable and spoke of what was there. Raw materials, in the way of original documents and rare printed works, for the first history of the war with Mexico to be undertaken in decades. He had already given two years to study and travel, and the subject remained alive for him.

"That must be an important part of it," she said.

"I tell you," he said vehemently, "to keep the large aspects alive in imagination while finding supporting fact—the daily excitement and challenge."

"Do you know all the places? Are there many?"

"Oh, all of them, but much yet to possess in detail—the Rio Grande for all its course, and northern Mexico, the border deserts, the inland battle sites, the capital city of Mexico, Washington and President Polk's campaign carried out on maps, and above all, the littoral of the Gulf of Mexico, where the first actual battles took place under Zachary Taylor in 1846."

"Do you know the Gulf?"

"Oh yes, as a boy I was taken fishing there by my father, and I have gone back since, especially lately. There is some odd magic about the thing, for me, even on a map. Yes, listen." He jumped up and went to his table and brought back an old book whose pages were limp as heavy linen, and said,

"Listen: I will read you something marvelous I found here in your father's collection. This is a compendium, published in London in 1604, of geographical reports of the opening world as explorers and mariners saw it. Here is an old map"—he showed it to her—"of the Gulf, and you see, it is charted as *Mexico Bay* by the man who drew the map. He was Nicholas Broughton the Navigator, who was there with Francis Drake on the voyage of 1567. In old age, Nicholas wrote some wise words about the Gulf." Howard read aloud:

"It is not a Baye in the guise of a shelter all compact from storme or pursuit, rather for its extent beyond the sight of manie

days sayling it is a greate sea the whiche voyagers from farre landes observe onlie in its diverse parts. Thus there are given to it as manie characters as there be chroniclers, for one saith that it is peacefull as a lake and another that it hath as manie changes in temper as a woman and still another that with hardly a warnygne it bloweth into tempests so vanquyshyng that any few who survive declare how never did they see deathe so close or are so humblie gratefull to see safetie returne in such sweete suddain calme as in a morning after feaver."

"Oh, those Elizabethans," said Diana. "Everything they wrote seemed to say more than the words."

Howard held his old book high. His cheeks had gained color with excitement, like a child in intense play, Diana thought.

He answered, "Yes: even this: it sounds like a statement about composite human life. How can geography be so richly suggestive? I've got to try for something like it in my small way!"

"Well," said Diana, "I had to read history in college. It was mostly gray print. I hope you plan to enrage your academic colleagues with evidences of human life in your pages?"

"Yes, yes. I'm after the soldiers, the individual men on both sides, their lost little lives, that weren't little to them. And here in this library I've found such riches—original unpublished diaries, letters, soldiers, sailors on the Gulf and the river, descriptions of the wrecks of ships, even some medical reports. Polk's war messages. A Mexican mustering roster—those very names become men to me. President Santa Anna wrote a propaganda pamphlet trying to subvert our troops—there is a printed copy right here! You can't imagine!"

He was transfigured. She couldn't help laughing with sympathy in his enthusiasm. The laugh brought him down.

"I'm sorry," he said. "I get out of my skin when I get to talking."

"Oh, no, it's fascinating. —What will you call your book?"

He hauled a deep breath which spoke of the uncertainties ahead.

[49]

"If I get to do it, it will be *War Southwest: The United States and Mexico, 1846–1848.*"

"Then," said Diana lightly, "we'll have to have this new war promptly over with, so you can get on with your old one. —I think I'll leave you now. I'm glad to have had the sense of your work. Good night—and good luck."

He watched after her, thinking, *I believe she means that both ways, though she didn't want to mention what I might be going off to.*

It was not yet late at night. He went to his table and worked several hours with special enthusiasm kindled by the interest of another in his quest.

The next day she left for New York without seeing Howard again.

※

In New York, lunching together,

"I've talked to Jack several times," said Gregory Blaine to Diana. "I assured him that I've been doing everything I can for you in closing up things here. You're leaving the end of the week?"

"Yes. Oh, so tired. *Details.* Where to send this, what to give away, what to do with that. I shudder to think of setting up another house all over again."

"Call it your war work. I'll ask you to take some proofs to Jack, *Day's at the Morn.* The last play of his we'll publish until after the war, I guess. It's holding up wonderfully, by the way—I saw it again last night. A dozen calls at the end. It'll run another six months at least. Disgusting, how rich he gets, year after year and play after play."

"He doesn't mind."

Gregory laughed and his whole ungainly bulk shook. As John Wentworth's publisher, and oldest and most knowing friend, he had a mocking fondness for him which was meant not to offend but to amuse Diana. She knew there was little about her husband, and herself, and their relationship, that Gregory did not know, understand, and worry over. His affection for her had grown to a point beyond admission. Thrice divorced, he was always seeking for love, and despite his heavy figure on short legs, wide face with its saurian gaze, and his unavailing attempts at improving all this through expert tailoring, he was used to success with women. Diana liked his company. She felt much unspoken between them which gave her content and comfort. Of all the busy society and the hectic comradeship of the theater to which her marriage had introduced her, it was Gregory Blaine in whom she found the truest friend. No extraordinary confidences had ever taken place between them, and her composed gaiety prevented any useless avowals from Gregory. They seemed to have agreed that their feeling for each other, and the knowledge that it rested on, must continue to be a comedy of awareness unspoken within civilized convention.

"How was Dorchester?" asked Gregory. "Were you homesick, being home again? Sometimes it works that way."

"Not really. My father was sweet and grumbling. He lost the peace, you know, and yet can't be against the war. I think he's secretly jealous of Jack, and proud of him, too, for getting into the war effort at all, and so quickly, at that."

"I must admit I'm amazed, myself."

"There was a young man staying at home, a teacher at the University of Texas. He's using my father's historical archives of the Southwest. He's gone by now, to report to the Navy. I kept thinking, if only the lasting things could be allowed to go on growing at the same time the destruction and ruin have to be carried out."

"Yes, if only. —What's he writing?"

"A Mexican War history."

"Is he any good?"

"I've no idea, except that he's all lighted up by his subject."

"Tell me his name. I may keep an eye out for him."

Diana did so, and Gregory scribbled a note on a scrap of paper from his wallet.

"You never know," he said, as a publisher. "—Anything else, now, about things here?"

There was nothing else. The last chores of vacating a place, and a life, would be done by Paco and his wife, the young Spanish couple who had been with Jack for several years as houseman and cook. They would follow to Washington in a few days.

"Me, I leave on the midnight train," said Diana. "You've been helpful and sweet."

"For love of you, and joy in Jack's reprintings," said Gregory.

"Yes, I know, you fool."

She kissed him on the forehead and left him. He stayed at his table, watching her make her way out of sight. What he would give . . .

Interlude

GIVEN THE GIVENS, Gregory Blaine sometimes reflected, the marriage of his old friend John Wentworth to Diana Macdonald had its puzzlements. Wentworth—Jack—was almost twenty years older than his wife. Diana despite her youth had always seemed sure of herself, according to Jack, because her father's nature was reflected in the daughter. If she was a long time in making up her mind, once made up, her will was fixed. Jack did not mean that she was blunt or stubborn—it was rather a sort of pride in her certainty that informed her actions, and he was pleased, though not astonished, when she had accepted him.

Gregory went beyond politeness when Jack told him the news. He asked, "But what does she—how can she take to your world without some difficulty?"

Jack was indignant.

"It's not all that outlandish," he said. "I live a reasonably civilized life. After all: how many people do you know, especially among your grubby authors, who are invited once or twice a year to stay overnight at the White House, in order to divert and distract the Great Man with readings aloud from their own work? Who belongs to better clubs than I? Or stays in better country houses in England? If you please."

"No—no, I never meant—actually, it's a pretty luxurious life, no, I meant all that about the theater, and the other side or your associations with a quite different set of values than she grew up with, as you describe her background."

"Well: after all: I met her in her own world, Dorchester, that rich provincial society, where I am welcome, I assure you. My plays often try out there, and it may come as a surprise to you, but the best people, so-called, are pleased enough to entertain me. In fact, I sometimes have to fight them off. —Aren't you going to congratulate me?"

"Of course, Jack. I do, I do, most heartily. I can't wait to meet her."

"But you have reservations. Well, if it's any comfort to you, so does her father. He tries to be civil, but plainly he has no idea of who I am and what my position really is."

"Is that all?"

"What are you getting at?"

"Oh, Jack, let's not get into it. Let's just say that marriage would be the last thing anybody might expect for you."

"You don't think I am in love."

"Well, no, if it comes to that. —Is she?"

"Very much so. She is entirely happy with me. I can see it. I believe quite surely that she will make a good life with me, and *for* me. After all, I have many good years left, and my position really needs a permanent base. I am tired of being an escort instead of a husband, and having to explain away my single state in interviews —all that. She will move into a circle of distinguished people, and she will do it quite naturally. After all, she's always been used to the best things. She's beautifully educated, that advanced New England college for women, she was a great star in their theatrical doings. She played Shaw's Joan, I understand she was splendid, for an amateur. She adores the stage."

"Did you represent glamour to her?"

"And if I did, what's wrong with that? Or don't you think there's more to me than that?"

"Oh, come off it, Jack," said Gregory, heaving his bulk about in his chair. "You know how I feel about your talent and your useful charm and your famous discipline at work, and the rest."

"Well, Diana has had a rehearsal of all my qualities. Don't forget that after her graduation she worked with me for six months as a production assistant. You can't know anybody better than through a hard, professional relationship. If she had stars in her eyes about me at first, there was plenty of opportunity for them to glimmer out before now. Well, my stout party, I am pleased to announce that the stars are still there."

"Well, of course, I wish you the best of luck and happiness. And please excuse my initial astonishment. I just never thought of you as a husband and householder. After all, in spite of your social-register lady friends, you never showed serious interest in a woman before."

Jack sat back. He had black eyes which could take on a hard gaze when he was emotionally challenged.

"So that's it," he said dryly. "Then let me tell you that what's past is past, and none of it ever lasted, in spite of promises, each time. Diana will not find me lacking as her husband. She has a wonderful kind of what: innocence: unawareness: rejection of vulgar surmise: which makes her ideally the person for me to want to spend the rest of my life with. Not to mention her style, which happens to fit perfectly into my own." He felt himself growing too intense, and he moved lightly into another key. "After all, my dear Greg, who has written more and wiser plays about the state of man and wife than I have, or more amusingly, or more truly? Just ask the public. They'll tell you. Just ask your bookkeeper. My royalties on my plays which you publish will tell you. —Oh, all this: why are we wrangling? All I wanted to do was tell you I'm engaged, and to whom, and to ask you to be my best man."

Gregory gave out his heavy paw and joined the conventions.

"I accept with pleasure," he said. "I hope I can be as close a friend to your wife as I am to you."

Jack's eyes swam for a second as he saw himself through another's eyes. He was, Gregory thought, secretly uncertain about the future, and so the more determined to force it into a frame of his own making.

"I knew I could rely on you, Greg. Let's drink to it, then I must fly."

When he was gone, Gregory, in honor of truth and discretion together, wondered who was the more innocent of many meanings of married life: Jack, whom he knew so well, or Diana, whom he then knew only through Jack's desire for an ornament to position.

PART THREE

EVERYBODY FELT IT, the vast surge of new energy and purpose, then, which the sudden state of war brought with it. In their various ways, people believed that "a just war" was upon them. With all its disruptions and early bunglings, the mammoth heavings of a new national spirit stirring alive, the war pulled the great majority into a desire to take part in any way. It made whatever went before in separate lives seem, despite the Great Depression and less ordinary troubles, trivial compared to the new challenge.

An ambitious and privileged throng of the population converged on Washington. For them, Washington became, for whatever motive, "the thing to do." Jack Wentworth, with his sense of public style, was one of the first to enact the imperative. He awaited the arrival of his wife Diana impatiently. He was already too busy to give thought to domestic matters; and Diana was needed to set up the suitable establishment in Georgetown.

"Things are best for us when we're both busy," he reflected.

In his new importance, Jack was looking younger than his years, and his associates, particularly his official subordinates, were alive to the charm which he knew how to apply in having his ideas carried out—the fruit of many years of rehearsing actors and using their very vanities to animate his imagined plots and people. His vitality gave wit to his mannerisms—the quick turns of his body, his black-eyed stare, intent as if fascinated, into the eyes of others, the sweeping gesture of his left arm as he sought to enlarge an idea, his habit in repose of standing with his legs apart, his hands, thumbs forward, cradling his hips. He was above average in height, slim and sinewy, stronger than he looked, and arresting for the combination of his neat, regular features with his white hair and his black eyebrows, matched by his narrow black mustache. He had the looks to go with his abiding confidence as a distinguished man. If he seemed to others—men, mostly—overly fastidious, they had to admit that he lived up to his standards in dress, speech, taste, and, above all, in his marriage to a wife so young and beautiful, so intelligent and friendly, in her cool way. Waiting for Diana to join him in Washington, Jack said to himself one evening, "I am at the height of my powers"—and then, even in his satisfaction, he thought of how such a statement would sound from an actor, and he burst into a rippling laugh at his own vanity, and the fact of his perception of it.

※

They were able to move, after five weeks at the Carlton, into their restored eighteenth-century house overlooking the Potomac from a grassy point at the end of a narrow street. The original portion of the house was built of rosy brick, to which a fieldstone wing had been added years ago. The whole stood in a miniature park, surrounded by a wall of faded pink stucco with urns at the gateway, in all of which Jack felt himself properly clothed. His pleasure in the new residence was crowned when one evening rummaging in a box of old papers hidden in a forgotten fireplace cupboard he came upon a fine original name for the place in a deed dated 1799: The Riverpoint Manor. He at once ordered stationery engraved with it. For the rest, Diana saw to the furnishing and the ordering of the establishment, and Jack had proper evidence of his new position with the wartime government.

He was now the Deputy Assistant Director in charge of the United Kingdom desk in the new agency responsible for war information—in effect, propaganda, with offices in the State Department building next to the White House. He accepted that his earlier habit of easy familiarity at the White House was now impossible as a regular thing; but simply to be so near to the summit of power was gratifying, and among members of the secretariat he found many friends who noticed that Jack, with all his faithful attention to duty, saw the war as a social opportunity. He meant to bring to it the highest style he could manage. In a way, he felt, this was also duty, for in times of privation, drabness, personal losses, was it not all the more necessary to keep alive the graces of life at home for those who would one day return from battle? Meanwhile, he was content to be a particle of that magnetic force which drew the attention, and in many cases persons, of all parts of the nation.

※

Once the national course was committed, George Macdonald of Dorchester, believing in his "country right or wrong," came to Washington looking for a commission in the military service. In his memory stirred images of his extreme youth, and the desert dust and heat when he had served in the cavalry for a few months on the Mexican border, and later in France; and though he would never say it, he thought of himself as a veteran. He still regretted the entry of the nation into this war, for he believed that even victory would bankrupt the government; yet his conscientious pessimism was an incentive to his patriotism, and he began the wearisome tour of members of the House and Senate, the Departments of War and Navy, talking to friends who were in a position to further his need to serve. But his long record of isolationism was too well known—even the President had spoken of him by name on public occasions before the war when denouncing with ringing scorn those who had "a parochial vision of civilization." George was now rebuffed on all sides.

Staying at The Riverpoint Manor with his daughter and her husband (he would far rather have been independent in a hotel but actually could not find a room), he grumbled forth his frustrations. He had no false modesty about his ability which would certainly be useful somewhere in uniform.

Jack said, "But why didn't you ask me to take care of the matter in the beginning?" But Jack knew that George did not care to be beholden to his son-in-law for anything. It was Jack's chance to overcome him. "Leave it to me, *beau-père*. I'll see what I can do. What should it be: Army or Navy? I think Army. I will sound out certain persons. I think it would be a scandal if you were brought in at anything below brigadier general, a man of your experience and position." *My father-in-law, the General,* reflected Jack.

But next day Jack discovered that nominations to the rank of general officer had to be approved by the Senate, and then submitted to the President. The aide was certain that even if the Senate passed George, the White House would strike his name off the list.

"Magnanimity, eh?" said George sarcastically. "I'm not amazed."

"Never mind, we're not licked yet," said Jack.

In another week he had found a commission for George Macdonald as lieutenant colonel in the Intelligence arm of the Army Air Corps, which did not require congressional or Presidential approval. George was to report to Miami Beach at once for training in the school for officers who had had previous military experience —the so-called "Re-Treads."

The Riverpoint Manor was ready and smoothly running.

"We'll give our first important dinner party for George's going away," declared Jack.

"Oh, I think he'd hate it," said Diana.

"Nonsense, we'll have a few good names for him to tuck away, you never know when mentioning them will come in handy in official matters. His old friends the Scanlons are here, and I will ask my chief and his wife, they're old Washington, Billy and Cecile Millard. Give Paco a nice menu."

Michael Scanlon was serving for a dollar a year on the War Production Board. He and Marjorie were installed in yet another Georgetown house. Marjorie Scanlon said they would be delighted to come and send George off to war but might arrive a little late as they had to go first to the British Embassy for cocktails.

"The Scanlons? At the Halifaxes'?" exclaimed Jack to Diana irritably. "I know nothing of a cocktail party there. I wonder why I—we—were not asked. I run the United Kingdom desk, after all. I must find out if the Millards are going."

It was a lesser problem than managing George Macdonald.

"I don't want a party," George declared flatly. "I want you to get Jack to call it off. All I want is to have dinner alone with you, Diny. We may not be in touch again for quite a while."

"Jack would be dreadfully hurt, Pappy, if I asked him. This means much to him."

"So the party is really more for him than for me?"

"Don't make me say so."

"Does he know there's a war on? —Parties. I suppose to save you a lot of hell we'll have to go through with it."

She felt, as so often before, the sense of being pulled apart between her father and her husband. George realized this too, and in fairness resigned himself for her sake. This obliged her to say, "No! If you really want me to, I'll call it off. We've invited everybody, but I can cancel. I would far rather be with you on your last night here."

"There would be a row."

"I don't care."

"No," he said, looking at her shining hair, the little twist of her lips into a line of humorous determination, so like one of her remembered expressions in childhood, "I'll have to behave. It will be easier, now that I know you'd rather have us alone. —But if Jack begins to crow about engineering my commission, I'll go right up to bed."

"Oh, he won't, I'm sure."

"Anyway, here's one of the things I wanted to talk about alone with you later."

He then explained that under the exigencies of war service, including its mortal possibilities, he had reviewed his will, making certain provisions: that his library, including all the rare books and manuscripts, along with an endowment for its continuous enlargement and maintenance, would go to the University of Dorchester; that the family newspaper, the *World-Times*, would be transferred to the employees as owners under an executive trust; that the family residence and its contents be left to his daughter along with a trust fund to yield a moderately prosperous income for her which—

"I mean," he said, "if you should ever be free of your husband, I mean, without him, for whatever cause, you will be provided for. No great fortune, for I know you would not want that."

She nodded in agreement, but she looked white. He took her hand and pressed it.

"How awful it sounds," she said.

"It is all entirely routine," said her father, wearing his severe administrative face to disguise his feeling, and deny hers. "Not to leave affairs in order in wartime is idiotic. Don't dwell on it."

They embraced and said no more about it.

There were twelve for dinner, including as a last minute addition Gregory Blaine, who in his turn was in the capital for a wartime assignment. Jack said to him with the amused condescension of one with a war seniority of a few weeks, "I wondered when you'd be running down here after a job. Where are you going to start looking?"

"Oh, they sent for me," replied Gregory, which did not sit well with Jack. "We're working out how many days a week I can give to head a service of books for troops overseas."

Contrary to protocol, and over Jack's protests, Diana sat her father on her right, and Jack's chief, William Millard, on her left. The rest were properly disposed down the long table. Jack had collected a major general from the staff of the Secretary of War with wife; the wife of an Army Air Corps general (he was overseas); a Washington hostess from Lafayette Square who had just returned from what she called her ranches in California; and Michael and Marjorie Scanlon.

"I can't stand it," said Marjorie. "It's too lovely, the house. How I wish I'd seen it first."

"I hope you're really envious," said Jack genially.

"Don't worry. I am."

The talk soon swelled on rumors, local and general, about the war. The danger of a Japanese invasion of California was not over. Nonsense, said the major general, the Japanese invasion if it came would spread from a landing in Mexico or Canada, and then a sweep along the coast. Mike Scanlon contradicted this with an opinion that airplane-production plants in southern California were on alert against long-range shelling by Japanese submarines in coastal waters. The wife of the overseas general—she was not at liberty to say where he was serving—supposed it was all right for her to tell that the Germans had perfected fire bombs, any one of which could wipe out New York or Washington.

"No," said Mike, "they'd go first for two other places: Niagara Falls, with its power grid, and Detroit, with its motor-vehicle production, including tanks."

"But do they have transatlantic aircraft?" asked Gregory.

"*We* have," replied Assistant Secretary Millard grimly.

What were our defenses then?

"Adequate," said the major general, underplaying the word, which gave his statement all the authority of the office of the Secretary of War.

The company shared an elevated feeling of being at the center of great affairs, though their assembly, and their opinions, could be duplicated at a hundred other Washington dinner tables at the same time. The reality lay elsewhere, in gray-walled, tube-lighted offices across the river, and in a small office lined with maps in the basement of the White House.

At the end of dinner, Diana called to Jack in high spirits, "Let's not divide, Jadi," and before he could object, she rose, taking her father and Bill Millard each by a hand and leading them to the long drawing room which faced the Potomac. Jack did his best to conceal his irritation at this maneuver, as he preferred the custom of detaining the gentlemen at the table for brandy and cigars while the ladies went off to be ladies by themselves.

"God, how soon can I get out of this?" muttered George to his daughter.

"A little while longer, Pappy. I've told everybody you have to catch a plane at four in the morning. They'll understand. I'll go up with you for a few minutes when it's time."

"Our grass on the ranches is dry as matchsticks," said the Washington hostess. "We have to watch like hawks for a spark. I wouldn't be here if I didn't feel it my duty—so much to do socially for the Allied missions who are in town."

"How was the party?" Jack asked Millard.

"What party?"

"This evening, before dinner, the Halifaxes. Weren't you there?"

"No. It was only for the supply people, war-production men from Britain who came over by bomber."

"Oh." Jack was visibly relieved. That explained the Scanlons. No snub.

Marjorie drew George to a small remote sofa.

"Well, my dear"—lifting her little coffee cup—"here's bon voyage and a safe return, whenever."

Try as he might to disguise it, George could not entirely mask the heightened feeling which held him on the eve of the unknown. He saw Marjorie, really looked at her, for the first time in years, and felt stir again something of the response so urgent so long ago. Her beauty was now mature, but no less moving for that, now that he saw her again. The hazy smile with which she disguised her sharpness of mind and the worldliness of her wit gave a mellow pungency to her nature. To this was now added a sense, unspoken but powerful, of the dearness of life itself as she gazed at George, who was headed for the common hazard of the war. Long recovered from the brief, driven passion of their younger days, they had entered the calm waters of harbored friendship, and in some ways the affection which expressed this was more enfolding than the reckless old love.

"Keep an eye on my child, will you?" said George.

"If she'll let me. I have a feeling that she's bent on managing her own struggle as a matter of pride."

"Struggle?"

"To hold on to what she feels for Jack."

[69]

"She does feel something?"

"Good God, yes. But if I know Jack, his real moments are rather widely spaced. Those are what she loves."

"I've given up trying to understand the whole thing," said George.

"It was—or something like it—was inevitable."

"What d'you mean?"

"Her marrying an older man."

"Why?"

"Oh, my dear"— as though this had to be explained to him of all people.

"No, really."

She shrugged. How could she tell him? He had enough on his mind, without listening to an opinion, given without judgment, that Diana's exclusive younger life with him had disposed her away from younger men, and drawn her to a man of settled years.

She said, "I keep thinking there might be a child, which would shift so many balances in the right direction."

"I've been hoping for it, too."

"*Alors, il est capable?*"

"How should I know? Diny and I have never spoken of the matter."

Marjorie sighed and slowly passed her velvety hands over her bosom. The gesture spoke of her own fulfillment through her children, now grown, and her kinship with all women. There was so much voluptuous satisfaction in this that George was sharply reminded of the empty places in his own life. He stood up abruptly, leaned down to kiss her cheek to say goodbye, and went to find Diana, who was working to extract merriment, however bleak, from William Millard, who was tall, sandy in color, with pale eyes behind silver-rimmed glasses, and who had made such a habit of impassiveness in his law practice that it was his fixed air at all times. His wife Cecile, whose high laugh could be heard across any room, made a point of providing animation for them both.

"I must say good night," said George.

"I'll see you to your room, Pappy," said Diana. "Excuse me, Mr Secretary, my father leaves before dawn. I have one or two things for him to take along. I'll be down again in a moment."

Upstairs, they stood silent in a fierce embrace for a long moment, shutting away doubts, and imploring blind powers for safekeeping. With another separation upon them, they mutely confessed and mourned their earlier one. There was nothing else of importance to make known to each other. Diana freed herself, looked at his packed but open suitcase, made sure her photograph in its little leather case was tucked under his shirts, and smiled at the neckties he had packed.

"You won't be needing these, will you?"

"I suppose not. Pull them out. I'm to be commissioned and in uniform as soon as I reach the OTC. I'll telephone when I can. It will be complicated enough, though I've had my physical here."

"Flying colors?"

"Fiddle."

"—Ah, Pappy, darling, let's not go on being silly and brave."

"Goodbye, my kiddy. Go on downstairs, now. Don't get up in the morning if you hear the car coming for me. We have to do like the millions, and accept the cutoff."

They kissed, he took her to his door, saw her out, and shut it. She was alone. Shaking her head against the knowledge of it, she took a deep breath, arranged her face, and returned to the warmly lit, pleasantly noisy room of her party.

Jack came forward. "Where is George? He didn't say goodbye to me. I'll run up and see him for a moment."

Diana held his arm. "No, don't, don't. He said to tell you goodbye, with fondest thanks, he really is tired, and yet too keyed up for goodbyes. Do go over and amuse Mrs General, who looks a little woebegone."

"Very well, if you think it—"

"I do."

Gregory Blaine was the one person in the room she would gladly talk to. He knew it and came to her. Leaving her feelings alone, and their reason, he said, "I've been having an idea."

"Yes?"

He didn't know in full detail yet about his Washington assignment, but he assumed he would have an office, a staff, and an assistant, and if she was free of other duties, and so inclined, do you suppose she might be interested to work for him? Everybody was doing *something*. He was to be in Washington for three days each week. He would need someone to keep an eye on things for him every day, and especially on those days when he was in his New York publishing house.

"Let's go to war together," he said.

She was grateful for his light tone. She wondered how he had thought to touch on a concern which had troubled her—to do something useful which would also in a sense liberate her.

"I would have to ask Jack, but yes, I would so much like to join you."

"You have to *ask* him?"

"Oh, Greg, you know him. Every decision 'made jointly.' "

"Does *he* ask *you*?"

"Let's say I am always informed."

They laughed together, having completed a composite portrait of Jack.

When asked the next day, Jack said, "I quite understand your wish to serve in some way. Do you think you can do it, and manage the house and all our engagements? My work, so much of it, is necessarily social, you know. Can you see to it, and also do a full-time job with Gregory?" His tone grew impatient. "He *is* such a busybody! Can't he leave anyone alone? Why should he come here to dine and end by upsetting you with this idea?"

"He had no such intention. He was doing me a kindness, and just working at his job."

But Jack knew this was an effort to give Diana a purpose beyond dressing his life. Since the effort was tied to the war, he could not very well dismiss it.

"Very well, Jadi," he said, caving in with one of his sudden radiant amusements at the dear wrongheadedness of women, "let's give it a try, and if it doesn't work out, you'll be the first to tell me."

He blinked both eyes at her with his smile.

❋

Within a month, Gregory Blaine had his Washington staff assembled and running. Diana worked under her maiden name, was paid like any other secretary, kept stricter hours than the others because she was Blaine's personal assistant, and was in charge of the office in his absence. Technical workers saw to the details of selecting books (to be reproduced in small format, paper-covered, in the millions of copies) and shipping them overseas to American servicemen and -women everywhere. Once launched, her work was unvaried. The days, the months, and, in due course, the years of the war seemed outside the measurement of time. Stages were marked by news of defeats—many defeats at first, and then by victories as the grand waves of energy made by the nation began to reach, and to grow, and to overflow with terrific power the enemy forces everywhere. Without speaking of it, there was a separate satisfaction for Diana in doing what she did as an anonymous individual unit of that energy; and tired as she might be by endless repetition and routine, and by the necessities of transforming herself after work into Jack's proper hostess, all grace, beauty, and animation, she felt equal to her two jobs, grateful for them both, for different reasons.

She often went to lunch with Gregory when his work allowed. They both knew that he wanted them to become lovers, and that to her it was out of the question. Actually the idea was vaguely attractive to her; his short, heavy body and his fleshy face with its penetrating eyes in their seeking gaze took on, for her, an appeal because they reflected so much experience of life—many varieties of life. It was something of a marvel, in her thought, that so ungainly a body and so coarse a face should contain a spirit so intuitive and sensitive. She felt that he knew her through and through, and desired of her more than he could see. She knew his reputation as a man who had a complete need of women, not only physically, but temperamentally—their turns of mind, their sensual chemistries of body, their appetites for the private theater of love as a game, and for the zest of mutual need. When he spoke of women his eyes watered slightly, and his heavy lips flattened against his teeth in the effect of preparing to taste.

One day he said to her at lunch, "The war is maddening, you know, in one way not much talked about."

"What is that?"

"The thing that is in the air everywhere—the frankly erotic aspect of it."

"Erotic? The war?"

"I mean actually the very sexual thing that is alive everywhere you look. You can't avoid seeing it, it gets in your own mind, you can almost smell it. Haven't you noticed?"

"How?"

"The men in uniform are twice the men they were before. The women with them everywhere rub up against this in every conceivable way. They don't care who's looking. They can't stay apart. It's in the very way every man in uniform looks at every woman he sees. They don't just kiss—they try to get under each other's very skins. Haven't you felt it?"

She had not considered it; but Gregory made her think of little incidents she had seen and to which she had now and then given a silent blessing, with a dim ache at heart. He saw that she was—in all but the technical sense—virginal. His long intimacy with Jack, and his own train of experiences had told him what her marriage lacked. He now took urgent pleasure in bringing ideas of sex into his conversation with Diana even as he knew nothing would come of it with her, as it would if he were playing on frank purposes with another woman.

"Yes, I have felt it," she said, "but I haven't given much thought to it. I just suppose men displaced are lonely."

"But the girls!" exclaimed Gregory. "They're as hungry as the soldiers, the sailors. —You know of course what's at the far end of it all."

"Not really."

"It's death. War devours. Men are going to die by the million. Women are going to lose them. Children must replace the lost. There is a great drive to have love, life, all of it, anyhow, anywhere, in the face of what will come when men go to war. It's a blind drive. Men are going to take lives and lose their own. They must replenish what they destroy. God! There is something blindly beautiful about it. Sometimes I can hardly watch a G.I. or a blue-jacket and their girls kissing in public, I get all bothered, if you know what I mean, wanting to be part of the kissing."

It was Gregory being more than himself. She felt a blush come hotly to her face for the summons of love he invoked. He reached across the table and took her hand and she felt his hand shaking before he let go.

"Yes," she said, steadying her voice, "yes, of course, I see what you mean."

It was, he saw, all that she was going to say about it.

But, alone, she saw with Gregory's eyes moments of wartime love in Washington. Giving it the stir of emotion which he had made known to her, she looked in contrast upon her own life.

One August night, late, when work kept her at her office (Jack telephoned every half hour to ask when on earth she was coming home, he had people there, they needed her), she could not find a taxi and was obliged to climb wearily into a bus on Sixteenth Street. The night was so hot that exhaust from the buses and cars strung itself out in the air and showed foggy around the street lamps. On a corner in a cone of heavy light three people were standing close together. Something had set them off laughing. It seemed as if they couldn't stop. One of the three—they were two sailors and a girl—wheezed his laugh in a comical way he had and the sound of it made the others laugh all the harder, until they thought they would die—especially the girl. The bus was waiting for a green light. Diana—she thought of how Gregory had put it—felt herself almost physically pulled toward the three on the sidewalk, for their youth, their trifling rapture, the sense of how they lived in each other's sensation. The girl was hanging on the arm of one of the two, laughing herself right into him, it seemed, by the way he must have felt her touch. A woman in a seat behind Diana said to her husband, "Look at those two sailors and that girl laughing like idiots." She paused, feeling perhaps what Diana felt, longing and solitary. Then she added, "Aren't they sweet, laughing like that, with this war going on. I don't suppose anybody knows *where* they'll"—and then she was shocked into silence by the other end of her vision. In a moment the bus ground ahead up the hot dark sweet sticky street. Diana had a sensation like a silent cry in her breast which said, *Let them be safe, let their moment of life be longer, they do not even think of what could be . . .*

When she reached The Riverpoint Manor, Jack's guests were still there. Her duty was plain—she even welcomed it for fear of falling into a morbid concern about which she could do nothing; and though she was tired and felt she must look almost haggard, she played "Jadi" with Jack before his guests so successfully that they were suddenly inspired to stay another hour or two, talking politics, war strategy, Georgetown gossip, and trying their best to measure up to Diana's animation and charm. One or two looked at Jack as if to discover how he had captured this very special woman, and grudgingly granted him his right to the air of patronizing content with which he treated her, calling her Jadi as a signal of devotion so deep that it could make a farce of itself in front of others.

But Diana's run of thought would not leave her alone. Love. Public love was everywhere she looked, now. It had appeared as a new sort of pride, and always her thought was completed by the awareness that young men in the land had made a deal with death; had put on the uniform of the armed forces like covers upon a contract. It was amazing how great a new dimension of health appeared. In place of the civilian's apologetic exercise or occupational pallor, there appeared in the soldier or the sailor a ruddy frankness of well-being. They walked with possessive and challenging ease along the streets. The uniform, designed for efficiency, had dramatic suitability to the body; and in addition to proclaiming that here were flesh and blood ready to be spent in battle, the uniform in unintentional ways revealed, accentuated, masculine splendor. Women saw; Diana saw; and understood and were proud of what they felt in return. Over all hovered the angel of the future, men's and women's conscious longings and dim duties to their species, for propagation and safety to spite the vast strides which death was making.

Walking to work one morning, Diana saw beneath the monument of Admiral Farragut—gray metal streaked with weather in the small park by the Army and Navy Club—a soldier and his girl reclining on the grass. The light from the sultry Washington sky was pearly—gray with pale reflections from grass and cloud, green and rose, softened by the summer air, close and hot. To her eye, the two of them had the pose of heroic loveliness. The classical painters of gods and goddesses—Mars and Venus—in the revealing raiment of love came to her memory; and the United States soldier in his khakis wrinkled from the hot day, and the girl in the wash dress, were lost to each other in attitudes of love. The soldier— thought and the little distance made him a boy in Diana's view—lay on his back with his head on the lap of the girl. Her legs were doubled back sideways. She was leaning down over his face looking into his eyes. His arms were crossed on his breast and he held her hands across his shoulders. His columnar legs were sprawled on the wilting grass. In the midst of the people who toiled along the walks in the heat, the soldier and his girl were unaware of anyone else. By the right of their overpowering duty they gave to the streets and the passing eye the love which in peacetime would have been theirs privately. Like a raffish tag to the immemorial tableau they made, the girl had on her head, at a rakish angle, as she bent over his face, the soldier's cap. "Like a claim," said Diana to herself, "like their being one and the same person." *Who had ever wanted, or would ever want, as much of her?* she asked herself. She shook her head against the unanswered distraction and walked faster to her office and the saving trivia of her day.

※

Because of the imposed irregularity of their working hours, Jack said, they should have their separate bedroom apartments. The Riverpoint Manor was spacious—there were several suites on the second floor. They could awake and go, or return and sleep, without disturbing each other. And of course, as he put it, there was nothing to prevent their coming together for a midnight chat, if either should happen to think of it. As often as their duties allowed, he believed, they must meet for breakfast in the semicircular glass annex to the dining room overlooking the river.

When she came in he was already immersed in his morning papers, where, reading with the speed of light, as he often said, he marked with a red pencil those items devoted to Great Britain which later might provide matter for his daily staff meetings in Pennsylvania Avenue. She would go and kiss his cheek, which he offered without losing his place. Presently he would look at his thin vest watch, rub the crystal with his thumb, exclaim at how nearly late he was going to be, and hurry smartly off with his marked pages to his waiting official limousine. Glancing after him, she thought he had never seemed so happy, and—she mentally noted— "I so full of care," though she was determined that nobody should be given a chance to notice this.

For different reasons, the Wentworths were pleased that they could ask Billy and Cecile Millard if they might bring along a young naval officer who was briefly in Washington from sea duty on a mission for his chief who commanded a carrier task force in the Pacific.

"How did you find us?" asked Diana on the telephone.

Lieutenant Debler replied, "I'm in Naval Intelligence, you know. We have our little connections here and there."

Diana laughed. "Jack says the upper Secretaries have a network of their own. —Anyway, I'm glad to hear from you. Will you be in town for long?"

"Only a very few days. Might we say hello? How is your father?"

"Running all over the place, I gather, with a very active general. Would you like to go to a party with us this evening? My husband's chief and his wife are having a party. I know they'd be glad to have us bring you."

It happened that Howard Debler was the only naval officer there that evening—other uniforms were those of the United States and British armies. It was not a large dinner party, but Cecile Millard marshaled it with her alert eye and her fixed idea of each guest's most useful interest.

When all came upstairs to the drawing room after dinner, Jack detained Howard in an unoccupied corner to ask questions with so much energy that Howard was hardly able to answer one before another came. They were standing with their brandy glasses and Jack's excellent cigar. Howard now and then looked beyond as though hoping to join other guests—Diana. But Jack, with rapid little steps in place, kept turning him around to face him, claiming his whole attention. Cecile Millard saw them from across the room, enjoying her own foregone conclusions. Diana, on an inner sigh, observed that Jack was spinning out all his flattering interest, and that Howard, looming above him, and looking down at him with a friendly, inattentive smile, was doing his best to be polite while trapped.

"How I envy you that most becoming of all service uniforms," said Jack. "I'd be in one myself but a certain Squire in the White House had other plans for me and here I am, stuck in the civilian nightmare. —Tell me, just what do you do in Naval Intelligence? My wife says she knows you, and that you are attached to the staff of my friend Admiral McGarrity; in fact, I took his house when he was ordered to San Diego to go to sea."

"I handle the decodes from Pearl when we are at sea, and I prepare the admiral's daily log of—"

"But where did you get all that highly technical training, it must be such a—"

"At Newport. It's quite different from anything I ever did before, but they thought that as a writer I—"

"Writer: how simply too perfect." Jack made his little steps to turn Howard away from the murmur of the party. "What do you write?"

"History. I taught history before the—"

"—war. Yes, and have you seen action in the Pacific?"

"Oh yes."

Jack's necessity to look up to Howard gave him a worshipful aspect, and Diana knew how he could make his eyes spark with interest, his hard black gaze shifting from Howard's eye to eye, his lips moist with engaged breath, and his shoulders a trifle lifted.

"Action: tell me:"

"Oh, my duty often takes me on flights from the flagship—it's a carrier—"

"Yes, I know, the *Concord*, but I'll never breathe the name to a soul. You mean you flew, observing fleet action against the enemy, or just reconnaissance, or what? How too fascinating. How can we ever do enough for you chaps! —Do you like flying?"

"Hate it. I'm a land-bound Westerner."

"But you go, and *do,* and you know?"—a little jig of possession— "it's fellows like you who confirm my conviction that we are going to win this war."

"I don't think many of us ever doubted it," replied Howard. He turned. "Oh, great. Here comes your wife."

Jack was deprived, but he honored all the graces, and greeted Diana.

"Jadi, my pet, this rangy old sea-going cowboy has been telling me the most fascinating—"

Diana said, "Let's take him to the others and let him forget the war."

Jack made a comic, forgiving face at Howard, as if to say that there was a woman for you, always concerned with the social aspect of the world, while men did the hard and hazardous work, out over lonely waters where life and death were like the very weather. (*Lonely Waters?* thought Jack, was this the germ, and the title, of a war play he would write about the Navy? In his habit, he quickly entered the words in his little gold-edged pocket notebook.)

They joined the Millards at the fireplace, where Jack once again gave Howard his endorsement, and they all saw that the tall, hardy man in blue and gold showed none of the excited gratitude so ardently hoped for. Because the facts of the matter made it necessary, Diana went to Jack's side and put her arm through his and stood by him.

The party shifted. Soon Cecile Millard had Diana to herself for a few moments. Someone once said that Cecile Millard was born with a smile which never left her face even when she was not being managerial, and especially when she exercised her talent for "understanding." She was a rounded woman, with an apple-like face that shone with health and looked solid in its fixed expression. Her pale eyes were halved by lids that slanted toward their outer corners.

"He's a very nice man, your Navy friend," she said. "Jack seems to have one of his instant crushes on him. Oh, Diny, we do think it absolutely beautiful, the way you run your life. I-mean, that dear combination of dignity and charm in the way you carry on no matter what."

Her smiling face could be so full of tolerance that those without her zest for "entering into people"—as she put it—sometimes felt like strangling her.

"We?" said Diana. "What do you mean by *we*, and what is so special about how I make my life?"

Cecile slowly closed and opened her half-lids.

"Oh, Diny darling, you don't have to evade with me. You're miserable."

"Good God, Cecile, what nonsense. Of course I'm not."

"No, I understand," said Cecile tenderly. "You needn't pretend with me. We don't have to identify anything you have never talked about and I expect never will. It's only that we—but if that offends you I'll say *I*—think it a good thing to speak out when there is something to admire in those we love. I-mean, people don't tell people often enough when they have reason to think somebody is a special human being."

"Good Lord, there's nothing special about me," protested Diana, with a little beat of heart which told her in annoyance that she knew well enough what Cecile was edging toward.

Cecile leaned back in her dove-silk sofa cushions and looked aside as though nothing was on her mind but the quiet luxury of her sitting room. She said to the air, "Well, I only hope Jack knows how lucky he is. There aren't many women, young, glorious-looking, covered with the hungry stares of countless other men, who could be so flawless in your situation." She hurried to turn and say, "But of course, Jack is so distinguished, so world-polished, older of course, and you meet his terms with such tact, I-mean, and Billy says he *is* superb at the Department."

Diana stood up. "I must be going," she said. "Do, both of us, forget this odd conversation, or you'll make me self-conscious every time we meet."

"As you like, dear Diny, not another word, but you can always be sure of my fond understanding, and so can Jack, but of course he'd never notice. Men never think, as we do, do they, about what others think of them. I-mean, perhaps Jack does, in his difference from run-of-the-mill men."

"He *is* special," said Diana in accents of pride, but with hidden anger that Cecile, in a mastery of indirection, had made her point, to no good purpose.

Assistant Secretary Millard came to Diana and said, "You may hate me for it, but I've just asked Jack to substitute for me on a trip beginning tomorrow—speeches out West, where they never seem to know just *what* Washington is doing for the war. You won't mind? Duty, and the rest."

Jack joined them and sighed comically. "A full day's flight to San Francisco on one of those tin egg-beaters. Billy is a slave driver."

They all four laughed like intimate friends on the best of terms.
"Collect your sailor," said Jack to Diana. "We'll drop him off at his hotel on our way home. I'll have to pack tonight."

At the door of the Hay-Adams, Howard said, "Will I see you again? I'm off in a few days."

"And I'm off first thing tomorrow," said Jack. "—Diny, why don't you give him a bite of dinner at home tomorrow or next day?"

It was arranged.

At home, Jack said, "Good night, Diny, I'll be leaving early, I won't wake you, I'll call you from California. Kiss."

"Good night, and goodbye, Jack. Be careful."

They smiled at each other, and parted.

Diana felt tired. She thought there was nothing she'd rather have than a week or so of vacant evenings, but Jack had committed her to the visiting Navy man. Her early sense of her husband returned to her with a rush, and she felt protective, and she said silently, *Oh, don't let him be hurt.*

❧

When Paco brought Howard into the crimson library at The Riverpoint Manor, Diana was amused, even flattered, that his suntanned face seemed to be darkened by a blush, though why, she could not imagine. His dark eyes were almost closed by a smile so broad that his cheeks rose up high. After they had shaken hands and sat down, his hands on his knees looked like boluses on tree limbs.

"My oh my," he said in his mild voice, "you do live in a magnificent house."

"I think it almost shameful," replied Diana, "in wartime, but my husband had to take what he could find, and it turned out to be too much instead of too little. I must add that he became used to it fast enough. —So did I," she added, for fear of sounding disloyal.

"I could use it myself," said Howard. "I'd write a different book in every room, all at the same time. To have a library like this, or your father's in Dorchester!"

Everything about Howard was far removed from the wartime atmosphere of Washington, with its grotesque mingling of the gravely fateful with hurrying self-importance. Over dinner they disposed of affairs in the foreground, and returned to the library.

"Have you dared think about your own Mexican War?" she asked.

He stood up and locked his hands behind him and paced back and forth, giving physical form to his long-repressed excitement. He made her think, with amusement, of an actor playing a country lawyer in front of a jury box, except that here there was no artifice.

"Well, sir," he said, "I'll confess: I stole a few hours from my mission here to sidle off to the National Archives for a look-see. I got drunk just on the catalogues, and I asked to see a handful of documents. Now, I'm not a mystical animal, or a philosophical one, but when I handle the actual papers of the men long dead whose actions I'm out to recapture, two remarkable things happen to me. One is, I begin to feel their humanity, and the other is, I begin in a greater degree to observe and feel the humanity of people around me *today*."

"Men in actual combat," she murmured.

"There. Yes. Lord, to actually face the meaning of *abstract policy* having power over flesh and blood, bodies like my own, the living, obedient young men I command every day, and the same young men perhaps torn and dying and dead in the next hours or days. If I don't get the sense of this, living men, in my big frame of the

[85]

Mexicans and Americans of a century ago when I come back to write what they did, I won't have much of a book. —I could talk for hours:" *Looking at her,* he meant: because it was she who listened.

He made her see the immensity of the northern lands of Mexico and the present United States Southwest, and how they were once all one. The great Gulf of Mexico; the fateful border of the Rio Grande; the endless flat lands of mesquite brush and cactus; the vast deserts to the south where mountains rose and fell in profiles like lines of distant, unheard music; the white and pink, blue and earth-colored Mexican villages where armies ebbed and flowed and families were victims; the righteousness that gave energy to both sides of the war . . .

"You must think you're in a lecture hall. I get carried away."

"But so do I, when there is that much passion in anyone's work!"

"Mrs Wentworth," he said, standing up, "I swear this has been the best evening I've had since I had to change my clothes for the duration. I do thank you."

She brought matters off their high plane and asked, "Have you a publisher?"

"Lord no. My first book went to a university press. I'll go after another someday."

"It wouldn't do any harm to discuss your work with a publisher —a first-rate man, a man I work with, who publishes my husband's work. Would you like to see him while you're here?"

"I would and I wouldn't. It's a danger to promise anything not yet written, or try to tell about the formless marvels I feel. I don't know. Maybe."

"My boss here"—and she told him about the old and distinguished firm of Adam and Blaine, and its head, Gregory Blaine. She could arrange a meeting for day after tomorrow, when Mr Blaine would be in town. "Perhaps without any binding commitment, it might be a comfortable thing to think about when you're back at sea, and you may need something to look forward to, now and then."

He thought about it with his thumb knuckle against his teeth for a long moment, and then, in one of his jolts, straightened up and agreed. He told her where to leave a message for him in the Navy Department, said good night, and called her "ma'am," which he made to sound pleasantly archaic rather than self-consciously regional.

Two days later Gregory came into her office and said, "Your friend has the makings of a good, maybe a great, book. I offered him a contract."

"He must have been eloquent."

"He was, in a selfless way. Not selling anything. The subject, the country of it, the personalities, are really alive in him. But he refused a contract. I then proposed an option for a first look. Oh, he said, that wasn't necessary, he'd just let me see it before anyone else. I don't quite know why, after thirty years of scrambling after authors, a notoriously shifty crew, but I took him at his word."

"I think you can believe him."

Lieutenant Debler telephoned Diana that evening to say goodbye —he was leaving at midnight to spend a week's leave at his mother's home in Texas.

"How did you feel about Gregory Blaine?" she asked.

"I'd trust him anywhere. He didn't ask a single question too much, nor did he interrupt, nor did he press me about any business ideas."

"He liked what you talked about."

"Well."

"Goodbye, and all good fortune."

He felt a sudden distance in her voice.

"Thank you. Goodbye, Mrs Wentworth."

As she rang off, she was glad—and felt a little treasonable about it—that Jack was not at home during Lieutenant Debler's first evening in Washington.

※

After a shaky flight in an old C-47 which landed for local military traffic many times after leaving Washington, Howard arrived in West Texas. On the vast plains again, he felt homesick for them while looking at them. He was their son, and to him they were anything but monotonous in their subtleties of color and distance. Their history, of which his family was a part, had given him his vocation. He was elated and looked forward to driving in a rented car to spend a week in the house at Grand Plains where he grew up.

Toward the end of his drive he saw with familiar feeling the distant signs of his home town. His highway converged parallel to the tracks of the Santa Fe Railroad. The tracks would go into town alongside his highway. Late in the day, long blades of light fell across the level plains and cast shadows from signal towers, a windmill of an outlying farm, presently the struts of the municipal water tower, and then the tank where the trains paused to take on water before pulling into the little town. Houses grew distinct. Those that were white gleamed against the dull gold of the prairie.

But why was it, he asked, that his spirit sank a little every time he returned home? Because a journey was ending? Because of memories so dim that only sensations remained of them, not their facts? Because, perhaps, he had escaped into another life and in doing so had become false to the simple terms of his beginning?

No such notions must ever show when he met his mother Clara Vetchison Debler where she lived alone in the square high house in which he was born. Her greeting would show a hint of general reproach, assumed to conceal a longing so great for his permanent return that neither of them could ever speak of it.

He pulled into the driveway alongside the old white house, shut off his engine, and sat for a moment to hear whether the side door would be unchained and opened, to her dry-voiced greeting. But there was silence, and with guilty relief he jumped out and ran up the front steps, unlocked the door and looked for, and found, a note which his mother, as always, had left on the narrow hall table. Whenever she left the house, she told where she had gone, what for, and gave any messages, in case, in her absence, someone should come home, no matter from how far away, or after how long a time.

"I am out leaving a few things," said the note, "here and there, across town. Will stop at the church hall on the way back, choir schedules. Fresh apple pie in pantry. Only got your telegram this morning. Your mail is on your desk upstairs."

He went up to his workroom, which occupied the second story of a wide square tower at the side of the house. The tower was an addition built as a lookout by his grandfather Major Vetchison (a courtesy title), who had lived through Indian threats as a boy, and had never forgotten the heart-stopping Pawnee whistle sounding at night. The threats were long over when the tower was built, but it was a monument to memory.

In the study, Howard sighed over evidences of his mother's busy efforts at "thoughtfulness" on behalf of his comfort. He regretted attempts by anybody to penetrate into his private workplace. He was not interested in neatness. If papers were disorderly, if books lay on the floor, he wanted always to find them as he had left them, for he knew where everything was in that room. As a principle, he did not object to flowers in pots, but if geraniums were set in a row on the Major's windowsill, it meant that he must water them and pluck away yellowed leaves while he occupied his room, which nobody was allowed to enter, and therefore, while he was away, that his mother must tend the plants, and so have the freedom of his cell. She liked to place his reading chair at a certain angle to the window, to give him better light to read by. He preferred it another way, handy to a window bench where he could prop up his legs while reading.

He went now and restored the chair to his own angle. He felt the earth in the flowerpots—freshly dampened. On his desk everything was now aligned at right angles and the whole top was covered by a transparent plastic sheet. He threw it off. At the portrait of his mother suggested by such details he began to laugh and shake his head. He was an ungrateful son. She must be as she was—but so must he be himself. He knew her hunger to be needed, most of all by him.

All I have left—this was the sustaining principle of Clara Debler's life ever since the death of her husband when her son Howard was a small boy, and it was Howard whom she meant by her thought. For all her time remaining, she had put away the idea of ever marrying again; though fugitive memories of her young married life returned at times to make her pale with desire and loss; rigid with determination to forget "all that," not only on her own behalf, but on that of others, including her son. As she so often reminded her circle of friends in Grand Plains, he was a model son. Her eyes would grow fierce and hazy at the marvel of how she, such a small, though always active, woman, could have borne so tall a man with a habit of such long thoughts and deliberate actions. Now and then she could read almost spiteful inquiry in the faces of certain friends: if he was such a model son, how did it happen that he lived far away, teaching at Austin, and even on his visits home, that he was so remote from all that Grand Plains meant to her? With her delicate gesture of feeling with thumb and third finger for drops of saliva at the corners of her mouth, she forgivingly let it be known that his privacy must be protected; he deserved the exclusiveness of celebrity, for how many other persons in that end of Texas had published an important history book? However, she was glad to report where he went when absent. No matter how busy he was elsewhere, traveling, studying, England, France, Spain, Italy, Mexico, she would show the picture side of his postcards. In the presence of strangers, she referred to him as Doctor Debler.

It was for his sake, she told herself sternly, that she kept herself so active. She would not have him thinking that she just sat around, luxuriating in her loneliness. Never.

Lord knew—everyone knew—she had enough to occupy her, beginning with the big, square, two-story house with its tower, and its portico of Doric pillars, where she had been born. In its turns it had been expanded from her grandfather's and father's lonely cabin, built before Grand Plains was even a village, out on the Staked Plains soon after Texan independence. Now strangers were often driven slowly past the old Vetchison place because it was part of Panhandle history, for President Lamar had once spent a night there expecting a dispatch from the expedition he had sent against Santa Fe in 1841. It never came, and the president moved on, returning to Austin, but not without leaving his signature, *Mirabeau B. Lamar*, on the inside of the front door, a memento now covered by glass framed in gold molding.

But as though housekeeping were all: she was a member of two ladies' clubs, she played the organ at the First Church of Christ Redeemer, and only she in all Grand Plains subscribed to *The Sunday New York Times*, which with her Bible studies, and the novels of Retha Glenn McCloud coming one every two years in a continuing saga about the Confederacy, "took care," as she said, of her reading. People envied her energetic kindness. Well: her local causes: her days full of rapid visits to one house after another in her old car (named Bessie after a patient buggy mare long vanished), usually to deliver a small gift, or a piece of news, or sensible sympathy for misfortune, illness, or death. In the Sunday *Times* she found matter to interest different friends every week, and she took out clippings, which she delivered with an air of informing a public.

"Wonderful, how Clara *keeps up*," they said, meaning her interest in the affairs of the worlds of music, books, New York society, Washington, and all. The years bestowed on her, if on anyone, they agreed, the position of the leading lady of Grand Plains. The best of it was that her position had nothing to do with money (they all knew she had just evenly enough of that), or show, or anything, not even her ancestral claim, but simply her own way of going about life.

When Clara Debler drove up to her house, which she herself thought of as *The Old Vetchison Place*, and saw Howard's car at the side, she felt a throb in her breast and put her hands over it for a moment. Her joy was so full that when she came in, to find him running down the stairs to greet her, she said, snappishly, "You might have let me know sooner when you were coming home!"

He laughed, leaning down to hold her. From the kitchen her large gray-and-white cat came bounding, and then stopped three feet short of his mistress, sat down, and began to lick his right forepaw instead of answering her call for a caress. His name was Nicodemus, because, as she could explain, "he often comes up the back stairs at nighttime: John III: 2."

"It's good to be home," said Howard.

"I should hope so. What are you up to now?"

"I have six whole days left, and I'm going to spend them in the tower with my papers. I hope you haven't told anybody I was coming home."

"Of course I have told them. You don't come home off that ocean every other day. But if you won't see people, then you shan't, and I'll take care of that. —My, you're looking well. Isn't it dreadful: war agrees with men. —What's it like?"

"Regular hours, except when we're being bombed," he said, hoping to sound funny.

"I don't want to hear about it if I want to sleep nights. —Do you ever see land?"

"We're ashore now and then, in Hawaii."

"Is it all that they say?"

"How?"

"Oh, those half-naked women, snaking their arms around and pushing their hips."

"Why, Mother:"

"Oh, I've seen them in the picture shows."

She looked earnestly at him to read any evidence of "women" in his expression.

He laughed; but he knew her abiding concern. When would he ever marry and give grandchildren to her—"grandbabies" as she would say in the local idiom—while she was still on this earth to enjoy them and love the future for them? On the other hand, she feared what she half knew or suspected about his "seeing" women otherwise, which he never talked about. But from time to time there had been long series of letters in envelopes with feminine writing, and long-distance calls, and she thought what she thought.

"Many of our young sailors," he said, "get married ashore, and then have to leave their wives for months, years, whatever. Then they come home to strangers. Wartime is no time for that."

"Well, so long's you're happy," she said, in her habit of elliptical remarks from which meaning could depart in any direction. "Come sit with me on the sun porch. I'm making a chase-ball for Nicodemus. He needs something to do while I'm out of the house."

She had a shoe box marked *Pieces of String Too Short to Use.*

"But you see?" she said, holding up two four-inch lengths of common white string, "they were worth saving after all."

She tied them together, and took from the box other lengths already joined, and began to wrap them around a neatly rounded ball built up by other knotted bits of string.

Watching her contentedly, Howard mused about relative importances in the tasks of life, and awarded no priorities in his thought.

At the end of his week with his files and notes in the Major's lookout, he resumed his uniform and returned to San Diego to be flown over the Pacific to rejoin his ship.

�✾

As the year grew deeper, Jack Wentworth carried himself more and more as a man of official substance. Diana noticed that lately he seemed preoccupied, though always polite when reminded of her. He walked with his elbows slightly flared; spoke of his official self rather often as "we"; and in general appeared to be incubating some matter of serious importance. He was tender with Diana but in a kindly way more suitable to attractive children than to his beautiful and knowledgeable wife who so ably entertained his official guests. These were increasingly drawn from higher and higher circles, domestic and foreign, of wartime Washington.

Her interest in what was concerning him was suddenly trivialized by the appearance in town soon after Christmas of her father, Lieutenant Colonel George Macdonald of the Army Air Corps, after his final training in the Intelligence School at Harrisburg, Pennsylvania.

"—With *us* again, old man, your rooms are always ready," insisted Jack.

"No, thank you, but no," replied George firmly. "I am already established at the Army and Navy Club, it is more convenient for the things I have to do here in town, and you, here, are all too social for me. Quite often I have to work evenings. Besides, my chief, General Chittenden, is also staying at the club, and like all generals, he has the genial habit of sending for me at all hours, day or night, to agree with his formulated opinions."

But Diana knew it was because her father wanted to be free to see her alone, and she rejoiced. They were able to lunch and dine together now and then, quite as in the old days when each had the complete freedom and joy of the other's complicity in things great or small. When she asked him now what he would do next, he shook his head.

"Can't say, even to you," he replied.

"Something's up."

"Yes. Don't ask. I couldn't answer. You'll know afterward."

She stretched across the table and squeezed his hand.

"I love it. You'll win the war and let others tell me about it."

He was more serious than she'd ever known him. His ponderous discretion brought them, in some odd way, close together again— perhaps because heavy security always implied some extraordinary danger. They did their best to keep their exchanges light and happy, as in the time when the world existed for them only. He was looking particularly well; harder, thinner, more alive with purpose. She often sighed over how the war gave men in uniform a keener motive, as though they had long been waiting for it in the course of their long years of merely doing for their own selves, families, and fortunes. Later, when she thought about those days with George in Washington that winter, she remembered thinking how, unspoken behind all their fond and easy times, she felt that along with all his new knowledge and position, the handsome smartness of his presence as an officer, there was in him a newly tapped depth of humanity which she could recognize sometimes as much in what he did not say as in what he said; and in his eyes there was sometimes a confirmation of this as though the precious-ness of life had taken on a new, wide meaning where before he had been in his abrupt way limited in his sympathies to what concerned her, chiefly. If before she had thought him the model of a father and companion, she now saw in him a glimpse of men at large, and what let some become, when need be, strong beyond their actual powers, and great for the sake of others' need. There was no way in which she could speak of any of this to him; but she always thought he had some notion of what she was thinking about him. They had never been closer or happier.

And then one day in January he was gone.

When she telephoned the Army and Navy Club all they could tell her was that he had checked out.

And General Chittenden?

He had also left.

She spoke of the sudden departure to Jack.

"We all get used to these dashes," he said. "Don't trouble yourself about it, Jadi."

But he wore a dimmed smile of superior information as he returned to the clipboard and fountain pen which were almost always with him, not now to write stage dialogue, but to draft memorandums, speeches, policy papers, or critiques requested by the State Department or the Secretary of War, whose mantles he wore by proxy and found appropriate and becoming.

During the third night after George's departure Diana awoke to the sound of a cry—her own name, called out twice, and then three other words. She put her hands over her ears and then took them away to hear whether she had heard a dream or not. But the cry did not sound again, and she knew with dread that she had heard no dream—"Diny! Diny! This is Pappy!"

Oh, no, no, she told herself, with breath gone from around her heart. Her tears streamed now, she swept them with the backs of her hands, and sat up rocking with grief, in the darkness which was relieved by an almost imperceptible glow that came off the Potomac at night—a few lights of anchored vessels in midstream, a few more lights on the opposite shore. George was dead, her father was dead, killed somewhere in the war. She was as certain of it as of her own life. She had heard stories of such a visitation as hers—a soldier at the instant of his death called to where his love was. He was bright and clear before her mind as alone in her room—how glad she was for that!—she knew him again. She slept no more and by daylight she was resolved to keep the secret of that night. To whom could she speak of it? Jack would make comforting remarks, wise allusions to dream projections, dear little worries rarely borne out by events. She carried dread in her breast like a formless weight, and tried to show a good face to the world.

Hiding her strain, which Jack did not notice, she tried her best to remember that countless thousands across the nation must live, as she now did, with the common knowledge of what was happening to those in the service whom they loved. At last, one evening, Jack was able to tell her why, if she had noticed, he had been more preoccupied than usual in recent weeks—less open with her, more (pleasurably) harassed by his work and its secrets.

"I've been in on it from the start of the planning," he said, "so much to arrange by liaison with the Prime Minister's staff, on behalf of the White House. You can imagine the million and one details! Well: now I can tell you, for it will be on the late news tonight. The President has safely landed in Casablanca with his people for a conference with Winston—we all speak of him that way, though I've not yet met him. At first they thought I should go along, but in the end Bill Millard was asked for, and of course I am left to run the shop."

She was properly astonished.

"But how did the President get there? Those Nazi submarines— the Navy must have taken him with a whole fleet."

"No. He flew."

"Flew!"

"You can't imagine how eager and excited he was at the prospect. Flew. —Not directly, of course. The North Atlantic sea lanes would be dangerous even to aircraft. I suppose there's no harm telling you now that he left on the eleventh, going by train to Miami. He took a Pan-Am Clipper from there, a flying boat south to Trinidad, and then Belem, in Brazil, and then: the great turning point: out over the South Atlantic direct to West Africa at Bathurst on the Gambia. There his party transferred to an Army C-54 and flew direct over-, land to Casablanca. They got there this afternoon, January 14. We had the cables this morning—the time difference, you know. You've no idea how hard I've worked at all this for weeks. —In his small way, your humble spouse played his part in history through all this. Let's open some champagne to celebrate!"

"How marvelous, Jack. I'm proud of you."

"And not a single security leak! —You see now why I couldn't tell you anything, though I was bursting to."

But a security leak there had been.

Soon after lunch a day later, Jack telephoned to Diana at her office.

"Diana, dear, please arrange," he said, "to leave your office for the rest of the day, and go home. There is someone who wants to see you there at three o'clock. —I just looked out the window. It is snowing. I'll send a Department car for you."

"What is it? What is it?" Foreboding held her.

"I cannot say more now. Just be ready and go, my dear. I will be home early."

The snow was gray rather than white, in the light of the storm. She had hardly come home when another car drew up and a lady came to the door. Paco brought her at once to Diana in the library. He handed Diana a calling card. It read,

Mrs Amos Gardner Chittenden

and Diana went forward to greet her.

Mrs Chittenden was a woman of late middle age, with a pretty face high in color, and light gray eyes. Her hair was brushed with gray at the sides. She wore a small fur hat and a fur coat to match. She was smiling over momentous feeling. She held Diana's hand a trifle longer than expected.

"May I sit down, my dear:" she said in a habit of speech slightly hesitant but cultivated in tone.

"You are the general's wife?" asked Diana.

"Yes, child." She paused and then resolutely went on, "Commanders' wives have as many duties as their husbands. I have one here today. It is hard to do, but as I share in what I have to tell you, I hope I will be of help."

Diana's heart began to beat and she went white. She put her fingers against her mouth and nodded. Mrs Chittenden continued to speak.

She said that as soon as she was notified, she was flown in an Army plane from Fort Benning in Georgia, where her husband had been stationed for a year, to Washington, where she was fully briefed by the War Department. On the ninth, two days before the President left for Africa, her husband and his aide, Colonel Macdonald, who was also one of his planning officers, had been sent by courier plane to Africa with duplicate materials for use in the Casablanca conference. Their plane used the same route as that planned for the Presidential party. On the flight from Trinidad to Belem, over water, the pilot had had only a moment to send a message by radio before he was silenced. The message said that a German submarine had surfaced and was shelling the plane. Then there was no further word. Patrol planes and surface vessels had immediately been dispatched from bases in Brazil, but no trace of plane or survivors was found. It was the conclusion of the War Department that the enemy had received information of the Presidential flight and its route, had stationed the submarine on watch, with orders to destroy the official plane. The enemy plans worked perfectly except that they went into action one day early, mistaking the courier plane for the one they were waiting for. During the next days there was no claim by the Germans, as they awaited confirmation of their great kill before sending the news worldwide. When at last it was clear that the Supreme Command had safely reached Casablanca, the enemy made no announcement, and so far as they were concerned, the incident and its failure were closed. As for word of those lost, only their immediate families were to be informed, with orders not to make the news public until released by the authorities.

"There will be a telegram from the Adjutant General, for you," said Katherine Chittenden. "But I wanted to see you first, myself, and all others whom I can find, who belonged to the rest of the men lost. Come here, my dear, I know, I do, I know."

Diana let herself be taken into the arms of the older woman, a stranger, also in grief. For some moments they said little to each other. Katherine made the formless sounds of older wisdom in sorrow, and Diana wept as silently as possible. Katherine tightened her embrace as though to hold life itself together within its familiar mold.

Presently Diana was able to sit away and upright. She said, "You are kind to come—what you yourself must feel!"

"Amos and I were married for thirty-one years. I used to think it a century, we had done so much together, but now I feel it was more like an hour or two, for all that we planned to do, more."

Her eyes, too, shone with tears, but she held them back. She felt obliged to keep her composure for the sake of enduring the grief of those she felt responsible for.

"My father," said Diana in the breathy voice of a small child, "was with me for the last few days before he went. I know now he was more aware than I of some premonition. Now I know he was taking leave of me in case of—" She could not continue.

"Oh!" said Katherine, "if I could even count the number of times I have felt the same whenever my husband left me on some duty full of chance!"

She took Diana's hand. Diana said, "Three nights after I said goodbye to him, I was awakened by him, he was calling my name—"

"That was the night," said Katherine. "Then you knew."

"Tell me how to bear this," begged Diana.

"He meant much to you?"

"More than anyone in my life."

"Well, my dear child, all I can tell you is nothing new; but it is something true. You must do your best, later, when it will begin to seem possible, to be as strong in accepting this as he would want you to be."

Diana nodded. It was age-old advice, and she had no idea of how to observe it.

Katherine Chittenden rose. She said, "I will settle myself at home, when I can, out of the Army. If ever I can help you you must let me know, at Woods Hill, Wilmington. Goodbye, child. You are not alone. I am glad you have your husband to turn to. He arranged for me to see you."

She left.

※

In wartime Washington, classified information, especially if it conveyed bad news, traveled fast through privileged circles.

Dressing for a dinner party, Michael Scanlon said to his wife Marjorie, "I'm ready for you to do my tie."

She came and stood behind him, reaching across his heavy shoulders to handle the ends of his black tie as though to tie them for herself. She watched the operation in a mirror they both faced. She still took pleasure in his florid good looks—his blond gray hair setting off the deep black of his eyes in his heavy, ruddy face which retained some hint of the wondering boy who survived within the shrewd, successful banker.

"I don't know if I ought to speak of it, now, just before we go out," he said, as she worked at the tie, failed, and began again.

"Why not? What?"

"I mean, not to upset you."

"Oh, Mike, what *is* it:"

In the mirror, he gave her a keen, black look. She knew he had a thought behind a thought, and she laughed lightly at him.

"All right," he went on, "if you can take it. George Macdonald was killed in a plane shot down on the way to the Casablanca conference. He was with his boss, General Chittenden."

Her fingers faltered on the tie and she exclaimed, "Oh, damn: I'll have to start again. —Oh, poor, dear George. How dreadful. Truly dreadful."

Mike learned nothing from her response to the news. What had he expected her to do on hearing of the death of her old lover—if he was her old lover? Never having been certain, her husband had thought this time that she would somehow through shock betray the fact he had suspected for all those years. But she bit her lip in concentration as she worked once more at his tie, and now made a perfect bow and stood away with a little pat on his shoulders, and said, "Poor George, our dear old friend—poor Diana. She knows?"

"I suppose so."

"How did it happen?"

"I heard about it at lunch today at the Pentagon, General Somervell had some supply people in and asked me to represent the WPB. —The plane was shot down off Brazil by a German submarine, evidently gunning for the President, but they were a day early. —Did George mention anything to you about going off?"

"Heavens, how could he? I haven't seen him, or heard from him, naturally."

She knew what Mike was doing; her heart was beating fast. Her throat dried but she kept her voice steady. She leaned to the mirror for a last critical look. She took the topic away from her husband, and changed it, and said, "Oh, it's too dreadful. He was such a superb friend to us both. —But I can't help thinking at once of Diny."

"Yes," he said flatly. "She will feel it."

"Feel it! —I think it will perhaps change her life."

"How d'you mean."

"Oh, not immediately, but I think George had a restraining effect on her, and yet it was one she had to escape. Hence Jack Wentworth. But you know what *that* amounts to! No, I mean, as long as poor darling George was *there*, she had to make everything work in her own home. But sooner or later, I think, a change may come, just how, who can say. It's all numbness now, I'm sure. Poor sweet. But in the long run—d'you see?"

"I'm afraid not. As usual, you're miles ahead of me. —I thought you'd be pretty cut up about the news."

"But I am: we loved George. —What will become of that house, and the paper, everything!"

"Well, we're in charge of all that at the bank, he arranged things before he left home."

He knew she was once again too clever for him. Obscurely, he was relieved. He did not really want to know for certain what he had probed for. He thought her beautiful. He reached to kiss her. She gave him her cheek, for now, but with a smile that said, *Later,* and she asked, "Ready?"

He lofted his jacket above his head like a student and let it settle on his arms. He smartened it about his waist, and sighed, and said, "Go ahead. I'll turn out the lights."

Throughout the remaining years of the war, Diana, after being told at home that there was no place in wartime for official mourning, maintained Jack's position in the household at The Riverpoint Manor, and continued her job downtown. When Gregory Blaine learned that George Macdonald was lost, he asked her if she would like a vacation for a little while.

"No, I'll keep on here. It doesn't matter. The war is more or less over, for me, so far as what I feel. The real things are blurred. I have Jack to maintain, and this mechanical job here with you is probably the best thing for me. But thank you. You are a dear."

In his own time, Jack said, "If I don't say much about it, Jadi, I want you to know how much I appreciate how marvelously you're doing. I know it can't be easy. You and he were so close. He never liked me, I was sorry for that, I sincerely admired and respected him. I'm afraid I show my feelings too easily and some people are put off by it. Do you think? Am I too good-natured?"

"No, Jadi, it's what makes people respond to you. I have never seen you so happy."

The total dedication required by his service in the war was his deliverance from himself.

He found most content in a secret to be told only to the most intimate handful of people who—there was satisfaction in this for him—could never share in it actually. It was this: as the war followed its heavy course, the Commander in Chief, to be diverted from his unthinkable daily burdens, liked to have brought to him in the White House at six o'clock in the evening two or three men at a time, in an irregular rotation, old friends or new, who would drink the martini cocktails which he himself in his wheelchair mixed with bantering zest. Then would come forty-five minutes of talk about anything but the war. Jack was one of those often sent for by a Presidential aide. Everyone agreed that he was a successful guest, with his racy anecdotes about the theater, or the best scraps from his current reading, or his skill at asking precisely the inviting question to stimulate the President's own best monologues. There was no more exclusive little gathering in town, and in a tacit recognition that for everyone the great value of the event was its privacy, it was not loosely spoken of by its members, several of whom belonged to the upper levels of the government. By his presence among them, Jack knew that they came to regard him as a person of consequence in an important post.

But the summit of Jack's pleasure in his position came to a shocking halt in his fourth year of service.

One April afternoon—a gray day but bright, with the effect of light edging all new colors of spring—he glanced out of the corner of his office facing the White House across the narrow alley of the west entrance. He was idling back and forth through a small arc in his high leather desk chair, his hands clasped behind his head, his mind working with fine clarity. Then something changed in the view out of his office window facing the White House: a movement of color, playing in a slow breeze against the late afternoon peach color of the Potomac sky.

He sat up sharply.

Great God, he thought.

The flag above the front portico of the mansion was slowly coming to half-mast. At the same time a few long black limousines swept up the drive to the west door and their occupants dashed inside.

Jack dialed his chief's phone. All its lines were busy. He ran out into the tessellated hallway and met a young secretary who was running from one office to another. She was in tears.

[105]

"He is dead," she gasped, waving vaguely, and disappeared.

From open doors down the corridor he heard the voices of several radios, and soon he was certain of the news. The President was dead in Georgia.

※

In the months following, even until the end of the war in high summer, it was a time for everyone in the vast vine-like organism of the wartime government to hold steady. Jack did so. He felt a sometimes visible grief in the President's death, and behind this was a depressing sentiment which he kept to himself: *I have lost the White House.*

But with the victorious end of the war Jack was momentarily lifted from his low spirits at the change in his world. He was lifted again when in the early autumn he was called to the Embassy of Great Britain to be decorated with a CBE for his "unstinting and loyal services to the joint cause of the United States and the United Kingdom during the whole of the recent war." When his unberibboned friends genially addressed him as "Commendatore," he ascribed the mockery of this to simple envy, and went on with the uninspiring task of gradually dismantling his section of the huge bureau which had been his official and—so he sometimes thought—spiritual home for four years.

"What are our plans now?" asked Diana.

She saw that, with war's end, an empowering time of dedication and goodness in Jack's life was finished. He loved Washington for what it had given him, and he wished now he could keep it all. But it was not the same Washington. His "élite" was gone. Another less to his liking was in charge. He was adrift.

There was only one durable remedy—Jack must return to the theater and begin work on a new play.

Thinking to read his own thought, she said, "Is it to be New York again, for us? Your other great life is there, in the theater, with a new play."

He frowned at any intrusion into his uncertainty.

"I have thought—but I never imagined it might be so hard, climbing down after the war. Yes, of course, I have a dozen ideas for plays drifting in my skull, but they're like little clouds that float away just when I expect rain. I *do* know something, though. It's not to be New York. I think we are beautifully *placed* here. There's no such thing as a Riverpoint Manor in Manhattan, and who knows? The same party is in power here, and who knows: my war record might just inspire somebody to bring me in again— undersecretary, Cultural Affairs, ambassador somewhere, you know?"

She must see him as he saw himself.

The climate changed one day when he found earlier notes for a comedy which suddenly reignited his sense of character and plot.

"What is it, Jack?" Diana asked.

"I can't say anything yet, but I think I'm on to something for a play."

His eyes shone with relief that his long dry spell as a playwright was ending. He laughed when he recalled the moment with which his new comedy had begun.

At lunch, several years ago, with Marjorie Scanlon in Dorchester, they had played verbal ping-pong with all their old pleasure. And yet, at one moment, he had seen in her, despite her retained beauty and worldly management, a sense of having missed something vital. Like so many middle-aged American wives, she unconsciously gave hints that she was living the question, "Is this all there is to my life, day after day?"

He had been struck by that sense of "all there is," and he said, to her, "Excuse me, Marjie, I just thought of something," taking out his gold-edged pocket notebook.

"Something I said?" she asked with lazy archness.

"Oh, I'm always writing you down. You make the best of all epigrams—you never know, or care, when you make them."

She raised her shoulders in pleasant satisfaction, while he treasonably scribbled the kernel of a comedy about a well-married matron who in the midst of plenty was still questing after an undefined goal. His problem as a storyteller for the stage would be to revive his conviction, invent the goal, and show his heroine as she went after it, passing through comic hazards, finally reaching it, and what she thought of it when she got it. He had his title: *All There Is.*

Diana was silently grateful that he seemed no longer adrift now, his days no longer fretful. She made it her purpose, then, to find new friends to replace those gone home from the war. She was so successful that their calendar showed few vacant days. Everyone enjoyed the charm, luxury, and propriety of life in The Riverpoint Manor: physical beauty overlaid with evidences of discreet but heavy expenditure. Diana began to look critically at her house, and had various rooms done over. Now and then she gave a suspicion of riding at a gallop—the place which the Washington hostess sooner or later had to fall into if she cared about keeping up. What would have astonished friends in older times was that Diana seemed to care. She became as attentive to protocol as the State Department, and as partial to ambassadors. Her health did not suffer; but something in her expression did. Was she whirling for the sake of it? But she and Jack continued to appear everywhere together, evidently in the best of humors.

How did people know what they knew? Everybody was a barometer, subject to little unexpressed pressures. The general notion came into currency that, without a single crack in the surface, Diana was now frankly making a job of her marriage. It was agreed that she did it beautifully.

She was clever with Jack among other people. He saw to it that preparation had its uses.

"After everybody gets here," he said, "and when one of those party pauses takes place—they always do sooner or later—I'll give you a look, and then *you* say to me, so everybody can hear, *Jadi, I was trying to remember what it was F.D.R. said to you when you were at one of his secret little cocktail hours, at the White House,* and then I'll say, *I don't know what you mean, Jadi, he said so many good things,* and then you say, *Oh yes, Jadi, you know, he told you about the time the Prime Minister walked stark naked into the President's bedroom to invent the United Nations?* and then I'll say, *Oh, that, of course, let me see: I remember: the President told me he threw back his head and roared with laughter, and said, 'Where's my harpoon, Captain Ahab, I've just sighted a great pink whale!'* —Don't you think they'll love it?"

So she manipulated his store of anecdotes to their best advantage. When the well-rehearsed point came at the end, she would lead the laughter with gaiety which caught up the other listeners. She sometimes flashed out with her own critical humor, revealing her true mind, which in those days had little to engage it. Did she have something else to engage her, someone else? Dig as they would, people never found anything. Those who turned to Diana received light. If anything was missing, it was warmth, which was puzzling to a few perceptive persons, who saw the promise of it in her.

Still, there were the vases full of peonies, and the silks of her rooms, the proper cacophony of her imperative parties, Jack's growing gallery of newly illustrious faces and signatures in silver-framed photographs, the best food in town, the unpredictable but rewarding presence of Mrs L, and talk of John Wentworth's new play on the stocks; a façade for everything.

PART FOUR

※

EARLY ONE AFTERNOON a heavy mist rolled in from far out over the Atlantic. It was a frigid day and the mist froze as it touched the earth. Streetlights came on in mid-afternoon, blooming in the heavy air. Under the ice storm, Washington turned into a city of crystal. Not until people wanted to go home for the night was it generally understood that the icy streets would prevent normal traffic for . twenty-four hours.

That was the afternoon when the Franz Bader Gallery opened an exhibition of war drawings by Ben Ives. The show was called "Men Alone," and carried the subtitle, "War Sketches by Benjamin Ives." About a hundred of the multitude of little drawings which the artist made during the war were selected and captioned for the show. They were drawn on any and every kind of paper, mostly in India ink with rubbings of spittle or swipes of pale wash. The subjects ranged through every imaginable attitude of the soldier. In their technical excellence, and their intense regard for the pathos of human beauty in disguise and in danger of destruction, they brought the reality of the war to eye as no other information did, for they had not only fact, like photographs, but feeling, present in every line and volume set down by the artist. Not many of the drawings were over a few inches tall or wide. They were often careless, as though they must catch an instant of life before it should be blown to bits. Their spontaneity was unmistakable, and so were their

[113]

compassion, their humor, and their merit in design and other values of art.

The men drawn did indeed seem alone, no matter what they were shown doing among their fellows. Digging. Sleeping. Marching. Writing letters. Bathing. Gaming. Making love to maddamozels or frawleens. Rotting in death. Receiving wounds like stigmata. Wolfing field rations. Staring in idiot fatigue. Jubilating or hurting over news from home. Hungrily caressing a puppy or a kitten or a small child. Urinating on a bonfire. Praying at field Mass. Dozens of subjects, done with flair and speed, as though Ives felt that the vision from the corner of the eye might receive more of human truth about men at war than could ever be set down in more studied fashion. Taken together, the little figures as they pursued from drawing to drawing their destined course had a powerful cumulative effect upon the viewer's emotions. The drawings were not priced very high, and on that first afternoon, nearly half of them were sold.

One who purchased a group of four was John Wentworth. He had arrived early in order to have an uncrowded view. The unselfconscious honesty of those soldiers transfixed off-guard in their hazardous masculine world struck Jack a series of little blows in mind and emotion, even, abstractedly, in desire.

When other people started to come in, he said he must go, but would return on a day less crowded; but just then Ben Ives arrived to attend his opening, and was introduced to Jack. They talked a few minutes, until Ben was taken away to meet more people.

Jack remained to watch him in glimpses through the growing crowd. He hoped for another word with Ben, and presently he had it, and found himself taken with Ben's openness of spirit and manner, by Ben's careless costume, and by the ease with which he met people, many of whom were supposed in Washington to be impressive in their own right. Jack stayed on in spite of the clamor made by opinionated voices in the crowded gallery rooms. Ben was dressed in dark gray flannel trousers, Army shoes well shined, a white long-collared shirt with a loosely knotted woolen tie of dark red, and an admirably made but frayed brown tweed jacket. People clustered about him as though he contained some healing secret. Vitality? Charm? Love of life? Good looks? They couldn't separate the components. All they knew was that when he was in the room, they wanted to be with him, men and women both, though for obscurely different attractions.

Jack finally found him alone for a moment just before six o'clock and said, "Look, if you have nothing better to do, you must be up to here with all this mob, why don't you come home with me for dinner with us in Georgetown? There will be—"

—a handful of people coming in, all very engaging, and Ben would interest them all, and they might even interest him. Jack wanted him especially to meet his wife, and to give advice on where to hang the four drawings he had bought and which after the traveling show closed he would be proud to have in the house.

"You chose four of the best ones," said Ben.

"I know. Do come."

It was an inspired kindness. As it happened, being locally unknown, Ben had nowhere to go, and thought he would return to New York that same evening in a day coach. He knew who Jack was. Jack was known to be very good of his kind—a generous, cultivated, hardworking man. Ben was interested in all expressions of life, provided they were wholehearted, and gave something to the world. He accepted the invitation. As patron claimed artist, it was to the credit of both that what never entered their minds was the fact that Ben would be richer by twelve hundred dollars after commissions, owing to Jack's purchases.

They did not wait for the gallery to close. Outside, the heavy fog with its freezing particles on branch and lamppost, wire and pavement, came to them as a surprise. Ben stopped still and gazed with delight at the wintry freak. It was bitter cold and the air was still.

The hushed streets were almost empty of movement. Cars were stalled at grotesque angles, unable to creep on the ice without swinging crazily out of course. People walking footed it precariously, and now and then someone fell. Mostly they were laughing at their plight. The capital was paralyzed and its residents, proud of their important city, took it as a great joke.

"We'll have to try walking," said Jack.

They set out. It was an enjoyable contest to beat their way over layers of ice. Ben invented a technique of running a few steps and then sliding as far as possible. Jack imitated it. They laughed like boys. Their ears and noses felt almost frozen. Once a venturesome cab crawled out of the mist, advancing sidewise, fighting for traction with its tire chains. Jack hailed it, waving his arm and giving an ear-splitting whistle—the kind made by putting two fingers against the tongue. It was a rude and unexpected accomplishment in one so mannerly. Ben complimented him and tried it too, but couldn't make the wild sound. The cabdriver acknowledged it, but called back that if he stopped he'd never get going again, and was only trying to make it in to the company garage. Ben amiably told him to go screw himself, and tried for its own sake to make the whistle again. He began to get the knack. They proceeded toward Wisconsin Avenue, a famous playwright and a young artist of remarkable quality, making unspeakable noises and laughing and skating on their shoes like a pair of juvenile gang members. The comedy of this was lost on neither of them. Jack felt a restorative excitement he had not known for years. Covering it, he said they would have to hurry, as he must dress before the guests came.

When finally they came indoors, the two realized how cold they were. Paco helped them out of their coats and spoke of the weather: there were fires going both in the downstairs drawing room and in the library upstairs. Might he fix them a hot whiskey drink right away, before anything else? Mrs Wentworth was not yet downstairs, as the guests were not due for half an hour.

"No thanks," said Ben. "I don't drink anything. I'll just thaw out by the fire while you dress."

Jack took him up to the library and gave him into a deep armchair before the fire.

"I'll come for you in half an hour."

"Thanks."

Jack left him and he at once fell asleep, his arms and legs flung wide, and his mouth smiling.

On her way downstairs, Diana went into the library to look over her flowers and prepare the room for after dinner—they would all come here for coffee. When she saw Ben asleep by the fire, she stopped still. As she regarded the sprawling figure of this stranger, she found herself irritated by its somehow possessive relaxation. When had she last seen any such repose? Ben was flushed and his clothes were rumpled like bedding. He slept with energetic pleasure, breathing in joyful gusts. His hands were clasped under his chin, his elbows supported by the arms of the chair. She was about to tiptoe out of the room when the desk telephone rang.

She went to answer it before it awoke the sleeper; but it made him start upright and she was forced to nod at him with a reserved smile. The phone call was from two of her dinner guests saying that because of the ice on the streets they found that they could not possibly come tonight. They had tried to start out in their own car, with laughable and dangerous results. No taxis. The radio was broadcasting police warnings to keep off the streets. The hostess and her guests consoled each other, and then she was obliged to turn to Ben, introducing herself.

He came and shook her hand. Making a joke out of being discovered and unaccounted for here, he spoke mildly, in a voice oddly light in someone so hardy in figure. She should have been amused and reassured. She was not. Her feelings were all on hair-trigger tension, these days. Her hand felt as though the shape of his had been printed on it. What did he bring with him that spoke straight

[117]

through the simple conventions he was observing so pleasantly? She asked herself what was the matter with her. She was in a fine state of nerves if, in her own house, she could not meet a stray guest of Jack's without feeling a sudden weariness—or did she mean wariness?—so heavy that she wanted to turn and go upstairs and shut her eyes. Instead, she asked Ben to go down to the drawing room with her where they might have a drink until the others came.

"I don't drink, but'll be delighted to come along."

They went down.

Ben sat facing her on a long pale linen sofa by the fire. He recited in detail the story of the silly adventure of getting here over the ice with Jack. In spite of his clothes he seemed well dressed because of the harmony and power of the body beneath. His hands were hardly clean, and probably never would be, no matter how much he scrubbed them. They had a surface like cloisonné with the many colors of paint and ink that had been impressed into them. She saw that those hands, chapped, scarred, stained, spoke of hard work. A little silence fell. He smiled. The big, sharp dog-teeth which bounded his smile made him inexpressibly young and at the same time quite irregularly good-looking—they made one of those details, flaws in themselves, which only confirmed by contrast an impression of general appeal. He wore a stubby haircut—pale with darkish underlocks—which showed the good shape of his head. His eyes were light brown and when he smiled they nearly vanished in little sickles of glee. He smiled frequently. His lips were broad and sharply chiseled. In repose they had almost a sweet expression, if that could be said about a young man with such a long, hard jaw line and a chin so blunt and shapely. The whole effect of him was one of physical appeal and capacity, but his plain egotism came not from such fortunate attributes but from inner energies of mind and conviction of talent.

In a moment, Jack came in, immaculate in a burgundy velvet smoking jacket.

"But you've already met," he declared. "I wanted to have the pleasure. But when I looked into the library, my bird had flown. —Jadi, are we going to have a small potation? We'll toast the drawings by this remarkable artist I acquired today."

Paco was already bringing the tray into the room. As he set it down before Diana, he said that he had taken a telephone message in his pantry. The remaining dinner guests had called to say that it was impossible to cross town.

"That leaves us only," said Diana.

"All the better!" cried Jack. "We'll have our very own special evening. I loathe parties, anyway, don't you, Ben?"

Diana knew he said it because he was guessing that Mr Ives was the sort of man who disliked parties.

"Oh no," Ben replied. "In streaks, I like them very much. There are whole months when I never get to bed till dawn because I am out on the town. And then again, I have times when I don't see anybody at all, really. I have never explained it to myself."

Jack told him with humor and style just why. "I know. You are like a great air-breathing plant, you perform effortlessly your necessary functions for growth and survival, you expand, you live on lights, pleasure, talk, personalities, the challenge of new and lovely women, and then suddenly your roots are saturated in the deep dark cool dampness of your reservoir where there is enough of the world to nourish you. When that happens, you have no more use for the world, and you leave it. And then come those splendid interludes of creation, alone, again almost thoughtless, but how sufficiently and triumphantly whole unto itself is that process of mining your own talent!"

If anyone had expected the florid address to end instead with the word "genius," they should have known that Jack was restrained in his appraisals of other people's ability.

Ben laughed out loud at the speech, and said, "It's great fun to listen to that sort of thing, you do it well, but it has nothing to do with the facts—*my* facts. I just go day and night until I get tired or bored, and then I quit. As for creation, I work all the time anyhow."

Jack closed his eyes for a second, smiling with a shade of pity and affection for those in the world who simply refused to be understood.

"You will see," he said, awakening from his tender self-communion, "one day you will not only do great things, you will know *how* and *why* you do them. We agree in essentials. I have won my way through to complete honesty about work—*my* work and everyone else's. It hasn't been easy, it hasn't always been pleasant. It is a daily grind. But what else is so worthwhile? Why should such honesty not enter into every phase of life?" He turned to Diana and laced his fingers with hers on the sofa. "Am I right, Jadi?"

She inclined her head a little to one side, and looked into the fire as pensively as she knew he wanted her to, while she answered, "Ever so right, Jadi darling."

Ben stared at one and then the other of them, and for all his politeness, he might as well have stated out loud that they did not fool him. This was all acting, and he did not blame them, for what it might try to conceal.

"I think we're all going to be tremendous friends," said Jack. "You two, especially, I'm sure. —Ben," he said earnestly, leaning forward, "people like us *know* and *live* things which take years for most others to get to. We met this afternoon, and yet I feel as though we've known each other for twenty years. You agree?" It was only civil to agree, and Ben did. "Your work: I saw it all there. Oh, so much of it tells a sorrowful story, a sordid story, about what human beings do to each other. And yet there is a vast goodness in the total effect of what you made in your pictures. I would believe in you, trust you, in any essential matter, Ben. I believe you see people as they are. I believe you are indifferent to prejudice."

There was a curious animation in Jack as he said this, and other things like it, during the evening. If Ben grew rather silent as the evening went on, and if Diana said little herself, and then chiefly to offer Jack a deft reminder of one or another of his best subjects, nobody felt ill at ease, for Jack was equal to the burden of carrying the occasion. He was in his element, with two attractive and intelligent younger listeners, and no threat of interruption or cleverness, and no necessity to prove himself anything but an appealing master of good talk. He kept their eyes and ears upon him all evening. Even when he would rise to go to the liquor tray to make himself another highball—Ben took nothing all evening—he held them over his shoulder, and as he came back to them in his neat pumps and his long-legged stroll, he picked them up again with his forefinger extended off his highball glass. A master of pacing, he would allow his speech to slow down as though in amused and penetrating estimate of what might be passing between them before his gaze. Sure that he had something in the back of his mind, Diana would lift her head and smile at Ben to show how she adored her husband as the most brilliant, distinguished, and cherished of men.

So it was that Jack knew, and established by his most elaborate indirections, that something smote Ben as soon as he met Diana. If he knew it before anyone, his intuition came from his own recognitions on meeting Ben.

Late in the evening, he said, "You can't go anywhere, of course, Ben. You'll have to stay the night with us and see what sort of weather the morning brings. We'll love putting you up, won't we, Jadi?"

Ben became for the first time a member of their household.

Oh, Lord, no, thought Diana when the situation began to be clear to her.

Ben was marooned with them. In the morning, he kept saying that he really must get a train for New York at the earliest opportunity, and then he would imply with a large smile that this was only talk, as nothing was as interesting to him in New York as seeing Diana right here in Washington. With an air of giving his blessing to life—"Life"—Jack made a great point of keeping to his morning's schedule of work, leaving the two of them together in the library, while a thickening fall of snow curtained the tall windows.

"You don't have to stay and entertain me, Diana," Ben said, "though I wish you would."

"A little while. I have loads of things to do."

"How long have you been married?"

"Six years."

"Have you any children?"

"No."

"Do you help Jack with his work?"

"No. He has a secretary. A most able and kind soul who has a crush on him. Miss Irene Borrowdale. He calls her Missie. It suits her."

"—And him."

"What do you mean?"

"Nothing. —Only, I think he keeps people off where he wants them with quaint little conventions." She frowned at him. "I'm sorry. I don't mean to make fun of him. He's awfully kind. It was most hospitable of him to bring me home and take care of me."

But Ben could not dissemble. He was eating her up with his senses. He seemed to press all his idlest questions against her with single-minded interest. She felt the aggression in every sound of his voice. She supposed that, if observed from a distance, the ritual Ben was enacting might seem a little comic; but such detachment was not possible for her. She felt a faintly sickening annoyance at Jack for bringing him here. She reminded herself that surely the weather would clear up soon, and nice as he was, and full of the vitality of freedom and simple direct wants, their guest would be able to go away. The reflection gave her a crisp sort of solace. She wanted no emotional tests or complications in the life she had established with a dignity which was not to be disturbed. She went to the radio and turned on a local station.

"What is that for?" asked Ben.

"I thought you would want to know about the weather forecast. It must be a nuisance for you, not knowing what to expect."

He grinned and swept her with his look. "I know what I'd like to expect. Perhaps you may want to know even more than I do."

"About what?" Her lips felt a trifle dry.

"About the weather," he said. He stuck his jaw forward in a candid sort of sensual relish.

"Nonsense. I long ago gave up on the Washington weather."

She caught up some letters from the desk and bent to the radio as the forecast began. The announcement was made that local officials expected the streets to be clear by mid-afternoon. She switched it off.

"I'll leave you to amuse yourself," she said. "You'll find all sorts of books here—Jack has all the latest ones every week. I have to see to the house, and answer some letters. We'll have lunch at half past one. Jack will make a cocktail at one. —But you don't drink."

"Almost never. I know better."

"Better?"

"Oh, I don't mean to be critical of you or Jack, or anyone else who likes to. It just isn't for me."

"Are you a reformed alcoholic?"

"I've often wondered. My friends say I'm drunk all the time on everything else. I don't need liquor. Or if I do, I need it too much. Mostly, I leave it alone. Do you have to go?"

"I really should."

"Why?"

"I have dozens of things to—"

"Everybody always has. The thing is, you ought to choose. Everyone ought. I do. No. That's not exactly it. I get chosen."

"Get chosen?"

"So it seems to me, mostly. Things choose me, really. It began long ago."

"Where?"

"When I was a boy. Just a little boy. I felt such excitements then, they struck me always all of a sudden; and I've been excited ever since."

She went gently down on the arm of a chair across the hearth from him. He continued to talk.

※

Ben Ives was born in Olympia, Iowa, the youngest of many children, and measured by their ages, his parents could have been his grandparents. His father was a farmer. Their place was on the outskirts of the little town of Olympia, far enough to feel lonely much of the time, near enough in to allow the family to join in the social doings organized by the churches, school, and ladies' groups. As a child, Ben felt most lonely when obliged to take part in these functions. His grown-up brothers and sisters spoiled him at first, and then when they saw that it was going to be difficult to account for this preoccupied changeling in their midst, they came near to persecuting him. Only his mother stood between him and social misery. She would proclaim his rights and powers to the listening family world in her muted horn-like voice, and they would bend under her authority.

The father was a silent and dyspeptic man. Ben always suspected that his father was at times positively ravaged by a sort of inarticulate, tragic poetry born of his farmer's frustrations and the pressing wonders of natural life. Long later, Ben said, he found his father in the *Eclogues* of Vergil. He knew some silent communion with the old man, who allowed him to come along on the farm jobs. At an animal birth, or a heavy loss of crops, or the disaster of a storm, or the breeding of a cow or a mare, the father would look like a gaunt prophet out of the Old Testament or the drawings of William Blake, lamenting and praising life and death in the same breath. Ben was already striking through to meanings with his essential faculty, that of seeing.

His life took a determining turn on a particular Saturday when his mother brought him to town while she went to the stores. She had many places to go, at her unhurried pace, and she turned him loose, making him promise to meet her back at the Ford Model A at a certain hour.

He wandered off, barefooted, clad in cut-down pants and shirt, his light hair tangled like wild grass. He happened into the small public library which stood in its squat, forbidding brownstone like a visual quotation from Richardson, under elms, on a corner opposite the firehouse. Ben gave the sense that destinies and revelations actually are, now and then, visited upon certain individuals with a force which marks them forever, as lightning strikes a tree.

(No one, thought Diana, had ever believed in his own living excellence more disarmingly than Ben Ives.)

In the library's storeroom, where he had no business to be, Ben came upon some old-fashioned folios of engraved plates reproducing famous works of art which had been willed to the library by a physician long deceased. Immediately, for the first of countless times, Ben forgot everything but that which spoke out in him and told him what he saw and how he must somehow make use of it. He was lost in the shadowy back room till the library was ready to close, when the librarian found him smudged with dust, and glaring like a cub disturbed at feeding. When he was on the street again and in search of his mother, he remotely felt he had a tremendous thing to tell, and then found that he had no adequate way to tell it.

The rest of his life, he said, was the history of trying to find that way. Other matters, scruples of behavior or custom, honestly seemed trivial or meaningless.

The meager cultural resources of Olympia oddly were enough for him until his middle adolescence. He could meet and magnify them with his responsive imagination. He would go to the Catholic church and there, even in a poverty-stricken parish, the ancient liturgy, the transfiguring vestments with their gold galloon, succession of colors, and change for ceremonies; the Gregorian chant, the antiphony of the little choir shrilling out over its foot-pumped reed organ, spoke much to him about the only living ancient culture in Olympia, as he listened to acolytes making responses in Latin. He grew beyond the impoverished music of his family Baptist church, the rural dramas of the occasional tent show which visited town, and felt, if he did not understand its need, the power of a spiritual tradition, and the fount of civilization in the Western world.

He discovered the great world itself in Olympia, Iowa, then, whenever he took refuge in the library, where the librarian, even as he mystified her, gave him the run of the place. He could read things at a glance. He knew what went on among his particular interests in New York, Paris, and London. He felt like a familiar of all cultivated and creative people alive or dead, and he believed that he knew their distant cities and countries with a dreamlike authority. He saw that the Olympians regarded him with awe and suspicion. He was their first and last sophisticate.

His mother never actually understood the nature of his gifts, but their energy moved her, and when he said he wanted to go to Chicago to study at the Art Institute, she gave him for the last time the embracing safety of her love and authority. Unable to defy her gaze, the family made up enough money to get him started and keep him for six months in Chicago, and let him go. The mother died a few weeks later. Ben did not return for the funeral, as he knew she would forgive him so long as he kept her alive in thank-fulness for all she had meant to him. She had given him life in every sense; and he believed that she would have silently agreed with him that there was no point in honoring death when life called so urgently. Ever afterward, his family exiled him.

"My education," he said, "soon took on the acquisition of experience through simple need."

When his Chicago money ran out, he found a few odd jobs, and returned to his classes between times. There were hard times, a few rather shaming but educational times, and then an imperative need to see himself in other worlds. He drifted across the country pausing here and there to earn enough money at brief jobs to get him along the road to his next stopping place. Always he filled sketchbooks with drawings, and here and there, at county fairs and the like, made extra money by setting up an easel and doing portraits in colored chalk at three dollars a head. What he wanted was enough money to go to Europe, and when he heard of the kind of pay given to hands on oil tankers out of Texas ports, he knew that was for him. He was signed on at Corpus Christi as a deckhand on a coastal tanker, deciding to work until he had saved enough to live abroad.

"There was another great benefit in that job I never thought of."

In his days ashore, sometimes as many as a week or two at a time, he became the possessor of the great arc of the sea edge of the Gulf of Mexico from Galveston to the Rio Grande. It was the landscape of all others in the country which seemed to set his inner vision clear before his eyes. In a borrowed car, sometimes alone, sometimes with a shipmate, he roved the great Gulf beaches of the mainland, and Mustang and Padre Islands. For miles of wild emptinesses in perspective, he would see no one. He might sit all day on a dune simply absorbing the brilliant green-blue of the sea on clear days, or watching the endlessly changing silver of the sky and sea in mist. He slept on the beach and in his joyfully confused senses made some abstruse union between the sound of the surf, *Thalassa, Thalassa,* with the slow round of the starry cycles in the sky, and he felt eternity in the repetition of those natural forces, always different, always the same. He sometimes rented a small sloop and sailed alone offshore, owning the waters with all his senses. He made innumerable little watercolor drawings, but never to his satisfaction. On his various rovings along the coast or on the water he found the very geography of independence from constraints. Whenever he had to leave the vacant beaches to return to his job aboard ship, he made vows to return, and he returned as often as possible until he was ready to work his way to Europe on a freighter, with enough savings to give him two years in Paris and London. But still it was the vision of the Gulf which long possessed him, sometimes in remote comfort, sometimes in acute longing.

"Have you ever been back?" asked Diana.

"No. But someday—"

In Paris he joined up with a band of five other young painters who called themselves Les Déracinés, and exhibited his work with theirs. He sold no pictures until his return to America. He settled in New York, found a small gallery which took him on, sold a few works, and had to look for commissions. A lucky one was a contract to design scenery for a ballet company. As could happen in New York, he became a minor celebrity through association with the members and patrons of the company, and was much photographed. The photographs made him rather uneasy because the projected selves of the fashion photographers seemed to be expressed through him. Until the war and the draft erased both his chance to work and the name he had made for himself, he ranged through the New York scene. In the Army he felt the monotonous humanity close about him with a sense of pity, but more, he learned to protect his essential privacy by giving, when prudent, a good imitation of being a roughneck, for which his days on the coastal oil tankers had prepared him. As an enlisted man, though asked to apply for officer training, he refused to do so. He took the position that as an enlisted man he might be killed, and that would be too bad; but as an officer he would have to order other men to be killed, which would be worse. In reflective moments he was amazed by the fact that he had come through the war unhurt, in spirit or body.

"Luck is a tremendous mystery," he said. "I wonder whether philosophers ever gave it their attention. Someday I'd like to do a courthouse mural on the theme *Justice and Luck*. Two great bitch goddesses in their own right. I'd say you have never felt the need of either. You have all the signs of a protected life."

Diana thought this somewhat impertinent.

"I wouldn't know what those are," she replied.

❧

They were interrupted by the age of communication. There was a house phone system which connected all the main rooms. Its buzzer sounded at the desk. Diana went to answer it.

"Yes?"

Ben could hear the voice at the other end. It said, "Jadi? What are you doing?"

She turned and smiled at Ben.

"Talking."

"Oh," said Jack upstairs. "Are you being nice to Ben?"

"I couldn't be nicer."

"That's good. He's a very lonely person. We must do everything we can for him."

This made Ben laugh out loud. Diana frowned at him.

"What?" asked Jack, as he heard the blurred laughter in the background.

[129]

"Nothing. Ben was laughing at being called lonesome."

"But he is. Lonely people, when they're *really* lonely, don't know it. That's what's so poignant about it."

"I'll just let you debate it with Ben. —He can hear every word you are saying."

"You need not warn me, I have nothing to say to you—or anyone—which he—or anyone—is not welcome to hear."

"Yes," murmured Ben, "that's part of the trouble."

There was a little silence in which a three-way relationship seemed to be suggested for the first time. Then, "I think I got it this morning," said Jack.

"What:"

"Ah, Jadi, you would never have had to ask that, a while ago." The electric voice was quacking with elegiac acceptance and patient understanding.

"What do you mean."

"My play, of course. The new ending for act one of *All There Is*. It came today so blandly, it simply rolled out of the typewriter. You'll love it. When the scene began to write itself I was half laughing and half crying. The audience will be too. It will play like silk. You'll see. I'll read it to you tonight. I have her do something absolutely unexpected, and yet perfectly true to her character. Unexpected and true. Is this the history of art in a phrase? —Ask Ben. I'll be down in a little while. Kiss."

"Kiss," she replied helplessly. She hung up the phone and once again started from the library.

Ben stood up. He was scowling in distaste. She did not allow him to say anything, for she was gone too quickly; but she knew he had overheard much about her marriage, and she had a sudden view of her life as Ben might see it. She ran upstairs with her head bent and her mouth against her fist. Only a few hours, and he would be gone. She would never see him again. She would manage. Only let him go away.

[130]

She reckoned without Jack.

The streets were passable in the afternoon. Ben went to catch a train. Jack insisted that they both drive him down to see him off. At the station Jack made a comedy about Ben's refusal to buy a parlor-car ticket.

"I never ride in Pullman cars," said Ben.

"You a rotten, charming, upside-down snob, then," declared Jack, with a jolly nod of forgiveness.

"It isn't that, but say what you will, differences in earthly possessions make a difference in how people show themselves. I prefer to see people nearer to their natural selves. I look at them, I draw them, I feel their lives in my own. I am not essentially a comic artist, yet if I rode in Pullmans, and bought other such privileges, I'm afraid my drawings would all seem funny. That is how the rich always seem to me."

"Rich!" scoffed Jack. "Nobody has to be rich to be comfortable these days. What's a parlor-car seat cost, anyway? And as to the rest of it, what's wrong with being another Daumier, anyhow? What's wrong with comic genius laid over compassionate vision?"

"Nothing, if it's what you have. I don't."

"Well, I do," said Jack, smiling to forgive himself. "You two wait right here. I'll go and get you the early papers. You may have reviews you'd like to clip."

He went off.

"I don't want them," said Ben to Diana. "If they're bad, I certainly don't want them, and if they're good, it'll be for reasons which will make me furious." He reached for her hand. She let him have it for only a second. "Are you coming to New York, Diana?"

"Oh no, we never go any more, unless Jack has a play to talk about."

She said to herself, *Have the train go, have it go, goodbye.*

"I'm seeing you again, though," said Ben.

Jack came back, comforted by accomplishment.

"Here," he said, thrusting the *Washington Star* and a ticket envelope upon Ben. "I bought you new tickets. I think you should know the facts of life and get over this self-important nonsense about classes in America. There are no classes. People like you want to create them. But you are really a born citizen of the world. Don't try to pretend you are humble. Here are parlor-car and railroad tickets. I shall expect you to have a great awakening to the beauties of self-indulgence. And:" he poked Ben in the chest with his well-gloved forefinger, "to use the return tickets, too, for I bought them round-trip, so you will have to come back to see us soon."

His own ardor made his eyes sting a little. He stormed Ben with his fond good nature, his new claim upon their great new friend, and the privilege of scolding him affectionately.

Ben hesitated a moment between tearing up the tickets on principle and accepting them to spare Diana a little scene. With a look at her which told her of this, he put the tickets into his pocket.

"Thank you, Jack. I'll be back."

"When?"

"I'll be back. Goodbye all." Ben shook hands and went to his train.

They both watched him until he disappeared in the vistas of steam alongside the cars in the wintry air. Then Jack turned and blinked both eyes at her drolly. What was he up to? Even wondering about it deadened her. They went home.

❧

When Ben returned for a weekend to stay with the Wentworths, Cecile and Billy Millard were giving a luncheon party. Cecile insisted that Ben be brought along. He was talked about, she had never met him and she wondered how he would "be," with Jack and Diana both. Billy had been asked after the war to stay on at the State Department and was now thought to be moving toward the Undersecretaryship.

The Millards lived in a tall, narrow deep house of pale stone with Lombardy poplars before it in a quiet side street half a block off Massachusetts Avenue in the embassy district. The front of the house was like a central slice taken from the façade of a palace and set by itself in lonely grandeur which seemed to call for one-half a fountain, a single gatepost, with one sentry box, a segment of carriage way. Once inside, the impression was complete—elegance, set off by big bouquets, stacks of new books, and two paintings by Monet from the Argenteuil period which made the long drawing room sparkle with color.

In symbolic embrace, Cecile Millard and Diana not quite touched their cheeks together, and Diana introduced Ben.

"But where is Jack?" asked Cecile, looking at Ben. She knew him well at once.

"Working," said Diana. "He said he would kill himself if you want him to, but he couldn't put away what he is doing. He sent us on. He might drop in later."

"How wonderful it must be to be a great man and as rude as you like," said Cecile, and took Ben to meet her husband. Ben gave an impression of accepting them with approval, which reversed the ordinary trend in that house. It was a party of nine, without Jack. Cecile took Ben around for introductions, with hardly an interruption in her own chatter.

"It is so pleasant," she said, working her eyebrows expressively, "to see pictures like yours, about people, I-mean instead of little pathologies dealing with machines, ideologies, refuse heaps, mad wallpaper, but not a line about men and women and boys and girls. I like your little human beings, Mr Ives. I've been twice to see your show. It must be very daring of you nowadays to be so honestly interested in bodies and acts."

Ben with charm and no tact beamed at finding such intelligent praise in anyone so importantly chic as Mrs Millard. He turned to make an open secret of his pleasure with Diana nearby.

She felt his look appealing to her to the exclusion of all the others in the room, and she frowned a little for the confidential confession it made of intimacy he assumed with her. She refused to turn and accept him, in spite of his ardent presence in the corner of her eye. Cecile Millard studied the incident with all her penetrative skill.

Diana was engaged in a lively and idle scene with General Francis McCartney, the youngest brigadier general in the Army, who was written up everywhere as the "boy wonder" of the General Staff. He was thirty-nine, a bachelor, good-looking, and, as Betty Beale put it in the *Star*, fuller of social tone than all the upper Navy put together. Today Diana astonished him by the fullness of her attention to him. Like all the others, on her arrival with Ben, he had habitually wondered—what was the degree of their relationship? Now, and all through lunch, General McCartney obtusely believed that he saw possible gossip confuted in front of him, for Mrs Wentworth hardly glanced at Mr Ives.

It was true she felt Ben's eyes upon her always, and his aroused bewilderment at her treatment of him. Yet something made her persist, and she carried on with the General as though they had not seen each other for years, with much to catch up on in the meantime.

"Cecile," said Millard, across everybody to his wife, "why don't you ask Mr Ives if he has ever painted anything out West?"

"Oh, yes: Billy: I will. —Mr Ives, do you know the West? We're mad for it. We took a new station wagon and simply drove there last summer for three weeks. Our first time off in years. Won't you let me see your pictures and drawings of the West?"

"I have nothing on hand," said Ben. "I did make some drawings as a youngster out there years ago, mostly on the Gulf of Mexico. I've always meant to go back. Mysterious and wonderful. Gulf coast."

"Oh yes, go, you must go back, Mr Ives, and when you return, come straight to us, won't you?"

There was a general feeling that Ben had made another little daily success, with everyone content about it. Diana felt it most sharply. She could not say whether it made her glad or sorry.

Later, in the drawing room for coffee, Cecile asked Ben to hand the cups around for her, smiling in the way to smile over a bright, promising, outlandish boy. He brought a cup to Diana and after giving it to her went springily down into a crouch before her. It was a moment everybody was waiting for. How would those two "be" together?

"Shouldn't we be going?" he asked.

"Is it time?"

He looked at his watch.

General McCartney said, "Oh? You have to be somewhere?"

"Mr Ives has to catch a train for New York."

"But not for hours, surely, there's one every hour," said the General, looking at Ben as though he were a map. "You were in the Army, weren't you, Ives? I saw your exhibition. Your pictures told a lot about all of it. It was all true, too."

"Yes. Thanks, General."

"Don't thank me, old boy. In wartime, if I had anything to say about it, I'd suppress your drawings."

Millard called to his wife, "How about that, Cecile?"

She flashed him a glance of suspended opinion.

"Why, General?" asked Ben.

"They're too true. They'd disturb a lot of people, even might to some degree undermine a war effort."

"But, Frankie," protested Cecile Millard, "you are interested in art. How could you do a thing like that?"

"Of course I am, but that has nothing to do with what might be necessary, from a military point of view, about morale."

"Oh, and I thought you so civilized, for a soldier," cried Mrs Millard.

"Expedient veneer, ma'am," said the General, grinning so like a brat, well-scrubbed and combed, that everybody burst out laughing, and Diana stood up.

McCartney stood up too, and asked if he could not take her home. Ben was behind her, but she believed she knew the look on his face when after a moment's hesitation she said to McCartney, "Yes."

Then she turned to Ben, held out her hand, smiled, and said he would be able to get a cab near here, and added, "Jack hopes you'll be coming back soon again to see us."

This was meant as a public lesson. He smiled a little hazily, didn't speak, but shook his head.

Billy, who rarely missed anything, said in a loud genial voice, "Cecile, why don't I just run Mr Ives down to the station when he has to go? Isn't your car still around at the side?"

"I think so, darling. Do. This will mean that we can keep Mr Ives a little longer. Sit down, Mr Ives. I am going to call you Ben. I am Cecile."

Diana and General McCartney left him with his lesson. But it was a lesson that turned out the wrong way for her later feeling, as so often when she made a move too positive. It shamed her to be rude to anyone so warm, strong, and unoffending as Ben. Why should she punish him, and make a fool of herself, because of something neither of them was responsible for?

Later, Jack said, "What did you do with Ben?"

"I let him go to the train."

"Alone?"

"Not quite alone, Billy drove him down."

"Why didn't you take him?"

"Francis McCartney offered to bring me home."

"But, Jadi!"

Jack was aghast. How could she. After all, Ben was their guest. What must he be thinking of them—of him—at this minute? She could see red glints of anger deep in his black eyes. What if her action today—rude and unfriendly—had severed the tie by which he had been binding Ben to himself—to their household? He acted swiftly.

He composed a telegram to Ben:

JACK SAYS DIANA SAYS WHAT A SHAME YOU HAD TO GO BACK TODAY
AND WITH NO MORE RED CARPETS AND FLOURISHES THAN THAT OYEZ
OYEZ OYEZ COME BACK FOR NEXT CONCERT WEDNESDAY WEEK
PHILADELPHIA ORCHESTRA WONDERFUL PROGRAM MARTINU VIOLIN
CONCERTO KREISLER HAYDEN 102 BRAHMS THIRD AND OF COURSE STAY
WITH US THEN THATS SETTLED HASTA LA VISTA

J AND D

Until he had an answer to this, Jack was restive and preoccupied. But it came the next afternoon, a telegram simply reading

O K THANKS

BEN

and the household was again at its arranged ease.

When Ben returned, it was not to stay overnight, but just to dine, hear the concert, and take the five-minutes-past-midnight train back to New York, where he was expecting a sitter the next morning.

"I loathe doing portraits, but I need the money, and my new dealer, Mr Rijkmann—Murray Hill Gallery—is able to get me commissions at fees I can't laugh off."

"How much, Benjy?" asked Jack, always frankly avid of other people's affairs, especially in respect of money. They were dining, the three of them, at the Manor.

[137]

Something was wrong with the tone of things. Ben was calm and polite, his usual animation gone. It was unlike him to be passive among people. Diana knew that it was all her fault. She had behaved toward him like an ill-bred schoolgirl ten days ago, and if he was here at all tonight, it was only to show that whether he came or went was of such little matter to him that he might as well come, this time, anyway; or so Jack perceived the mood. His gaze when it touched upon Diana held disguised anger.

"How much?" he repeated, leaning forward into the candlelight about the white carnations and polished green lemon leaves that stood in the middle of the table.

"Ten thousand," said Ben.

"My golly!" exclaimed Jack, and sat back with comic admiration.

"But the dealer gets a third," added Ben wryly.

"But that still leaves you nearly seven thousand. I'd no idea."

Ben stared at him, and then burst out laughing like himself for the first time that evening.

"Jack, you do like money, don't you."

"Nonsense," said Jack, scowling like an actor. "I don't like money. *I love it.*"

Ben turned to Diana. "I think he now thinks me a really good painter, for the first time," he said in an effort to break the strained relationship between them all.

"You do him an injustice," she replied, looking at Jack with one of those looks out of their beginning together which used to signify that in her eyes he could do no wrong. "He was just pleased, as I was, that our Ives drawings will be so very valuable one day before long."

They had, all three, agreed to accept the game.

So, when it was time for the concert, there was nothing to do all over again when Jack said, "Now here are the tickets, you two run along, be good children, and think of me rewriting one line from act two seventeen times this evening."

"Jack!" cried Ben, "aren't you coming?"

"Lord no, my bravo, where would anybody get an extra ticket for one of the Ormandy concerts? They are sold out in August every year. They're practically hereditary—I'll will you my pair."

"But you asked me—"

"I certainly did, and here you are. Now shoo! Psss! Get going!" a burlesque impersonation of a fussbudget dismissing two adorable children whom he loved but who at the moment exasperated him beyond endurance; though at the same time he looked at them with his sleek head on one side, his eyes moist, his mouth in a downward smile which must say nothing more for fear of saying too much; his hands joined by their thumbs, waving them out of the house with comic impatience.

They went.

But not without one last tug from Jack, who after all could not bear to let them go entirely. He opened the front door after them, to watch them into the cab, and to call, "Jadi darling, this time you do the proper thing by Ben and see him off at the train!"

She promised with a wave.

Only afterward, on the way to the station in a taxi with the splendor of the orchestral evening beginning to recede into recollection, did Ben find his ease with her again. He reached to take her hand, which she took away.

But he had touched her for long enough to feel something in her even if she managed not to let it show.

In the occasional light which fanned over them from the street-corner lamps as they drove, he looked at her, grinning as though to recognize their enlivening predicament, to find it sweet and imperative.

At the Union Station he said, "Let's have a drink. There's time."

They went to the long restaurant which was in general darkness but for spotlights which shone separately upon little groups of people at spaced tables. Smoke from cigarettes made the cones of light pale blue. A face caught in that illumination was modeled into a mask and Ben half-closed his eyes to memorize it. There was a common grace over everything in that vivid light which made private and intimate that which everyone could see. Beyond the big room the trundle of trains, the glisten of throngs on the waiting platforms, the roll of carts, gave a pulse of life which could be felt in the bones. The place was charged with emotion, the sum of the comings and goings that happened there.

"Do you feel it?" he asked, looking around.

"What:"

"Everything that takes place here. One of the places of significant feeling. A great railroad station."

"Ah, yes."

"This, and a hospital, and a Catholic church, and a Landing Craft Infantry, and a prison—places where you see people inside out. Who could not spend two minutes in any of them and not be full of love?"

"Love?" she repeated, adding to herself, *Oh, don't.*

He put his hands on hers on the table. "How are you, Diny? Where are you?"

"Splendid"—taking her hand away. "Here."

He shook his head and hung loosely over the table for a moment like an exhausted and panting athlete. "It's awful," he said. "I don't know how much longer—"

The light from above crowned his hair with golden glints. She looked at the gold. She looked away.

He reached into his pocket and produced the railroad envelope containing his tickets. He slipped the tickets out and patted them flat on the tablecloth. With his forefinger he nicked one of the tickets over toward her, and said, "Look at it."

She took it up. "What about it?"

"See what it's for."

"Yes. I see. It's a Pullman ticket."

"Yes, but look at what it says."

She pretended to look again, and then breathing shallowly, said, "It just says Bedroom C, Car 171."

He nodded.

"Will you?" he asked.

"Ben: what:"

He took back the ticket and leaned to her. "Oh, for God's sake, Diny, will you come with me? Why else do you suppose I would get a room ticket? —This has gone on long enough."

He was no actor. His face was contorted with both impatience and tenderness. He seemed almost to scrape across her face with his eyes.

She imagined the train and in it that little room locked against time and darkness, distance and reckoning. This was the first time he had made an open avowal to her.

With shaken lightness she said, "What on earth would you do with a lady in a rumpled concert dress at seven o'clock in the morning in the Pennsylvania Station, in New York? There's where the train would end—end, you know, Ben."

"All a joke, then, to you."

"Hardly a joke, no, not at all, Benjamin." And she wanted to go on to say that he could not understand anything except what *he* felt, but the banality of the remark halted her. She fell into misery in her thought, and kept silent.

The next thing she knew, he was standing, glancing at his watch. "I think my train is made up. I might as well get on board and go to sleep, then. You can get a cab here easily enough. Good night."

He walked off.

She had not expected this—that he might suddenly turn stiff and offended. But as she watched him out, and the thrust of his shoulders as he strode, she was reached by a sense of his fleshly self, and also by a weary relief that she had done what she had done. But this did not prevent a confusion of feeling as she went out to

Georgetown in a taxi. Where could she go?—and she did not mean to what house, to what material frame: to what heart; what life.

She said his name to herself: "Ben": and then she said, "No."

Soon enough,

"Such a splendid concert, and such a pleasant time. —Yes, Ben enjoyed all of it."

In the next few days, Jack could hardly help wondering, then, why Ben had not scribbled him the smallest scratch of thanks.

Still.

These children of nature. They had no laws. He smiled with insistent penetration and allowance. They would hear from Ben in his own time and way.

In another week he was back.

Exhausting as it was to endure Ben's arrivals, Diana did her best to preserve a light and amusing surface for the three of them. When Jack, in the name of wholesomeness and belief in the ultimate goodness of mankind, made occasion for her to be alone with Ben, whom he trusted so blatantly, her heart sank again. Yet she would not admit to herself that her husband was false to her in a way which grew more complicated whenever Ben appeared. He sent her with Ben to parties without himself; to more concerts; to exhibitions. Jack would plead press of work—*All There Is* was going superbly (but he was a slow and careful worker and harvested every moment of his inspiration)—or he would announce a headache which could be borne pluckily, or admit an errand of kindness which ("You know Jack") nothing on earth could keep him from, and almost anonymously at that.

Each time, Diana was amazed at her endurance. Without formal religion, she believed and tried to act in harmony with values to whose sum other people gave the name of goodness. It was the George Macdonald of her childhood speaking silently in her. For Ben, her goodness, beautifully embodied, only made her more desirable—so much so that he tried to hold patiently to her terms, and found a certain zest in a course so different from his usual pursuit of love—or, "peer, pounce, and depart," as a rowdy friend once described it.

But he was as he was; and one day during one of their visits to the National Gallery he returned to the hunt. They had wandered slowly through the spacious vaulted rooms. He took her arm and she let him, only intent upon the pictures they lingered before. They came into the west garden court of the museum and seeing a marble bench in a shadowy corner, where tubbed trees arched over, and where the broken melody of the fountain at the center of the court made a hushed little echo, Diana said, "Let's stop here for a while. I am never tired in this wonderful place, but I often want to halt and think about what I've been looking at."

They sat down. A fall of pale light came from the coved ceiling. It touched the trees and plants about the fountain, and the passing people, with what she thought of as classic light, brightening the upward surfaces of everything, and muting with shadow all undersides. An echoing air in the high ceilings told of the drifting humanity below. It was like the sound of stirred branches and leaves, as in some great space where she might appear only to herself. She set her head on one side and narrowed her gaze, and felt the joyful transport of vision from the commonplace to the heightened—the theatrical, which always lifted her spirits. She sighed.

Ben said her name. She was, he thought, never more desirable, even abstracted in mood as she was.

"Yes?" she said.

"Are we thinking of the same thing?" he asked, taking her hand.

"I imagine so. Of all the ones we've seen today, can you guess which painting stays most in my eyes?"

"Oh." It was not what he hoped. "I can't guess."

"It is the still life by Fantin-Latour—the blue book on the table with pink and white carnations, and apples, pears, and a peeled orange. All that against dove gray. If I had to show anyone the perfect elegance of simplicity, I think that would be it. —What is yours?"

He sighed. If she wanted this game, he would play it. As he entered into it, his energy grew, and the game became important.

"Do you remember Saint John in the Desert? Domenico Veneziano? That scene with wild rocks like tall, frozen waves, and prickly greens, and in the center, the young saint wearing his halo and casting off his clothes? A moment of decision of some sort, but so strong, so content, so calm, in a world beyond ours. I think he is on a little plateau on a high mountain, and behind him mountains higher still cut way up against a new blue sky beyond our old blue sky. The whole thing is monumental, an immense place, a huge innocence, a mortal fact of the bare human body, and it says more than paint, more than image. I don't know what it says, but what it says is piercing. The panel is only about a square foot in size, and I would give the rest of my life to have painted it!"

His eyes seemed full of flecks of light. As she looked at him, her face glowed with color. He took her roughly into his arms and murmuring her name against her lips, her throat, he kissed and kissed her with the force of power long held back. Passing people smiled at each other for young lovers.

She folded her arms upward against him, and could speak only on little takes of breath.

"No, Ben. No, no. I—"

He let her go and she bent over, away from him. Her heart was skipping like a bird with a broken wing. She hid her face with her hands. He touched her shoulder. She shook her head. After a while, she sat up again and faced him. Her face was hot and flushed. When she spoke, her voice was unsteady but she tried to even it out.

"You must never again—" she said.

He stopped her mouth with his fingertips. "We both know it," he said. "I don't care how or where. I have waited and waited. Surely it's time, time."

She stood. "Ben, we have been friends. If we cannot still be friends, you must never come back."

"But you feel—your heart went wild, I felt it. I know it. How can you deny it?"

"You startled me."

"I had the truth out for us."

"You must not speak so. We must go now. You must promise or not return."

She walked away from him. He followed at a little distance until they came to the street. It was late afternoon. Lamps were just coming on in the long perspective of Constitution Avenue.

"Jack will be expecting us," she said, reestablishing her world.

"Jack!" he said half aloud, but she caught his mocking tone, and said,

"He has been very good to you."

"Yes," said Ben, now formally. "We must have a cab."

He hailed a taxi. They rode in silence to Georgetown, and Ben stared out the window, grinding in his thoughts the word "love," and in precise terms saw himself pulled into it, though how differently, by two people. He left her at the door.

With no one to speak to about her troubling state, Diana resolved that in some way or other she must remove herself from Ben. She began to wonder how to do it. She knew Jack would enact virtuous outrage if she ever suggested that Ben's constant appearances and attentions were a threat to the inner peace of the household, and must end. Should she declare an end? She shook her head. Peaceful rescue did not lie that way.

It seemed suddenly to come from an unexpected quarter.

Jack said one evening in late May, "The most unbelievable luck."

She inquired with a look.

"Yes," he continued, "the Millards are going abroad for the summer. Billy has offered us his place up on Lake Ontario for July and August. He said gratis, but I insisted on paying. It's expensive, but perfect. You will see."

He showed her snapshots which William Millard had given him. The house was a long, rambling white wooden cottage at Point St Albans on the Canadian side of Lake Ontario. It was surrounded by pine woods. The property ran right down to the lake. There was a power boat, a staff of servants—college students on vacation jobs who had been with the Millards for two summers and were already reengaged. The place was miles from the nearest summer-resort cottages, and there was a flawless beach, all private. The nights would be cool. Jack had decided to accept the place, bury himself there, and by a supreme effort of will and talent finish *All There Is* in time for autumn rehearsals. If Diana liked, he would give Miss Borrowdale the whole summer off with pay (poor thing, she adored him, it would kill her), and once again he and Diana would have those happy daily hours of work together. How would she like that?

It was a promise of peace and restoration. She was grateful. They made their plans.

Three weeks after they had been settled in the big cottage on the lake, Jack said he had a happy surprise for her.

"I'm afraid you are getting a little lonesome. It is pretty selfish of me to whisk you away without anyone else to see."

Anyone else! she thought. No one else, was all she asked, for as she said to herself, she was catching her breath, and beginning to feel secretly well again where she had been secretly ill.

Jack went on, "There is only one person in the world who fits in with us like velvet. I can go right on working, so can he. There is ever so much to paint around here. He once told me that water is his real element. I've asked Ben to join us."

"Oh, Jack, no!"

"But yes. Why. Why not? Aren't you pleased? Why not. I thought you were devoted to him."

She turned cold. She couldn't answer. Jack continued:

"He's crazy about you, plain to see. It will be amusing for you, you are so much nearer in age"—he did not specify than whom— "and we all talk the same language; and we never *really* had Ben to ourselves in Washington. Always those parties, and those *women* reaching for him in their dozens of little ways. We can have picnics, and take the power boat out fishing, and listen to records in the evening, or play backgammon, or I can read to you both. We can swim. I'm sorry if you are not pleased with my little surprise. I did it for you. —Not that I deny that I am awfully fond of Ben, he delights me with his relation to life. I've observed him, made notes— I've described him in one of them as a great beautiful animal who sees what he wants and simply takes it. He makes no demands on anyone, you see. He is never in my way. I think he will love the woods, the lake, the air, all of this. —I hope you can be nice to him," he added rather sardonically, in the face of her lack of enthusiasm.

A whirl of wild longing made her think of running away— though where, and to whom, she could not think. But somehow if there was yet time—she found her voice.

"When does he arrive?"

"Today. I sent the boat to Point St Albans to meet the train from Belle Plaine. It gets in about noon. It'll take them twenty-five minutes to come here in the Chris-Craft. I thought it would be more fun for Ben to arrive by water than by car. We can have drinks on the terrace, and a late lunch."

It was a beautiful day. The calm lake was the color of aquamarine. High clouds made long lines against the pale blue sky. The sand of the beach was a golden pale pink with sunlight, and the dark pines along the ridge behind the house were full of copious shadows which promised coolness and the smell of damp earth, velvet moss shot with little shafts of escaped sunshine. The lights and airs of such a day came freely into the house where there was every comfort to make people happy, in terms of easy and judicious taste.

But to Diana it seemed like an overcast day, the big, open house like a confining prison. If Ben was arriving in an hour or so, escape was impossible. The sound of the little waves lapping up on the beach was full of the monotony of unending sadness. She had the feeling that her strength—her physical strength—was leaving her. How must she arrange to look at him when he came? What should she say to him? How long might her spirit hold out? What seemed to her the final humiliation was that she loved him.

※

"Oh, how civilized we are," thought Diana.

Jack loved luxury and well-run houses. He came from a background quite as simple as Ben's, but what a climb he had made—poor dear, Diana reflected. They went on dressing for dinner, excepting Ben. Diana was grateful for whatever shred of formality was left to her. There was an effect of false stillness in the air in the first day or two after Ben's arrival. Finally, "What's the matter?" he asked Diana. "Why are you so—so unlike yourself?"

"But am I?"

"One minute so distant, the next so high and free?"

"I don't know," she replied untruthfully. "It is a strange summer."

"We are never alone."

"You should be left to yourself to paint."

"You know why I'm here."

"If I only knew *really*."

The household seemed to be waiting for the first thunderclap of a storm.

Diana wondered if Jack must be living with an elaborate melodrama in mind; something complicated, hard to believe, yet powerful enough to affect others. Only in such vague terms could she account for the kind of thing that was taking place. With nothing said about it, Jack—she tried any explanation which occurred to her —seemed to be tempting her with Ben's very presence.

One evening on the grassed terrace overlooking the lake they dined by candlelight in the still air, which was scented by roses that climbed profusely upon lattices against the white wall of the house. Jack put some records on the music machine in the sitting room and left the long glass doors open. The music came to them enhanced by distance.

After their coffee, Jack said, "I am going to have a glass of brandy. Will you join me?"

"Yes—lots," said Diana.

He stared at her. "Have we an emerging alcoholic on our hands? —Ben, how about you?"

"No, thank you."

Jack stopped in his tracks on the way to the bar tray which stood by the dining-room doors. "I must have you drop this nonsense about not drinking, Benjy," he declared. "We are all adults. We can drink like civilized persons. It is really a trifle churlish of you not to join us now and then in a drink. I'm going to bring you a glass of brandy and I'm going to see you drink it like a little man and prove to you that a spot of good brandy never hurt anybody."

"No, thanks."

"But why? Why. Why won't you accept my hospitality to the fullest?"

There was excitement in Jack's eyes by the candlelight.

"Jadi, don't insist," said Diana more sharply than she intended.

"I don't really like it," said Ben. "When I drink I get distorted."

"Distorted? What do you mean."

"I look and act like what I used to paint in Paris. Rooftops upside down and nudes with selected members much exaggerated."

Jack laughed as if involuntarily. "You mean liquor does things to you. Breaks you down? You like it too well? You do mean it that way, don't you:"

Ben shrugged. "If you want to say it that way."

"But you're so wholesome, Benjy. Just a little—"

"For heaven's sake, Jack, let him alone. If he doesn't want to, he doesn't have to."

Jack faced her with an animal smile—raised nostrils, revealed eye teeth.

"Oh yes," said Jack, "oh yes, it all adds up. When people are afraid of life they kill something in themselves. How do you suppose I keep going? I know pretty much the worst in people. God knows I am called upon often enough to help when someone goes down. I simply trust the life principle, that's all. It will persist. Life will out. It will repeat itself eternally. If you know this, there is nothing in the whole range of existence that can scare you. Admit everything, and you can govern anything. Am I now obliged to get quietly squiffy by myself?"

Having made his cross little joke—for it was his known habit to drink sparingly—he went to the tray and came back with his drink and Diana's. On an impulse he extended his drink to Ben. Ben put his hands in his pockets and looked at the brandy in which swam the golden reflections of the candle flames. Jack caught a deep breath which sounded.

He said, "You love it. You know you do. I can see it. It makes a whole other world in your head and your belly. Here. Take it."

Ben looked at him with a severe grin. "If I took it—and I don't intend to—you might be sorry. I'd probably take another, and then another, and then the bottle. And then I'd probably do something regrettable."

"Like what, like what!" demanded Jack. His voice was reedy.

"For no reason at all I might beat you up."

Jack's excitement flared out like static electricity. Even then, he was not forgetful. He looked behind to be certain that the servants had retired to their part of the house, or had gone to the village. Nobody was about.

"If you tried, you'd get quite a surprise," said Jack, with a sickish, ardent look about his mouth. "I'm in pretty good condition. I work out all year at my club. I've got the reach on you, you know. I may look to you like an old man, and a skinny old man, but I could give an account of myself. I'm not scared. Here. Take it. I'll prove it to you."

He rolled the brandy around in the big snifter and the fumes came up delicately and powerfully. Ben looked at him and blew out a big breath. He reached for the glass. Diana reached forward.

"This is nonsense, and very unattractive nonsense," she said. "Jack, I cannot think what's got into you. I don't think Ben ought to take it. Give it to me, Ben. Give it to me."

Now Ben was peacefully content to have the glass—in a sense relieved of responsibility. He bent slightly over Diana, holding the glass away from her. With his head on one side, he gave her a smile of inquiring sweetness. It turned her heart over. He was like a boy committed to dear folly. Putting his hand out to hold hers away as she reached for the glass, he drank it empty in one long, luxurious, joyful draught.

The act seemed to dissipate some precarious tension which had been gathering in them all for months.

"There!" cried Jack. "That's my boy. You see? You couldn't drink a bad brandy like that!"

Alcohol did little to Jack—only made him more elaborately talkative. Ben was drowsy and content, until Jack opened a new bottle. Ben then got up from his chair, took the bottle from him, and shoved him away. With an air of wit and achievement, he drank, holding a finger up to call attention to his prowess. After a prodigious drink he handed the bottle back to Jack and threw his arms apart in wild well-being and let out a yell of simple joy.

Jack began to laugh in excited approval. He acted drunker than he was. He pointed weakly at Ben and tried to talk but failed and only went on laughing. Ben went close to him.

"May I ask," he said in comic distinctness, "who—pardon, whom —you are laughing at?"

Jack poked him in the chest, gasping with laughter. Ben gave him a shove. Jack fell down. Ben hauled him to his feet, and said, "If only we were all nothing else but friends. How happy we should be. Sometimes it is a bore not being just friends."

"Why, Ben, what a strange remark."

"Nothing strange."

"Tell me, Ben. This is very interesting. What are you getting at?"

Ben waved a forefinger before his face and said, "Oh no you don't. I'm not that drunk."

"You're not drunk at all, my boy."

"Ha."

Ben's happiness with his liquor was suddenly gone. His eyes looked smaller. His cheeks looked gray.

"Sometime," said Jack, "I'll have to get you really drunk."

As suddenly as before, Ben's mood changed. A grimace of glee came on his face. "You'd be sor-ry," he chanted.

"Why? Why should I be sorry, Ben, tell me, fella?"

Ben did not answer that, but turned to Diana in a loose lunge as though to excuse himself to her with a plea on his face. Then he returned to Jack, and said with a studious assumption of reasonableness, "No, Jack, old kid, old kid, too many things come back. I should never drink."

"Oh. Oh, *that*, Benjy." Jack bravely lifted his head and waved at invisible chimerae. "That's the only way to get rid of them. —What sort of thing? What comes back?" His eyes gleamed and he edged forward in his chair.

"There's nothing in your life to parallel it," said Ben. "You'd never get it. You don't know about anything real."

"Me? Of course I would. Of course I do. Ben: if there's anything you must believe about me, it is that I want to grasp all there is in life. If I ever achieve even a little of that, I will have the right to forgive, for myself, and for everybody else—*anything* that can happen to men and women."

"Well, they never tried to stop you," said Ben. Clouds of past regrets were rising and falling behind his thought.

"No—yes—something always tries, life keeps trying everywhere," declared Jack pedantically.

"Yes, you are right. But they couldn't. They would have had to kill me. Maybe they thought they were doing it, in one way or another."

Jack asked softly, urgently, "How, Ben, how:"

"Well, sir, I'll tell you," said Ben, with his forefinger making drunken loops in the air. "I was the changeling, you see, and the rest, brothers, cousins, the village of Olympia, would not forgive that, no, I know. They had no *way* to forgive that. So I knew oh so early that I had to re—to repudiate them, all of them, and I did it, and I lost them by finding myself. I lost her, but they didn't know what she really was—"

"Who, Ben, who:"

Diana wanted to tell Jack to be quiet; but there was an intense, drunken concentration between the two men, and she could not break it. She was silent.

"Why, you damned fool, my mother, and they thought I didn't love and respect her. But it had to be everybody or nobody so it was everybody and I left, never to go back. But let me tell you something, she took life as an honor, she had the honorable modesty about the huge fact of containing life and being alive—they all took it for granted. Except me. And maybe my father. I can't speak of that. No son can. Grand mystery, one of the creative secrets of the world, you know—what any mother sees in the father of her children, and what she hears from him. Maybe the old man had enough unformed poetry in him to keep her spirit glowing. Don't know. Red barn. Dark maples. Ducks on a pond. Our cows in the marsh that drained to the crick. Brown carpet in the parlor. The town like a set of cracker boxes except when the first sunrise light or the last sunset struck it from the side, and made it as beautiful as Paris. Was the place innocent, or was I? Who knows. I left it because I had to know more about it than they would let me know. By *it* I mean any place, of course. Don't pretend you knew *that*. I didn't even go back to her funeral. Why didn't I? They never forgave me. I never could go back at all." He looked around hazily and sweetly. "Who ever said I wanted to?"

Diana found it hard to bear. Whether or not this was the revelation of a real betrayal did not matter— Ben thought it was real, and suffered accordingly. She wanted to comfort him. She made no move.

"Yes, Benjy, my boy," said Jack quietly, in his most resonant and cultivated tone, "I can be there with you, feel it all with you, suffer it with you, and *still* say that nothing matters but what we learn from the past, good or bad, rich or poor. You are the great man you are because you—"

Ben straightened up in his chair. "This is not a Bowery mission meeting, in a gutter, and I don't require any fellowship, thank you," he said.

Jack was too elated to quit. He put his hand toward an airy vision and said, "Yes, the white farmhouse under the big trees, and the orchard, perhaps? and all life teeming, with animals, yes, with young people aching with wonderful, terrible, sex, and I can see it, Ben, because I can see you there, and feel your amazement at your boyhood's grown flesh burning to spend its love—"

Such an invasion could have been tactfully misunderstood sober. Drunk, Ben had to recognize it for what it was. He rose and grasped Jack by the front of his velvet dinner coat, and hauled him to stand. Jack began to laugh with excitement. Ben shook him for want of words.

"Ben, Ben, be civilized," cried Jack. He poked Ben in the chest in a comradely spirit. Ben pushed him off. Jack fell, striking a chair which nudged the glass table from whose edge the second brandy bottle fell to the flagstone terrace and broke into bits. It made a sound of triumphant disorder. Ben pulled Jack to his feet again.

"O.K.," he said, spitting on his thumbs. "O.K."

Jack played up to what the scene called for. He pulled off his jacket and wrenched his collar open. He knew acting.

"Ho-ho," said Ben gleefully. "Some fun, eh?"

He threw down his own jacket, and then still feeling constricted, tore his shirt off down to his bare skin.

They began to fight.

"You idiots! This is so stupid!" cried Diana. "Stop it, stop it, do you hear?"

They ignored her. There was uncomplicated joy of physical battle in Ben's face, and in Jack's there was a loving sort of excite-ment mixed with delicious fear. They struck out at each other with all their might. Ben showed a fierce playfulness which was in itself funny and attractive to watch, except that something else hiding down under the alcohol disturbed Diana.

Jack retreated slowly before the superior onslaught. Ben's youth and powerful body threatened and fascinated him. They knocked lamps off tables, overturned chairs. Now and then they grappled and fell together to the floor, shaking the wooden house. When Diana went again to separate them they did not see or hear her. She was astonished how Jack survived the attack this long. They were not boxing. They were exchanging kicks, shoves, as well as blows. They threw their whole bodies at each other. Jack was shaken by the elemental force which was expending part of its full self against him. For the happy and raging Ben he felt love and envy which he must wreck if he could.

Diana was sick at the spectacle.

She turned and went outside to the long lawn which led down to the beach. Light from the house gave way to darkness, which she welcomed. She could still hear the struggle as it progressed to the front hall and then up the stairs.

In another moment she heard a tumbling fall and with a great racket something crashed its way down the stairs and ended with a house-shaking impact. Silence followed. She ran back inside. At the foot of the stairs Ben was lying inert against the square wooden newel post. Over his closed eyes he wore a fixed frown. He was unconscious. At the head of the stairs, breathing painfully and staring down at his achievement, was Jack. His face was drawn and gray. His eyes were almost blind from sweat but he saw enough to know that incredibly he had disposed of the goading image. When he saw Diana he seemed to start awake. He ran downstairs and knelt with her over Ben. He began to babble with fright and remorse, trying between heaves of his chest to explain and justify what he had done. Ben was chasing him up the stairs, Jack was barely getting away. At the top of the stairs Ben suddenly crouched, and lunged upward beyond balance. Seeing his chance, Jack kicked him in the belly and sent him thundering down the steps. It was all unintended. He didn't think. He misjudged his force. Good God, how badly was Ben hurt?

It was lucky that Diana was sober, and from shock Jack nearly so. They must take Ben to Point St Albans to find a doctor. As they worked to raise Ben, he dimly came to his senses, and they managed to take him out to the car. A deep cut in his head was still spouting blood but Diana had given Jack a cold wet napkin to hold over it. She drove as fast as night and the country road permitted. The inn at the village was still lighted downstairs. They found the address of a doctor and drove to his house. He took many stitches in the cut and dressed it. Jack and Diana watched like parents who suffered with their child in surgery. The doctor's office was old-fashioned, everything beyond the circle of his working lamp seemed dark brown, and shadows moved as he worked. Despite the pain deadener, Ben now and then could not suppress a swallowed grunt or curse. Brandy fumes reached the doctor. He worked with unhurried skill and in silent reproof. When he was done, he dryly stated that Ben would have a headache tomorrow, perhaps from something in addition to the cut itself, and later there would be a scar on the forehead. An old man, he had his opinion of summer folk.

※

The aftermath was almost more difficult for Diana to endure than the disreputable night. Jack was now playful about it.

"Can't say I didn't give you fair waaning," he declared in his imitation of a sly New England farmer's speech, swaggering over a smart triumph.

[157]

Ben chose to remember nothing. He let Jack enact his comedy of dangerous strength. There was no contempt in Ben's attention to the recital of what had happened to him. In a few days the cut was healing rapidly.

"You'll have a fascinating scar," said Jack, "running down from that tousled hairline. You'll make up splendid stories about how you got it. I can provide thrilling scenarios for you if you like. Marseilles waterfront. A German grenade you picked up and threw back half a second too late. A missed step climbing out of a window before somebody's husband came home. Females will want to touch the scar and imagine everything."

They resumed the life of a well-ordered household. Ben went wandering in the woods and far along the beach. Presently he began a picture. When he worked, he was alone, completely, whether anyone was about or not. It was hard to remember and to believe that other creature of wild power who had appeared in his likeness that night. He never drank again in that house.

※

A long spell of heat lingered over Point St Albans. Lake Ontario was glassy. If clouds appeared, they hung way out over the lake, thin, and high, never yielding rain. The villagers of Point St Albans, girt on three sides by pine woods, began to worry about forest fires. The vacation crowds enjoyed the calm blazing weather heedlessly, especially the nights. The nights were superb—still, with moonlight at all phases which seemed destined to linger forever upon all it touched. Many a pair who had met casually on vacation were pierced by the sweetness of such nights of opulent moonlight and air that hardly trembled, many a pair lost themselves in illusions of eternity and extremities of desire, until in the daylight of their last allotted time they had to go their separate ways.

At the big white cottage way out along the beach, they were not immune.

One evening Jack remarked, "I think it is absurd."

"What is, Jadi?"

"Absurd to come up here to the peace and wild of the Canadian lake shore, and sit down to dine every evening by candlelight, with silver and crystal, and two maids, and a houseboy in a white jacket. After all, what did we do all the rest of the year but live this way? I've been selfish, but only my work must be blamed, I forget the daily foreground of others. I am reminded of what the Goncourts said somewhere in their journals—'Theater is a disease like prostitution or beggary.' I'm hopelessly corrupted by it. But we must make amends. Don't you think? What we must do, we must have a picnic, and soon. Tomorrow night. There will be a full moon. We'll take hampers, and all go in the station wagon, with a radio, and lanterns, and some light Rhine wine in ice, and if the light is good enough—heavens: you could read by moonshine these nights —and if you're both really interested, I might read you a few scenes from *All There Is.*"

They assured him of their interest.

"And perhaps you could see things, Benjy, to draw or paint, beach nocturnes? That silvery dark water, that silvery endless sky? Why not plan a whole show of such atmospheres?"

"It is always edifying," said Diana "to see Jack roughing it."

Chiding her with a forgiving wink of both eyes, Jack rang for the college-boy butler, who came in wearing his starched white jacket. He was a tall, blond youth eager to please, but full of reserved opinions.

He said, "Yes, *patrón?*"

The form of address was agreed upon early in the summer. Jack had arrived at it with his domestic staff. He thought in their informal life he would be bored to be addressed as Mister. At the same time, "Jack," considering his seniority and his position in the world, was too familiar. "Maestro" would be affected. As he was the *papa* here, he told them, "let's say *patrón*" (he had been in Pamplona during his Hemingway period and had admired the ancient deference shown to the head of the house in Spain).

"Yes, *patrón*?"

"Guapo"—Jack had named him "Handsome" in Spanish—"we've decided on a picnic for tomorrow night. Put your head together with Cindy and Bella and plan everything. We want *everything*, and we want you three to be part of our picnic, too, so plan for all of us. If any of you can sing, practice your scales. Have you a guitar? Bring it, or a uke, or a jew's-harp, or anything, say, but a tuba. We'll have a bash. Chill a half dozen of the Liebfraumilch. We're all going to be your age tomorrow night. Wonderful? Be ready to leave at half past six. Wonderful."

They drove as far up the beach as they could before encountering boulders and driftwood too large to get around. Guapo stopped the car. Everyone took on a share of the load—rugs, hampers, ice buckets, cushions, Coleman lanterns, flashlights, radio, and the kit of materials with which to start a campfire. In the last daylight, stars were coming out and the moon grew in power. Jack in command led the party a way farther on foot, until they rounded a point and came upon a symmetrical little cove where moonlight, black pines, and shoreline all trembled in the pure water. Wavelets sounded like hushed laughter on the pale sand. It was the most appealing spot in the several miles of Jack's private beach. It gave an illusion of wildness and tenderness, as if nature though untutored were essentially gentle and good.

There on clean sand which winked like diamond dust in the moonlight they had a luxurious picnic. When done with serving, the collegiate servants were swept with an invitation to sit down and join in by Jack, in one of his officially humane moods. What with the wine, the charm of the place, and Jack's presiding kindness, it was not long before they all began to sing. Cindy had a guitar and a light high voice. Bella owned a pair of *sonajas* from Mexico and kept time. Guapo was a natural leader in the kind of song that belonged to campfire and beach, and led them all in a husky crooning voice which expertly reproduced the style of male radio stars. If his voice was unmusical, not so his spirit. Smiling in awareness of how he muddied the musical waters, he gave with conviction and glee a good share of the party's simple joy. Diana felt delivered by numbers. What genuinely nice young people they had working for them. What did they want? She wished she might give it to them for their lives.

But Jack always knew when enough was enough. At half past nine, he said cheerfully to them, "Well, children, you have absolutely made the party, I can't thank you enough, so now, if you will, please gather everything up and take the car and go on back to the house. The rest of us will stay awhile, and come back later on foot. It's not all that far. Bless you, my chicks. We must have another one soon."

The party fell apart. The moonlight now seemed to belong not to all of them but to Jack, who had allotted their proper share of it to those in his employ. As rueful as children, but better at concealing their feelings, the servants did his bidding; though there was a momentary threat to Jack's arrangements.

"Here, I'll go help them and ride back with them," said Ben.

"Nonsense, Ben. They can manage perfectly. —Don't you want to hear me read, after all?"

Even Ben could not ignore such a claim on his politeness. He fell back upon the sand and took a nap while the gathering up was completed and the others marched away.

But when the three were left alone, Jack riffled his pages doubtfully. "I don't know. I've always wondered if it's a good idea to read unfinished work to anyone—even ones to whom I feel so close as I do to you both. The first two acts stand pretty well as they are, and yet, and yet. It's not that I'm not sure of the work, but after all, this is a picnic. Why should we waste this wealth of moonlight, that liquid silver in our tiny bay, this warm night? I feel it caressing us all. Much better to use all that in innocent play." What did he mean? they seemed to ask in silence. "You know what I mean? Obvious. We should all get up and go swimming, here and now."

Diana sat up and looked at him. "But we didn't bring any suits," she said.

Jack laughed wholesomely at her qualm. "What difference should that make? What's wrong with going in without any? Aren't we who we are, to ourselves, and each other?"

Diana felt a thump in her breast. She could imagine how under other circumstances she might have gone swimming by moonlight without clothes, and no second thought about it; but with all of Jack's other devious measures to expose her and Ben to one another, for what purpose she could not, or would not, say, this was too explicit. For a moment she was unable to answer.

"Yes!" cried Ben with delight. He ran down to the water's edge, threw off his clothes, and with a great booming splash took to the water. He turned and slapped the water like a beaver and called to them. "Hurry up! It's marvelous. Come join me!"

"You see?" said Jack, turning to her. "Isn't that it, to be that natural and simple about what you want to do?"

His voice was a little dry and as he awaited her move his excitement could not be disguised.

"Oh, Jack, what are you thinking of," she said to him in a low voice.

"Hey! Come on!" bellowed Ben.

"Thinking of?" said Jack. "I'm not thinking of anything, except that we're all grown up, and closer than friends, and warm, and there's water and moonlight to be made use of. What are *you* thinking of, Diana?" he said, and into his voice he put reproof and sadly recognized depths of suspicion in her. He made her seem indecent. He was gentle and regretful, like one whose happy impulse has been falsely made shameful.

She put her hands to her face, shook her head, and ran off up the beach toward the way to the cottage.

Ben swam inshore to shallows and stood up; wet and gleaming in all his length. "What's the matter?" he called. "Why did she go?"

"Ben," said Jack in a voice held steady, "Ben, stand there forever, like a young Poseidon." Then he turned and busied himself with gathering up his possessions and said briskly, "It's nothing. The party's over. Stay if you like," and in his turn began the walk back along the beach.

Concluding with a frown that what occurred to him was true, Ben dressed and after a while began to idle his way after the others. When he reached the cottage, it was dark, but for a light on the terrace to guide him.

꙲

Not much was said the next day about the end of the picnic, but it was in the air when they all met again.

Jack bit on his pipe with a grizzled smile and winked his eyes at Diana as much as to say, for Ben's benefit, that as long as he lived, and as much as he had written about women, he would never understand them, bless their queer, wonderful, unpredictable hearts.

They were all supposed, according to the day's plan—Jack had a plan for each day—to go out after lunch in the motorboat, which Jack had christened the *Queen Mary II*. Diana was trying to make up her mind whether to say she had a headache and would not go, when Jack announced that the morning's mail had brought urgent matters to which he must attend without delay. Let Diny and Ben go without him, and be back in time for dinner with a full account of their adventures: a fine day for a ramble up the lake in the smart little cruiser.

It was still possible for Diana to make her excuses; but she was too tired at heart to do so.

"Good. Ben," she said a little stridently, "I'll go with you."

"Perfect," said Jack. "Guapo has seen to the boat. The girls have packed a hamper. The *Queen Mary* is a little beauty. You'll have a lovely time, while I slave away on drafts of committee letters for the Old Actors Relief Fund—I'm the new chairman."

As they set out, Diana felt dread and relief. Ben ran the boat. Once out in the open lake, she fell into a kind of numb peace.

"Would you mind if I slept a little while?" she asked. "If you see any interesting sights, you must wake me."

He waved his assent, smiling at the lake ahead where his bows were cutting a fine twin wave. He was alive with the spice of desire. She went to sleep lulled by the silky tearing sound of the water, the even hum of the engine, and the wafting motion of the hull.

She did not know how long she slept, but it was a long nap, when she was awakened by silence.

They were drifting.

"What is it?" she asked, sitting up.

Ben was below, leaning over the motor.

"I can't tell," he called. "We simply stopped."

They were miles from shore. Nothing was in sight but a long freight boat hull-down on the southern horizon, with its smoke standing idly in the still air.

"We should have plenty of gasoline," said Ben. "Jack said the tank was filled. It would be good for hours."

He went to sound the fuel tank. In a moment he called again, "Dry. Not a drop."

"It cannot be."

"It is."

He came on deck, smiling happily.

"I didn't do it," he said. "I've never used a stale joke."

She turned scarlet. "No," she said, "someone else did."

"I suppose the young man forgot."

"No."

She was pale with anger and certainty. Was there no foolish and wretched resort which Jack was ashamed to use?

"What do you mean:"

"Haven't you ever guessed—my husband."

"Oh, nonsense, Diny," said Ben. He was astonished and a little alarmed at her idea. "What on earth would he do a thing like that for?"

At the end of her resources of humor, tolerance, self-respect, she turned aside and broke into tears. She was humiliated as never before. She sobbed for her own weakness and for her barren life. Ben came and sat by her and took her in his arms. He made comforting sounds in which his bewilderment encouraged his joyously leaping flesh. She turned into his embrace. She held to him like a lost child. She could not speak or think. When he sought her face and kissed gently, and kissed her again in a surge of possession, brushing her tears with his lips and pressing her cheeks as though to engulf her, grief and all, in his being, she lost herself to his strength and simplicity. He suffered her to recover herself in her own time and way. They could not have been more alone, in that rimless circle of quiet water, under the sun, and the fleckless pale blue sky.

Soon she was at peace. She straightened away from him.

"Thank you," she said.

"No, no, nothing about thanks. Here:"

He took her to the secure little cabin below. The white cruiser drifted, rocking, and lifting and falling in its element.

The afternoon was falling with the sun. Slow ripples on the lake began to take on opalescent shadows. Ben came up into the cockpit to survey the horizon. Nothing yet in sight. He called to her. On the deck at the stern a bolted line lay neatly coiled. He threw its end overboard.

"The lake is warm."

He helped her over the side and followed. They held each other in the laving caress of the water.

"A wonderful light in your eyes," he exclaimed.

Cleaved to one another, they floated in the embrace of the moving, summery lake. She felt a lightness like the air itself.

The cruiser drifted a little distance away. They swam to it, he caught the lifeline, went aboard, and helped her after him. They went below to dress. He turned on the running lights. The sky was going from peach color to golden rose and the high heaven was already darkening.

In the locker below there was a wicker hamper filled with food and drink quite up to the Wentworth standard. They were hungry. Catching each other's eye, they laughed at the same moment when it struck them whose picnic they were enjoying—paté, chicken in aspic, chilled chablis, black bread, iced scallions and radishes. Ben ate rapidly in animal pleasure.

His appetites, she thought. *All related.*

As though he read her mind, he said, "Can we always be natural? It is part of freedom. Don't ever let me hurt you if I stay free. Love itself is freedom. I've known it ever since I left Olympia in my imagination, as a boy. *What* I loved had to change as I grew up. But love was always there."

He spoke lightly, his face aglow with his feeling for her. He was bestowing freedom upon her even as he claimed it for himself. If there were undermeanings in his creed, she did not then hear them. The hour was enough.

At dark, Ben turned on the boat's searchlight and beamed it into the sky as a beacon. The stars came out. Now and then they thought they could see shore lights, but these turned out to be only reflections of some of the larger stars near the horizon. The moon rose later than last night's. There was poetry in their feeling equaled by the night, the ancient repose of the lake waters at peace, and a detachment from the immediate world such as lovers ordinarily had to invoke for themselves but which now seemed to enfold them with all elements of the empty scene.

Late at night rescue came. Their failure to return by nightfall led to the organization of a search party from Point St Albans. A little tourist launch with striped awnings bore down on the drifting *Queen Mary II*. From a distance the two boats signaled each other with their searchlights. Everything was admirably thought out. The rescuing launch *Arrow,* from Mead in the inlet opposite Point St Albans, was stocked with blankets, life preservers, whiskey, hot coffee, extra gasoline, and Jack Wentworth. His courage had never flagged, and his high spirits and happy relief were a joy to behold when the boats touched hulls and both parties exchanged animated reports of how the adventure looked from each end. Nobody was the worse for the experience, and the village had a happy ending to talk about for days, together with the generous fees Jack had privately pressed upon the villagers who so selflessly had helped to find the crippled cruiser. To Jack's gratification, everyone made a point of behaving in the most considerate fashion. After a sound night's sleep, everyone would be as good as new.

When Jack came downstairs the next morning, he saw neatly stacked in the front hallway all of Ben's gear—his box of paints, his easel, some stretchers and canvases.

[167]

"What on earth!" he demanded heartily when he found Ben at breakfast on the grassy terrace.

"I have to get back to town," said Ben. "I should not have stayed so long, but it has been splendid. A fine place. A fine change."

"Oh, my," said Jack, sighing with fortitude, "it seems only yesterday—we all three were coming to a new and wonderful intimacy. —Oh, I know, I know," he added, shutting his eyes and holding up his palm, "nothing will persuade you to stay on. But as I've always said, the only way to hold your friends for life is to grant them complete, but *complete,* freedom. We'll all come together again when I come up to town for my rehearsals—the play will be finished, I'll need you then, you've no idea of the strain, what relief one needs between off-stage scenes with actor folk and stage-hands. Dear Ben. I hope it has been happy here?"

"Oh yes."

"You're not furious because the wretched little boat gave out?"

"Oh no."

"You know what you mean to me."

"Of course. A pal."

"I hate that word, it really says nothing. Never mind. Let it go. Some things mean more unspoken. —Does Diny know you're going?"

"Yes. I told her last night. She seemed relieved."

"Relieved! —But I know what you mean. Sometimes I wonder if she really likes you."

Ben's reply to this was silence, with a smile which he ground between his jaws. Jack, sure of yesterday's success, was positioning himself for a luxurious, long exploration of matters which had never yet been brought to light, but Ben left him to unwelcome silence.

Diana did not come down for breakfast.

Nolens volens, said Jack, he must work, even if his best friend was about to take his leave. He said goodbye to Ben with a conventional handshake but kept his eyes looking deeply into Ben's even while turning away to part from him.

Hurriedly, he said, "Goodbye, Benjy. Guapo will drive you to the dinky-train at Point St Albans. I'm sorry I can't go along—work, work, work. Don't ever be a slave. Yes. *Be* a slave. It's the only way. Nothing else matters but work. Can you learn to give everything to it, no matter what else you want?"

"You want the future. I want the moment. *Chacun.*"

"—*à son goût,*" said Jack brightly. With a smile of conscious bravery, he briskly turned and went to his future.

On the drive to the train, Ben asked, "Did you fill the tank yesterday in the Chris-Craft?"

"I certainly did," replied Guapo. "What's more, I saw the *patrón* go down to the boathouse after lunch and personally check the tank himself. Somebody must have emptied out more than half the gasoline after that. It burns me up."

"So it does."

"The train's in."

"Yes. Thanks. Goodbye and good luck."

"Mr Ives, does it take a long time to become an artist? I've thought of becoming a painter."

"If you didn't begin half your lifetime ago, I wouldn't expect too much of it now," said Ben, but kindly.

"Golly. I see. Starts early?"

"Everything does. *Adios.*"

The little two-car train began to move, Ben ran to catch it.

※

A fortnight later the Wentworths closed their lake household. Diana said to Jack that though they would leave together, she planned to stop off in Dorchester for a few days on the way home to Washington to see friends there, and to talk to Michael Scanlon at the bank about her father's estate.

Jack said, "You must of course do as you feel you must, but don't be too long about it. The Manor will be a hollow rockery until you come back."

She smiled dutifully.

"Besides," he continued, "I need you there when all the photographers come to take the publicity pictures for the production of *All There Is*—it *looks* so much better when you're in the pictures with me."

Meantime, he would take the bulk of her summer luggage on to Washington with him, if she liked, since she would need only a few things for a few days.

"And then, after you come home, there will be time for one of our talks."

"Talks?"

He smiled with both eyes closed for a second. "One of our little talks. No wide-eyed evasions, please. The one thing we have to agree to keep bright and shining, ever, is complete honesty. That adult understanding upon which if upon anything our life must stand."

He knew.

He wanted her to know that he knew.

He was preparing to reap luxuriously the emotional harvest of his long implanting. He was as sensitive to silent messages as a cat.

His smile looked, really, a little like a cat's when he took leave of her in the station at Dorchester to pursue his distinguished way alone to Washington. She could visualize how in a very short while he would have alerted the whole train to his presence, with a special kindly word to each of the porters, waiters, trainmen, whose happy job it was to convey him on his journey. If one were shy or surly, she knew how Jack would pull at him with claims of good nature and fellow feeling until—indispensible condition—he had found a new friend, and with him, fresh reassurances, confirmations, balm, for whatever it was in Jack which could not rest in its own peace. The Gentleman in Drawing Room A, Car 770, would have and must have the best, and have it happily given, even if only to repay flattery enfolded in five-dollar bills.

The same night, she took a local train to Batavia, New York, where Ben was to meet her. She had no doubts or regrets, but she did ask herself what really she knew about him. In those times when she was not with him, what did he do? Whom did he see? She had known him only in her world. He spoke much of freedom. How did he define it? No matter. Freedom was now hers. It was enough.

He was waiting at Batavia that night with a remarkable car, "bought second-hand two days ago in Albany," he explained when there was a moment for words.

"Where are we going?" she asked.

"I've no idea. We'll go until we want to stop."

A few days later she wrote a little note to Jack from a darkly wooded village in Kentucky telling him that she was motoring south with Ben Ives, and that he need not expect to hear from her again. She would make no claims upon him. He could be assured of her discretion so far as his own secure reputation might be concerned. She had resumed her maiden name as Diana Macdonald. There was no point in trying to tell him where she would be, as she did not know.

When John Wentworth read this message, he felt stricken and ill, for his two losses. Change was terrible. Love was both treacherous and abiding. In scheming their lives, what had he done to his own? For a moment of thought like vertigo he wondered how he could survive this pain.

He did so when his eye fell to the open engagement book on his desk, and he saw that this was the morning for the publicity photographers. He must not let them down. He must rise above private concern. He blinked away his visible distress. There would be time for grief later, and for decisions.

Interlude

Later that year, Howard Debler wrote a letter:

Dear Mrs Wentworth,

It has been a long time since we have been in touch. I hope it is not an intrusion now, or that you may think of me as a total stranger, as we met last time during the war when I was in Washington on temporary duty. But I have two purposes in writing to you now.

The first is to send you my sympathy on hearing of your father's death. Though it happened all that time ago, during the war, when I was at sea, I knew nothing of it until lately when I wrote to him asking if I might spend another few days in his library at Dorchester. My letter was answered by the manuscript curator at the University of Dorchester library, who told me that your father had been lost on a wartime mission, and that his library is now at the university. I was given permission to use it. I know how wonderfully close you were to him, and I know his death must be sorely troubling to you. If you'll let me, I'll say that it pains me in a particular way to think of you as having to endure suffering. As for me, I never met a man for whom I had greater respect—some immediate sense of getting to the central energy of anything we might be talking about. Though I knew him only briefly, I shall miss him, and particularly, the idea of him.

My other interest in writing to you is to ask if I might see you in Washington before the end of the month. I'll be going on to

*Washington after I finish working at the university library.
In Washington I need to collate some references at the National
Archives and the Library of Congress. Perhaps you will remember that I have been readying for several years (interrupted by
my war service) my book on the Mexican War of 1846-48.
When I emerged from the Navy I immediately went to work
again on the book, and it continues to take shape.*

*I have resigned from my teaching job to work full time on
my old war. If I'm lucky, I'll find another university post when
the book is done. In the meantime, I am living and working at
my mother's home, my own old home, actually, in Grand Plains,
Texas, where I am barricaded behind a fortress of books, photo-
stats, maps, old American and Mexican engravings, discarded
drafts, and a pyramid of unanswered letters. I may have something to show Mr Blaine (thanks to you!) before too long.*

*I would be ever so glad if you could let me call when I am in
Washington.*

Ever sincerely yours,
Howard Debler

He addressed the letter to Diana at The Riverview Manor in
Georgetown.

It was returned, with the envelope stamped in purple ink,
ADDRESSEE UNKNOWN. RETURN TO SENDER.

He knew then how much he had counted on seeing her. His dis-
appointment made him gloomy for days, though he tried to show
only his habitually preoccupied even temper. He did not deceive
Clara Debler.

"What is it?" she asked flatly one morning at breakfast.

"What is what?"

"It isn't your work—I hear your typewriter going day and night.
But you don't have a word for me, and you even push Nicodemus
off your lap when he jumps up to take charge of you."

"I'm sorry, Mother. I suppose I have been out of sorts. —I'll be glad for a little change when I go East." To make up for his behavior of recent days, he added, "Would you like to come with me? Perhaps a change would do you good, too."

"Change! What would I want with a *change*! Heavens, no. I have too much to do right here."

The furious energies which tied her to her world were, he saw, of the utmost importance. What could she do for anyone in Washington, D.C.? He laughed outright for the first time in a week, and went up to his lookout tower for the day's work.

PART FIVE

AT THE GULF OF MEXICO, the sea itself seemed a vast act of meditation. No matter what ships slowly rose on the horizon and dwindled from sight, or how many shuttering flights of seabirds united sky and water and vanished into light, the sea was always a limitless solitude.

Diana took the idea to herself at those times when she was alone waiting for Ben to return from one of his absences—"to paint," "to shake himself up," just "to *see* alone," as he so often put it in trying to make her accept the separate existence of his work as a painter. Little as she liked these brief abandonments, she knew they were true needs in him; and when he was gone she would see him, think of him, with a sort of double vision. She could feel a shiver of engulfing tenderness over how she loved watching him when he was unaware, rather as though she were watching a beloved child. But she could see also how he was with other people, with other women, exactly; and, denying good sense, a recognition would burn under her heart and heat her thought and tell her:

When you are in the presence of any woman even passably attractive, your eye takes on an almost comic shrewdness, your mouth becomes a line of calculating want, and you set your fine head on an angle of invitation and challenge. Oh, often enough all this stirs women to delight, or desire, or something more blind than either in the pitiless design of nature; and this shows itself to you even if you are met with shock or propriety, for response of any kind is proof of your power, and you like it. Yes, nature demands more of you than of other men. I dwell on this belief until forgiveness itself becomes a voluptuous passion, and I feel new heartstrings in me which are set to quivering with desire so great that I cast my inward eye away from it. And yet when you are here, sometimes I lie awake beside you and ask myself where you are. While you sleep content I ask myself, after all the other years of my life, "Am I truly like that?"

When alone, at night, in the midst of such moral storms, she would think of the sea, its lift and fall, and she would woo comfort from the memory of the lightness of heart which was hers if he but touched her in passing, or smiled in a certain way.

❦

As the days advanced and the warmth of the Gulf winter began to yield to the hot light of spring, the weather brought forerunners of the summer people to the beach.

One morning while Ben was gone for the day to paint in the salt marshes to the east, she was glad to hear the grinding of gears behind the dunes and know that the soft-drink man had arrived in his truck to arrange for her summer supplies. She had been feeling dowdy. Now, more for her sake than the driver's, she quickly smartened herself before her little mirror, and when he bounded up to the porch, she was ready to greet him. She came out and stood behind her oilcloth counter as he climbed up on one of the tall metal stools placed for customers.

"Are you the lady of the house?"

"Yes," she replied, laughing. "If that's what this is."

"My name is Pud. I aim to make regular calls here to supply you with Coc'-Cola. My boss said you left an order."

[182]

"Yes. This will be my first summer so you must tell me what others have bought on a regular delivery. —What happened to them after last summer? Did they just leave?"

"They just up and left. Sort of a crippled man and his old lady. Nice folks, but I never did get them to talkin."

Pud was as unconsciously expectant of life and happiness as a baby. He seemed compounded of glee, confidence, and content. His hair, the color of a new penny, was thick where it escaped from his Coca-Cola cap. His face was mostly occupied by his smile, surrounded by large freckles in white skin. He made Diana smile just to look at him, for if his features were lumpish and plain, his self-regard proclaimed him as one of the best men you could find anywhere.

"So what do you figger?" he asked, taking out his order pad. "I've got to write your name down?"

"Miss Macdonald."

"You alone?"

"Oh, no. I have a friend with me. He is away for the day. How much did you deliver last summer? Was it every day? Every week? How?"

"I waddn't here, ol Jody made this run. But I've got the figgers."

They bent together over the order and worked out a schedule of deliveries Monday, Wednesday, and—because of the weekend crowds—Friday.

He did his job well, and had attention left over with which to ask unspoken questions all about her, the shack, why she was there. She was disproportionately grateful for the visit of so cheerful a young man, one so glad of his place in the universe, and so much at ease with himself. He brought from the truck a first consignment of bottle cases, and in a gallant gesture proposed that they have a Coc'-Cola together to seal their business arrangement. When he drove away, it was with the air of leaving a close friend. It made Diana laugh with simple pleasure to think of him.

He had not come a day too soon with his supplies. By noon the beach was dotted with picnickers. They soon discovered that the board shack on the edge of the dunes gave assurances of refreshment. Diana found her cigar box under the counter filling up with small change. She was thankful that the beach parties stayed near to the surf, some distance away. The dunes were not comfortable to idle in, and the sounds of voices and music from portable radios were far enough off not to invade her place too insistently. In her turn of life, she had come to value her solitude, but she had to admit that, for the moment, anyhow, the lives along the sand, resembling scattered confetti if she blurred her vision looking at them, gave her a curious remote relief. When Ben returned in late twilight, only a few people remained; but they made campfires, at which his indignation was sharp, even when Diana reminded him that the soft-drink stand was part of their plan from the start, and that it presupposed customers.

"But it's my beach. I acquired it years ago," he said. He hugged her tightly. His painting had gone well today. She mustn't believe anything but that he was glad to be there with her. Even so, she could not help asking, though she regretted doing so, "Oh, Ben, truly?"

❦

Ben Ives almost never thought of safety—or the lack of it—for himself, or anyone else. As the days and nights heated up in June, he thought of his prewar times in Corpus Christi when his tanker used to put in to load oil. He felt like the same youth who then had "taken over the town," by which he, and his shipmates, meant ranging through the waterfront dives, to sample whatever license they offered. Memories tugged at his loins, and visions of the seafront and the great slope of the land down to the harbor gave him notions for how to paint what he might now find in Corpus Christi. He would have to look for it alone—at least, to start with.

He said lightly to Diana, "I won't be long—a few days. You won't mind staying here alone for that short while?"

"I'll try."

"What will you do?"

"I'll think of things."

"Maybe your Mexican War addict will happen by again."

"Howard Debler?"

"He had an eye for you, you know."

"Don't be silly. —No. I'll read my Brownsville library books, and sleep, and write down my most searching thoughts and then tear them up. I can lie in the sun out back near the dunes. And I'll sell my carbonated delights to man, woman, and child, who ramble up in wet bathing suits with salty sand sticking to their behinds, and who regard me as their well-paid servant. The worst thing will be their portable radios. —But never mind, we'll be getting rich."

He hauled her into his arms for making him laugh. She would send him off with an easy mind.

She already knew the kind of lingerer who wanted to lounge across her oilcloth counter and talk, and she had already proved that her Eastern United States air was better protection against un-specified nuisances or even dangers than displaying her pistol casually on a shelf behind the counter. Still, humanity on holiday had a greedy heedlessness which was not pleasant to look upon, and though unafraid she was always more at ease when Ben was home.

"I'll bring you something nice," he said. "And if Corpus turns out to be wonderful, I'll come back and get you, and we can find ourselves another shed. What fools people are who tie themselves down with possessions."

He kissed her.

What a poor dissembler he was. She measured his frailties and his powers with the same loving intuition, knowing the latent exultation at escape—he could not conceal it—which was both his hunger and his nourishment.

As he was turning to go, she felt a sudden piercing ache like some finality; and she drew him back in stormy silence. Ravished by her want of him, he returned it in kind, and they made love in a private weather which in their little scale was as universal as the ocean endlessly desiring the earth.

※

Ben's war, ended over three years ago, had made differences in the Corpus Christi he once knew. Taller buildings. New piers extending into the port harbor behind the dredged ship channel which led to the Gulf. Bayside roadways reaching out to the North Beach area where sailors spent money. The overall light he remembered. It made him eager to paint.

He found a room in a tourist court in the North Beach section. It was barely a shelter. Cracks let in the weather, a gas heater smelling of old fumes was set into the powdering plasterboard wall, the blankets on the bed were worn thin. He didn't care. Spanning years and meeting in joy, his late boyhood and his present headlong life were joined in memory. He must rake through the town for the past before he could absorb and own the present.

Most of the bars he remembered were gone. He found one where he could drink beer with sailors from the Naval Air Station; or, if he had brought his own bottle of whiskey, order setups and treat his new friends while he quizzed them about their lives. Mostly they seemed to him very young, some of them awkward, a few self-consciously tough. Officers never came to places like this, they said, only the enlisted men and civilians who had day or night assignments at the air station. The planes had to be kept in the air, mainly for training purposes, but also, they had patrol duties, though what for, no poor bastard in the hangars knew. Corpus was a hellhole, they said; but admitted they'd say so about any place where they might be stationed. They had a few places to dance, there were movies, up North Beach way was a visiting carnival with sideshows, "concessions," and "rides"; and a little ways uptown there was a roller-skating rink where you could sometimes find someone on the loose and get to her. It was called Roller Heaven. Something about going round and round, fast, dreamy, to music, and the sound of the steel rollers of the skates, the ball bearings, the smooth, hardwood floor echoing—there was something about it like forgetfulness.

But who would want to forget, asked Ben of himself. Nothing should be lost. And then he reflected that having no freedom, these fellows had to forget why.

He found Roller Heaven late on his second night in Corpus Christi. It was a long, wide shed in a street dark except for the big electric circle where lights chased each other round and round, enclosing the name of the rink. The admission charge was fifty cents. To rent skates cost a dollar. Every half hour another fifty cents was due, unless the customer came simply to watch, sitting in the bank of seats on a stepped platform along one side of the hall. If gentlemen came unaccompanied and desired to skate they were permitted to introduce themselves to ladies who attended alone, but were expected to pay for the ladies' skating tickets and after their allotted half hour—marked by the silencing of the strident music from loudspeakers at each end of the hall—were asked to escort their partners back to their seats at the edge of the floor.

Ben went into the observers' seats. A half hour was in progress. He figured that some twenty-odd couples were skating, and a few men or women who skated alone, in order to demonstrate fancy evolutions, weaving in and out between less adventurous pairs. If nobody paid the solo skaters much attention, they seemed not to mind, but enacted their spins and one-legged glides, their leaps and backward pirouettes, for their own dream-fixed pleasure.

He was spellbound by all who floated past him, circling the wide floor, lost in motion itself. The sailors in the bar were right. It was mindlessness in swaying oblivion which went by him. The faces were vacant. The eyes saw nothing. There was no sign of willed movement. He half-closed his eyes. The movement became abstract. The pathos of human deliverance from daily acts of need and purpose struck him with a pang. What lives those must be! to have recourse to this mindless motion. Need of them filled his breast. Rolling over him, the sound of the skates and the hugely amplified music put him in another world. *Mr Sandman,* sang a girl's voice on the record, *bring me a dream, Make him the cutest I've ever seen* . . . Great God, he thought, how to get this feeling into paint! If that were impossible, perhaps it was enough simply to feel it. He must feel it.

The music ended. The floor was cleared.

He went to the counter where the skates were rented and took a pair. He had not skated since he was a boy. He laughed to find how uncertain he was. He was whirling his arms to avoid falling when he felt a steadying grasp at his shoulder.

"Just move nice and slow to start with," said a calm, rather smoky voice, and he turned to see a girl looking at him with a downward smile on her prim lips. When he was steady, she released her grasp but continued to hold him with her eyes.

He reached toward her, saying, "If you're alone—?"

She nodded.

He promised himself a fine time. Crossing arms, they held hands, and with beautiful ease she led them off into a slow glide, ignoring the faster rhythm of the new recording, which played "*Three o'clock in the morning.*" Talk was not possible and in any case would have been meaningless. Ben like everyone else was lost in the chaining oval of the skaters. It was like being undersea, swayed by tides unwilled; drowned upright in the sustained roar of the rollers; made one with whose hands were in his; bodies innocent and subject.

They skated for another ticket's worth, and then she looked at her drugstore wristwatch and said she had not much more time. She must soon go home.

"Do you come here often?" asked Ben. "What's your name?"

"Willa Mae. Well, I come here, and I go out to the carnival, where they have those amusements, you know, I like it and I feel my stomach lump up when the ferris wheel starts down, you know?"

"Do you have to go right away?"

"Pretty soon."

"I have a room near here."

"Where."

"The Texas Star, my motel."

"I know the place. —I don't know. You really want to?"

"Only if you do."

He gave her the dignity she must establish. She was no common pickup, if she had to say so herself.

"I wish we could," said Ben gently, close to her face. She had a kitten-shaped face with small features and large gray eyes. If she was not pretty, she was young, with a questing look about her which touched him. He ran his hand lightly across her hair, which was close-cut, standing out in shiny pale ringlets.

"If we hurry," she said. "My car is outside. I'll follow you."

Her car was a Chevrolet pickup truck, shined and gleaming. In his old black Ford he led her to the Texas Star.

"I can't stay long," she said. "Who are you?"

He told her his name, and when he said he was an artist, she seemed relieved to undress with him, for that was what artists had girls do. He held her standing for a little while. When he held her closer, her belly caved in with a qualm of desire. He was fascinated by her nostrils—they were tiny; he traced them with a finger. He marveled at these doors of breath, and when her breathing grew shorter and faster with his embrace he was flooded with tenderness at the simple fact of aliveness as he felt the warmth and heard the gust of her breath against his face, and in the same moment he thought of life and death, and the power to give both. On the thin blankets he took her with him out of mind.

A little silence followed, but she could hear the strong, abating thump of his heart. The light in the room was like cloudy acid, but he saw her shape softly modeled by it, and he said, "I want to make a little drawing, will you let me? Don't move, you are as turned in to yourself as a nice little bird."

"This way?" she said, a little shocked now, meaning nude.

"Yes, yes, you are wonderful to look at."

"I am?"

"Didn't anybody ever tell you that?"

"No."

He was drawing with joy. She watched him in fascination. She reflected that she did the strangest things, and when she asked herself why, she couldn't say.

He showed her the drawing.

"Do I look like that?"

"Yes. To me, you do. Do you like it?"

"It's lovely."

"Do you want it?"

"Oh, I don't dare. T.J. would find it, he looks at everything to see things are neat. He wouldn't like it. He would ask me who did it, and how I did such a thing, and you know."

"Who is T.J.?"

"My husband, T. J. Hassett. That's why I have to go, I don't hardly have any time already."

She dressed rapidly, explaining that T.J. had a civilian job until midnight at the Naval Air Station. She always had to pick him up at five minutes past midnight, that was how come she had a lot of time to herself, so she had to look for ways to kill time? Lots of things she did not tell T.J., because he had a funny temper, because of his wound, in the war, they said. But he was good to her when he felt good. She had to go now.

"But I want to see you again," said Ben. "You gave me a wonderful evening."

"I know. Well, tomorrow after five I can be somewhere."

"Let's meet by the ferris wheel at the carnival."

Ben spent the next morning looking for something to draw which was not picturesque in the matter of all harbors and seaports. He finally decided to park his car on the bluff above the city and make a watercolor drawing of four distances—the buildings of the main part of town just below him, the protected deep blue of the inlet this side of the breakwater, the paling blue of the Gulf receding to the almost invisible horizon, and finally the limitless sky in golden light. He thought Diana would delight in it, and he finished it as a gift for her.

At five o'clock he was at the ticket booth of the ferris wheel. A moment later, Willa Mae Hassett saw him, and broke into a little run to meet him.

"I thought you weren't coming," she said out of breath. "I can't meet you any more. I nearly got caught last night. T.J. wasn't at the gate waiting, I was late. He got a ride home with someone else, and when I came in, he slapped me in the face, see, look, I'm a little swollen there. But when I began to cry he was sorry and he said never mind, he was just tired, his headaches are always there, and when I explained, he said it was perfectly natural for me to stay through the double feature, only please don't let him just stand there any more, while everybody else goes tearing through the gate going home. So I just don't feel right about it."

"Weren't you glad to be with me?"

"Oh, I was glad. T.J. comes home just so tired, and when his head hurts, he doesn't want—" out of delicacy she paused.

"Why does his head hurt so much?"

"It's his war wound. He got hit in the head in Normandy. The doctors think it will clear up in time. He has to be careful. We got married when he came home. He was my high-school sweetheart. He wanted to be a famous surgeon."

"What happened?"

"He couldn't pass the tests to get into college after the war. It was awful. He said he had nothing to cling to but me. He was *real-real* sweet."

"Are you sorry, now, about last night?"

"No, but I can't ever again."

Ben grew hearty. "Well, I don't know how to make you feel better, but we might as well have a ride since here we are, and so few people around. Don't you want to?"

The ferris wheel had loaded a few gondolas, and when Ben and Willa Mae stepped into one, the gate came down, the whistle blew, the music began and the wheel began to turn. Their gondola rocked. The world fell away, the sky descended, the Gulf looked like a tabletop slowly lifting and falling. Willa Mae clutched Ben's arm with both hands and at the apex had to close her eyes out of fear and ecstasy. She cried out, "Oh! my insides!" as the wheel turned into the descent. A steam calliope made music to celebrate these rounds in the sky. Ben pretended to be as thrilled as Willa Mae at their danger and closeness; but his thought said to him, *Her poor ardent dumb little heart seeks every machine to give it voice and escape. Great God, what a world separates everyone from everyone else!* The wheel started upward again, and Willa Mae cried out in extremity, "I can't stand it! I can't stand it!" Her eyes were wild with delight. Thought Ben, *Am I too seeking something in my way that I cannot express, yet which drives me on?* He shook his head and she thought he was sharing her joyful terror. *Opposings. Reconcilings ever? The violet from the muck. The work of art from the rank betrayal.*

When they descended to the ground, Willa Mae looked for a moment at her set of opposings; and then she said, "I guess we better just get apart."

"I won't see you again?"

"I guess not."

"Can't we even just go sit somewhere later?"

"Well, I know a place, but T.J. and I go there together a lot, especially on his night off, and they know me there, so we can't go there."

"Where is it?"

"It's a club called the Tux 'n Tails, they have a Happy Hour, from five to seven, but if we went, somebody'd be sure to see me with you. You really want to see me again?"

"Yes, I do."

"Even just see me, *you* know, without the other part of it? —You drew my picture, if that means anything."

"Yes, I like to look at you."

"Well, I'll show you where the Tux 'n Tails is, and when T.J. is off this evening, we'll probably go there as usual, and you can come in and sit near us and you can see me. But you mustn't let on you ever saw me before. Promise?"

She was hungry to be in command of her virtue again.

"When?" he asked.

She told him, and said, "You be there, so I can see you, too. We have a favorite booth and you can sit at a table just across from it. Come on, you follow me this time, and when we come to the club, I'll wave at it, and you'll know where, and I'll drive right on." Her manner suddenly became formal and polite. "Thank you very kindly for the ferris-wheel ride. I always relish it"—erasing by manners any admission of what went on the night before at the Texas Star.

She drove away, he followed her, until passing the nightclub, she waved at it for him, and then increased her speed to leave him behind.

In the white sunlight, the place looked faded and cracked. A display sign showed a man incessantly tipping his top hat, twirling a straight cane, and making a jerky dance step, in pink neon light. The front of the building was painted pink over stucco. A canvas canopy much frayed led from the curb to the front door. Its scalloped edges were being whipped by a rising wind. Dust came up from the gutters. It would take nightfall to hide the decay of the Tux 'n Tails and give brilliance to the image of glamour and pleasure believed by its public. Ben felt a stir of pity for the terms of joy sought by so many people in the world. At the same moment he had a surge of desire, and knew his kinship with them.

He wrenched the old black Ford truck about and headed for the Texas Star. He was perversely in need of purification. He checked out of the motel and drove to the harbor.

There he had seen a boat-rental service. He longed for the water. He could see funnels and masts beyond streets and sheds. The main turning basin in the harbor lay just over there.

He would take a boat, be his own master, live aboard until he was ready to return to the shore at Boca Chica and Diana; and he would make paintings not from the docks but from the water side of the big tankers that waited at the tank farms to be filled with oil, then to take their way from the turning basin and go slowly across the Corpus Christi Bay along the twenty-mile ship channel to Aransas Pass and out to the open Gulf.

At the boatyard a small fleet of power craft was tied up at the slips of the U-Pi-Lot boat rental. The moored boats were rocking and nodding to the disturbed waters: a Coast Guard bulletin was coming over the radio predicting that a tropical storm, early for the season, was passing Florida westward, and would probably bring a small-craft warning. The turn of weather gave Ben added zest for his plan.

After half an hour of inspecting the available craft, he rented a sixteen-foot inboard cabin cruiser that could sleep two. She was called the *Millie P.*, after the proprietor's wife. Ben became her master under a three-day contract for which he made a deposit of one hundred dollars after filling out a form giving his name, home address in New York, car driver's license number, line of business, and next of kin. The last blank on the form had to be left empty.

"You goin fishin?" asked the proprietor.

No, he was just going to cruise around the harbor, and the inland channel, and sleep on board instead of in one of those stifling motels. The man nodded—they was no better than two-bit cathouses, specially on Satdy nights.

"I'll be right back," said Ben, "after I buy a few groceries and maybe a blanket. —Can I park my jalopy here during the three days?"

"Sure nough." The Ford was added security for the rental of the old, much repainted white cruiser.

Within an hour Ben was slowly touring the harbor. He entered a turning basin where a tanker deep in the water with a full cargo was making ready to face the ship channel and sail out. She was the *H. W. Roddy*. She looked familiar. He came close enough to exchange wavings with some of the deckhands, one of whom might have been himself a dozen years ago. His elation was like a boy's when he remembered that he had once shipped out on the *H. W. Roddy*.

He made a quick drawing of her while his own boat drifted. He brought the scudding sky right down to her masts. He could smell her oil, her thin drift of funnel gas, the sour essence of the bilge water spewing from her battered hull. She looked almost too old to have been his. He wished to be on board her. Then he laughed at himself and said he was not hankering after an old coastwise freighter but after an uncomplicated self long outgrown.

He had a horn in his cruiser, and as he came alongside the *H. W. Roddy*, he gave her a two-blast salute. Her mate, high above him on the bridge at the rear of the ship, answered with a formal return salute by the ship's deep voice, which, so Ben thought, included a measure of wit. He watched the towering stern and its rusted white castle recede. It would take the *Roddy* much of the night to traverse the channel and reach the Pass and the Gulf. Her house flag and other buntings were whipped straight by the wind. She was doing the right thing, he mused, to be taking to the open sea if the Florida storm was heading this way with a chance of turning into something. For his work, he necessarily belonged only to himself; but there were moments—this was keenly one—when he wished fleetingly that he belonged to a working world alongside other men.

But the swiftly changing sky, now shafted with vast blades of light from the broken clouds, again silvered over by low mist, soon had him back where he belonged in his desires. His general wellbeing was given an obscure comfort by the oiled regularity of his boat engine—the rhythmic tappets made an elegant running assurance that he was free, in charge, and content. Why should he and Diana not get a boat—buy it with an advance from Mr Rijkmann of the Murray Hill Gallery on all the new paintings now stacked in the lean-to at Boca Chica—and live on board, cruise the Gulf, even as far as Mexico, perhaps settle in Mexico for a year? Beyond all such drifting plans and notions he had a calculating interest in the Happy Hour coming late in the day at the Tux 'n Tails. He had not had a drink in months, even at the Paloma Azul in Matamoros. This might be the night for a drink—as if it could *be* only one, when he got started, he reminded himself lovingly.

In the evenings and nights when the hour was too late for fishing, there would be beach supper parties, and couples came to lie under the stars in the allowed privacy of their joined flesh. They brought portable radios which they turned on and ignored. Now and then Diana had trouble with late stayers who wanted more Coc'-Colas to mix with their liquor. At such moments she longed for Ben's protectiveness. Still—she laughed over the relativity of values in human concerns—she was rolling in wealth, what with hundreds of nickels and dimes stowed away in a cardboard carton under the cold stove.

One afternoon toward sundown a pair of youngsters came up the beach to the shack and leaned on the counter. The girl carried a portable radio which she set on the counter with an air of pride in the power it gave her over the supports of her life. Music attended her wherever she went. Her flesh and that of her boyfriend made half-conscious, joyful quivers to the jerking jazz. They ordered their gaseous drinks and leaned their bare shoulders together and dreamily drank and communed in their bathing suits, which matched. They were both blond, bleached by sun and sea, and their tanned skins exhaled a salty animal essence. Now and then they exchanged approving comments on the music they had brought along, and which exactly expressed the music within them.

"Get that jive."

"Solid."

But their attention was not selective, and when in a moment the tiny radio left the music and began the six o'clock newscast, they let it alone, content to ignore the confident voice just so it continued to issue forth. Diana listened with lonely interest.

Presently she listened with horror.

Brightly "turning to news closer to home," the newscaster's voice, reading from a press dispatch, stated that coastal Texas was the scene last night of a brutal murder which took place in a Corpus Christi nightclub, when a fight broke out between two men, one of whom, according to eyewitnesses, had been threatening the other all evening. The victim was T. J. Hassett, of this city, who died almost immediately from the effects of injuries inflicted by a man later identified by the victim's wife, Mrs Willa Mae Hassett, as an artist named Benjamin Ives, who had once tried to accost her at a skating rink.

"According to the bartender at the nightspot," quacked the voice, "which is called the Tux 'n Tails, located in the North Beach district, Ives had been drinking heavily. He was unaccompanied. Hassett, accompanied by his wife, occupied a booth opposite Ives's table during the five-to-seven Happy Hour. Few other patrons were in the place. Early in the evening Ives apparently invited the Hassett couple to have a drink with him as he had brought a bottle. They were drinking beer and did not care to join him. Some time later, according to the bartender, the invitation was repeated, but this time directed only to Mrs Hassett, who then asked her husband to leave with her. He refused, while cautioning Ives to cease his unwelcome attentions. During the floor show which followed, while a girl vocalist trio called the Bluebonnet Belles were giving a song number, Ives was observed to get up and attempt to enter the booth occupied by Mr and Mrs Hassett. Hassett pushed him away. Ives fell down. Claiming he had been attacked, he got to his feet and seized a chromium and Leatherette chair from a nearby table and struck Hassett with it, raining blows about the head and shoulders.

"While Mrs Hassett and others went to the aid of her husband, who was prostrate and unconscious, the assailant made his escape, and when the manager of the Tux 'n Tails, Cy Grady, followed to overtake him in the street, he was nowhere to be seen, though Grady saw a black Ford pickup truck pull away from the curb a little distance away only to be lost in the evening traffic.

"An ambulance was called, but Hassett was dead on arrival at the emergency room of the nearby Shoreland Hospital. Mrs Hassett, queried by reporters as to the incident, stated that the blow that killed her husband must have struck a silver plate which had been placed in his skull as a result of receiving a head wound in France during World War II. She is under sedation, in a state of shock, at the hospital. Some hours later the black Ford truck, carrying a New York state license number J-325-345, was found abandoned several blocks away from the Tux 'n Tails. Police have issued an all-points alert for the apprehension of the killer, who was described by Mrs Hassett as of more than medium height, solidly built, with dark blue eyes, medium-colored hair longer than usual, and dressed in dungarees, a gray sweat shirt and blue sneakers. A coroner's inquest is scheduled for Mr Hassett. Funeral arrangements, by MacQuoddy and Sons Twilight Parlor, are not final, pending arrival of the victim's sister Mrs Adolphus Rinckman, of Fredericksburg, and his parents, Mr and Mrs Hurlburt J. Hassett, of Knott.

"And now, after an important message from our sponsor, I'll be back with today's baseball scores."

The boy at the counter reached across his girl and picked up the radio.

"You want to hear the baseball scores?" he asked.

"Nuh-uh," she replied.

"O.K.," he said, tuning in music from another station. "You want another Coke?" rubbing his chin on her lifted shoulder.

"Nuh-uh, let's go find Betty Jo and ol' Goob."

"O.K."

He fished in the small money pocket of his trunks and fetched forth two nickels, which he flipped in the air at the same time and, to the admiration of the girl, caught them both. He slapped them loudly on the counter and without a glance at Diana the two went

down the wooden steps. On the boards their bare feet made a busy
little thumping sound sharpened by the whisper of sand which they
tracked with them. Diminishing with them, hot trumpets celebrated
them as they withdrew.

Diana went to the other side of the counter and removed the
props which held up the wooden awning of the shack. She dropped
the awning and fastened it. Alone, alone, to be alone with what had
happened. She went to the room and the lean-to beyond and
fastened the windows there, closing the board shutters. Outside on
the growing wind rose the myriad sounds of distant people ending
their play and going home before weather. Heedless world. She felt
as though her blood had been withdrawn from her. She felt heavy,
so heavy that she could not support herself. She fell down upon the
bed and stared at the ceiling. Her heart seemed like a mass of
knotted strings each striving to come free. She began to cry for the
ugliness and pity of the world. Ben's likeness inhabited her like a
dream. She must reach him. But where? He was not coming here—
he had abandoned his car. All buses, trains, airplanes, out of Corpus
Christi would be watched.

Until late evening, people occasionally came to bang on her
boarded front. For their journeys home they needed a supply of
what she could sell them. She put on no light but only lay in the
darkness hearing the innocent selfishness of the voices, the fists,
outside. She did not sleep but revolved in mind what she must do
when morning came. With pressing gratitude she counted on the
arrival at eight o'clock of the soft-drink truck. It was all she had to
cling to. She would ask the driver for a ride to Brownsville. Behind
all her practical schemes ran a refrain.

Oh no. God in heaven, let it not be! In the formlessness of her
anguish she called upon God without the realization that she was
doing so. But as every heartbeat seemed like a blow shaking her
breast, the only thing that kept her mind and her actions reasonably
together was the presence, ignored, taken for granted, even denied

in all her life, of the power she called out to in her appalled being. Tears stung her eyes like blown particles of sand.

During the night, the wind grew. It shook the hut. The loose tins of the roof sang. She could hear the risen surf pounding. Grimly she thought the storm was like an overtheatrical sound effect for her racing thoughts. With daybreak, she opened one of her shutters and saw that huge combers, ruffled white and brown, were rolling and washing high onto the beach. No people were visible. She went every few minutes to see if the big yellow truck was approaching; she turned her head to listen for its laboring gears as it crawled over the sand behind the dunes. Each time, hearing nothing of it, she assured herself that it would be hours yet; and yet again and again she went to listen and look for it.

She dressed herself for travel and packed indispensable things in one of her traveling bags. Whatever was left over she said goodbye to. She heard imagined sounds. It seemed to her that the very fabric of a life she loved had been torn violently apart, and she could almost hear the sound of that rending. In childhood fairy stories, hearts could talk. She could hear her own and she could hear Ben's. They said what they had to say three times, as everything was said in tales and legends.

It was after eight when she finally heard, woven in the rushing of wind and sand across the tin roof, the approach of the truck. It came grinding in compound gear over the dune. Her relief brought new tears to her eyes and then she realized that she wanted nobody to know who she was, where she was going, and why. She smartened up, refreshed her lipstick for the fourth time in an hour, and went out to the rickety porch with her luggage to greet the young driver. In one of her cloth shoe sacks, she had all her money in small change, and in her purse a small secret fund in traveler's checks.

Bending his head against the howling sand, Pud came around to the porch and set his first crate of Coc'-Colas on a low step while he looked up at her.

"My, my," he said, "don't we look like somepin this morning." He pushed his company cap with its shining black visor back on his wavy copper hair. "You fixin to go away somewhere?"

Yes, she was, for a few days, and she wondered if he would mind taking back the crate on the steps, and giving her a ride to town?

"I'd be mighty obliged to," said Pud, "if you don't mind a couple of stops for deliveries on the way back?"

Oh, thanks, thanks. When she returned, she would send word about when to resume deliveries.

He took up her bag and they leaned against the wind as they went to the truck. Swinging open his cab door, he helped her in, and lifted her luggage in after her.

"What you got in 'at little ol cloth bag?" he asked playfully.

"All my wealth. About two hundred dollars in nickels and dimes."

"Oh me, oh my. Beautiful *and* rich. Honey, how you know I won't run right off with you?"

He went back for his crate of Coke, and then they started away. He was good for her. He talked all the way back to Brownsville, with brief halts for his remaining deliveries. He had a happy belief that the most interesting thing in the world was his own life, and it was inconceivable that all its details would not be of absorbing interest to everyone else. She was grateful that he felt it worthwhile to talk about himself all the way to town. He was saving his money to go back to school and learn to be a radio announcer. He showed her how already he could talk like one. Leaning with charm toward his steering wheel, he made a microphone of it, he smiled and talked through it at the uncountable and invisible ladies and gentlemen of the radio audience. She clasped her hands in her lap and hoped fate would grant him his desire, since he knew it so clearly, and without any awareness of trouble in life.

He let her out downtown by the bank where she would change her coins for bills.

"You get back," he said, "you tell the distributor you want Pud to keep on making your deliveries, hear?"

She promised. She thanked him. They shook hands. If she would never see him again, she knew that now and then she would wonder about him.

By noon she was on a bus for Corpus Christi, in a tropical downpour which blew the high fans of the palm trees straight out like flags. The bus was not crowded, but she knew the habit of people to sit alongside someone for long confessional chats; and she asked the driver to arrange for her to sit alone, as she felt unwell. He was obliging. She tilted her seat back and mercifully slept for hours, lulled by the monotonous grind of the tires on the storm-lashed road. At Corpus Christi she asked a taxi driver to take her to a hotel. He left her at the Plaza. She registered as Miss D. Macdonald, of Brownsville. Her room was high in the front of the hotel, which sat on the bluff overlooking the streets and tall buildings below. She could see the T-head pier reaching into the protected harbor, and then the breakwater, and the stormy Gulf, which was revealed now and then by torn rifts in the howling torrents of rain from the tropical storm predicted two days earlier, now throwing its increasing fury on the central Gulf Coast. It was much the view which Ben had painted in a day of dazzling calm.

She had no notion of what to do. To be near where he had been seemed to her the only sensible course; so much, so large, had happened so fast that even her thoughts took on unreality. She felt that her life was a shadow—all that she saw and felt came to her as the vision of someone else. Wide awake, she lay host to daymares which seemed to put past events outside natural time. The present world was one she seemed to gaze at through a pane of glass. The sensation frightened her. For Ben's sake as well as her own, she must keep her wits about her, her strength to do what at any moment she might be able to do for their common safety.

[203]

But what was there to know? To rejoin the simple world, she turned on the radio beside the hotel bed to hear the evening news, wanting, and fearing, what it might have to tell her.

The first topic was the weather. It was expected that the tropical storm of near hurricane force would be moving along the coast toward Mexico. Last night it had damaged seafront settlements, and abnormally high tides and torrential rains had combined to flood many low-lying areas. No significant damage had yet been done to local shipping, though warnings had been in effect for twenty-four hours.

One violation of the warnings, however, was reported by the pilot who had taken the *H. W. Roddy*, an oil tanker, out the ship channel to the Gulf at Port Aransas. On returning home early this morning, the pilot, Captain Burton J. Phinizy, stated that the *Roddy*, proceeding with care, had been passed about ten o'clock last night by a sixteen-foot white cabin cruiser moving at high speed toward the Gulf. Assuming the occupants of the boat were unaware of the Coast Guard warning, Captain Phinizy had ordered that several short warning blasts be sounded on the ship's siren, while the ship's searchlight was trained on the motorboat and flashed on and off continuously. There was no response from the small craft, which soon disappeared in the mist. Probable identification of the cruiser was given shortly afterward when Cap "Babe" Poteeg, proprietor of the U-Pi-Lot boat rental service, informed police that a craft answering the description given by the *Roddy* pilot had been rented for three days by Benjamin Ives, of New York City, the man sought by police for the murder of T. J. Hassett in a fracas at the Tux 'n Tails nightclub of this city. In spite of continuing searches conducted at Port Aransas and Gulfside areas of the outer shores to the north and south of the Pass, there had been no further reports of the fugitive boat, which according to Mr Poteeg had not been returned to his docks. Mr Poteeg was meantime holding as security a black Ford pickup truck left in his parking area by Ives.

The heedless prattle and good humor of the radio following the news throbbed like her head until she turned off the switch. She had eaten nothing since morning, when a cup of coffee and two aspirin tablets had sustained her. She felt faint. If she remained in that hotel room for another moment she thought she would no longer belong to the human race. She must be like anyone else among strangers until she could know herself.

She took from her handbag her mother's small circlet of pearls which never left her possession, placed it about her throat, touched up her face, and went downstairs to find the public dining room of the hotel. She carried her head high and wore a faint smile, to control if she could the spasms of the little nerves which though invisible yet felt so enormous about her lips. If her beauty was strained, it still proclaimed its style; and the headwaiter, bending slightly forward, brought her to a corner table which had a small vase holding a yellow rose for Texas, and a little lamp with a yellow silk shade which cast an intimate circle of light like a zone of privacy. With a hurried glance, she saw gladly that the dining room was not yet much occupied.

There was a table across from her own, where without directly looking she was aware of two persons seated side by side on a banquette. They were just out of ordinary earshot. She felt that she could be of their kind, yet alone; and she knew a moment or two of suspended feeling—almost of peace.

But her feeling was treacherous. Trying to keep an air of lightness as she gave her order to the waitress, Diana suddenly felt like calling for help—for what and to whom made no difference.

Something must have shown in her face; the waitress said in a friendly low voice, "Are you all right, honey?"

Diana nodded and let her go. Her eyes were blurred. She winked them clear and saw the two at the opposite table. The sight of them at first gave her heart a strike of joy for so much beauty and delight in the world. They were a young pair. She could not take her eyes off them. They did not see her staring at them. They were lost in each other, their eyes, their lips, making messages nothing could interrupt. They shone with the light of their happiness, incandescent, like ripe fruit in a shining tree. The girl had long satiny blond hair which fell to her shoulders. Her face was pale with intensity. With her eyes she watched the mouth, the brow, the eyes of the boy with her, and her union with him was impregnable. He leaned close to her. His cheeks were brilliant. He seemed compact equally of desire and command. They could not say enough to each other. Their words overlapped. Diana could not hear what they said, and was thankful; it would have been too much to hear in her state. She longed to know them both. She fell in love with them both. She desired to be invisibly a third party to their joy together. She hungered to taste their youth and kiss their beauty, to race with their devouring thoughts and escape into their lives, never to let them change, or to let them leave her—she who was so bereft, in a sorrow which haggardly disgraced her and set her outside any such world of absorbed happiness as she stared at. So the world continued to be fair? Beautiful creatures hardly more than children fell in love and used each other's flesh, traded each other's lives? She said to them in thoughts which swept through her mind like cold mist, *Why can't you hear my silent cry for help? How can you be so beautiful, both of you, one so strong, the other so willing to feel that strength, when here I am almost near enough to touch you, and ready to die of what I know and don't know? How heedless you are in the safety of each other when I am so forlorn!*

She was then aware of the waitress bending near, whispering "Honeymooners!" and she tried to smile, but shook her head, silently excusing herself. She put a bill of money on the table and left to go upstairs, in dismay at the hysteria which had overwhelmed her in the presence of the two young strangers on the edge of the dear and dangerous, the unknown course of all life.

Again alone, she thought the onslaughts of rain thrown against her hotel windows by the shrieking gale were like the confusion of her thoughts.

She begged to be unconscious and so great was her exhaustion that she was lost in sleep beyond reaching. The great storm had not even an edge in her dreams. When next she knew anything, morning was calmly blinding off the enclosed harbor and the far Gulf.

She lay still, smiling in the delicious atmosphere of a dream which she thought had kept her all night. Behind her closed eyes lingered a vision of joy. She could not remember what the dream was about, but in it she was transported to a happiness so great that it filled her like the breath of life. How beautiful to feel so happy, she thought drowsily.

And then she felt the runnel of tears down her cheeks, and she came fully awake to her true state, and what had come to Ben and herself. She began to shake as though she would come apart. She half rose and sat on the edge of her bed, shrinking against the shock which gripped her. She held her breath to still her bones and flesh. Hardly able to stand, she went to a mirror to see who she was. She was white and drawn. Someone looked back at her from within her image. It told her that this was the worst possible time and therefore the most needful of strength. Slowly the tremors went away. If she must wait, wait, for any news of Ben, she must be sensible at the same time. She did as George Macdonald always used to do. She made a list of what was known, another of what might be true, and another of what to do about immediate circumstances, such as, where should she look to find Ben, how much money did she have, and how long would it last.

She looked in her handbag and saw that her first move must be to leave the hotel, which was too expensive for an indefinite stay, unless she went out to pawn her mother's necklace. But, sentiment aside, there might be danger in disposing of it—it was so valuable that any attempt to raise money on it in a place where she was unknown might lead to questions, perhaps by the police. She must conceal the pearls, remain private, and as soon as she was ready, go out into the hot, newly calm, white daylight, to find somewhere else to live in her vigil.

※

By late afternoon every day Howard Debler was ready to stop working in his lookout tower at Grand Plains. He was aching at the neck and shoulders from bending over his typewriter; but it was a virtuous ache, and in this summer he was held almost viscerally by a grand conviction: after the years during which the scheme for his book had remained alive and true for him, he was now at the point of giving form in his mind to the final phase of his huge narrative.

When he had the need to free his imagination and find a blank page for it to write upon, he always knew where to go. He put paperweights on his manuscripts and notes, stretched his body with a few wrenching exercises, ran downstairs, and entered his car to drive out on to the plains as the sun was beginning its descent over the endless plains into fiery twilight. Seeing the vast laterals of the land under the clarity of the open sky, he entered into limitless spaces for thought. Along back roads he drove at high speed. The spaces, earthly and heavenly, and all their changes as the light changed, held his sight; while in his inner space of thought his book forecast its conclusion. Next to him on the car seat he kept a large clipboard with heavy paper and as he drove he scribbled in large letters the ideas, phrases, sequences of action, which came thronging into his freed mind. He was blessedly alone. Physically occupied in the mechanical act of driving, he was liberated for concentration that was like a state of abstract prayer, he would tell himself. The splendors of the sky darkening in the east as it turned to pouring gold and fire in the west, and the gradual emergence of the brightest stars at the zenith, were joys of his whole lifetime in that place; and without saying so, he felt blessed by powers that made common wonders belong to him like private visions.

He drove for over an hour at random, but he knew all the roads, and how they would take him home when it was time. His note pages were black with ideas. Driving back, he saw lovingly the first little distant lights of Grand Plains, and on the horizon the silhouettes of a windmill here or there, and far away, traveling fast on the highway, the lights of a car now and then, and finally the water tower of the town black against the peach-gold glow of the last light. His drive had been short in distance and time, but he felt like a traveler happy to be coming home after a great journey. Clutching his notes, he ran up the back stairs of the house and into his watchtower. The light was on.

Instantly he saw differences. His mother had taken the chance to come up there and do some housework. He could read her action, though she had tried to replace everything as she had found and moved it for her dusting. It was her purpose in life, as she would say, to "neaten" her house, even in spite of his many requests that she leave his work room alone.

Once he had said, "I may have to lock my door."

"Not in my house, you won't," she replied with such vigor that like a son who had never grown up he answered, "No, I suppose I won't. But please:"

He repaired her order as well as he could.

She had put on his desk the drawing of Diana given him by Ben Ives, which he always kept on the windowsill of the watchtower, so that when he looked out over the distance he could pretend that his sight reached as far as the Gulf at Boca Chica, where she lived, in that weather-beaten shack, which she had made so inviting. He would say to himself that he must stop imagining himself there:

with her: in the circle of her charm: she was in the life of someone else. How odd. He had been there with Diana and Ben for only one evening, but he felt he had imagined the place years ago, and lived in it on his own terms, which meant, with her.

Now he picked up the framed drawing and looked at it close to. The act was like saying a word to her. He took it to the windowsill and set in its proper place. How was it that his mother had neglected to replace it herself? Or did Clara never do anything without a rapid calculation of a result which anywhere but in her busy thoughts might seem preposterous, if at times endearing?

"And who is she?" she asked her son weeks ago when he had set the drawing up on the Major's musket sill. "She's really rather pretty."

"Someone I met several years ago, and lost sight of, and then saw again near Brownsville when I was there this spring."

"Well. Do you like her? I suppose you do, or you wouldn't look at her picture all day. Well:"

But Clara was unable to make what she wanted out of the meager evidence she turned this way and that. *Nothing but that infernal typewriter, all day long,* she would reflect.

He briefly thought of asking his mother once again to stay out of his study, but his irritation disappeared in an abrupt awareness that the house was silent: she was not downstairs making the usual kitchen sounds preparing for supper (they had dinner at noon, in the manner of Grand Plains).

He went to look for her. Instead, he found one of her notes on the dining room table: YOU PROBABLY FORGOT BUT TONIGHT IS CHOIR PRACTICE I'M OFF EARLY TO PICK UP SOME MEMBERS YOUR SUPPER IS KEEPING WARM IN THE OVEN HOME BY NINE O'CLOCK WE CAN WATCH MAJOR BOWES.

"Yes, I forgot," he said. A small throat-greeting from the kitchen door made him turn to see Nicodemus arching his back and quivering his tail to say that it was his suppertime too.

"All right, you ravening tiger."

He went to fetch a saucer of milk, which he placed on the back porch. He then wandered back to the oven, looked in, and decided he was not yet hungry. In the dining room his place was set— *Never in my life have I ever served a meal in the kitchen, not in* MY *house*—and he found next to his napkin that day's Amarillo *News-Globe* neatly folded. On page 1 he saw the story.

Within fifteen minutes he was in his car, driving as fast as he could on Highway 287, heading for Brownsville and Boca Chica at the Gulf. He hoped he had not forgotten to lock the house, in his hurry to go. On the hall table he had left his note for Clara Vetchison Debler—*unexpectedly called away on an emergency, will telephone or write soon as could, was driving, Nicodemus fed on back porch, there were new notes on upstairs desk please not to disturb as had no time to put anything away, don't worry, love H.*

His thoughts went like his rush along the Texas highways as he drove all night, with nine hundred miles to go. How would she hear the news if she were alone, there, on that beach? Or if she had heard, to whom could she turn? He came before midnight into high winds that blew dust and tumbleweeds across his way. His car was pressed sideways and he fought the wheel but kept going. Within an hour, immense rains drove down and should have halted him. But he went on, unaware that he was hungry, until near Fort Worth in a gunmetal storm of rain and cloud he stopped for fuel and when he left took with him a paper cup of coffee and a hamburger.

By mid-morning the storm lessened. By noon the sky was open, and the world looked newly created and innocent. In the peaceful air his car radio was clear and he heard that the near hurricane which had passed that way was now dying along the Mexican coast to the south.

In early afternoon he came to the dirt roads leading to the dunes of Boca Chica. Driving was slow, for the new heaps of sand blown across the way. He halted behind the dunes. His heart trundled heavily. Would she be there: would she mind his coming: he trudged over the crest of the dunes where clumps of the hard grass had been either buried by sand or uprooted by the gale. At the top, he was stopped still by what he saw.

The shack was a random pile of weathered boards. The porch was gone, the side walls were thrown down except for a few timbers standing crazily. Parts of the tin-can roof clung to some two-by-fours on the ground. Other sidings and rafters still stood with sheets of the roof hanging like stiff curtains. The only portion of the shack still undamaged was the lean-to at the rear, but there the door had been blown open to hang awry. The storm must have taken the shack with a single blast.

He called her name. He ran down the dune and lifted a couple of boards aside to enter and look for her. Amid the rubble of intimate life there was no one. He felt an expanse of relief. Behind him a voice from the dunes cried out, "Gret God Ammighty!"

He turned. A young man ran down toward him, calling, "I've seen bad, but never worse. Thank God she got away before."

"She did? How do you know?" asked Howard.

"I have the Coc'-Cola run for these resorts, and I gave her a ride to Brownsville. —My name's Pud Michaelson?"

"Howard Debler. —Is she there now?"

"I can't rightly say. She said she had to go somewhere for a few days. —When my distributor heard I let her go off without paying up her account, he like to taken my ears off. I came by to see if mebbe she's got back, so I could report. It isn't so much she owes, but I'll have to make it up till she returns."

"How much?"

"Sixty-seven fifty."

"I'll take care of it. I'm going to be seeing her. She can pay me." Howard handed him the money.

"Boy, you sure saved my skin. Let's look around."

[212]

"Where did you take her?"

"To the bank. She had a jillion nickels and dimes to change for money. Said she was aimin to buy a bus ticket, last I saw of her. She sure is a honeybun. I just b'lieve she liked me a *little* bit."

Howard went to the lean-to. When he touched the door aside, it fell down. He looked within. There he saw against side walls two stacks of paintings. He lifted them away one by one. They were finished paintings—Ben's work of the past months. Howard did not think of them in terms of art; they were property, and should be saved and returned to the owner. He asked Pud Michaelson to help him carry the paintings over the dunes. They put them in the trunk of Howard's car.

"Well," said Pud, "I sure do thank you. Tell her ol Pud will be watchin for her to get back."

Howard nodded. Pud drove away.

Back in the wreckage, Howard gave a last look around. Under a low pile of crossed planks an edge of gold shone dimly. He leaned down. It was a corner of the frame on George Macdonald's photograph. He took it up. She must have it.

In Brownsville he went directly to the bus station. *Yes. On the morning when the storm hit its first licks along the Gulf hereabouts, a lady that she sounded like the one he described got a ticket to Corpus. It was raining a gullywasher, but the driver took off anyways, and got through to Corpus safe enough, but an hour late, for the visi-bil-itih was nigh unto zero at times. You couldn't help but remember her, for she had a suitcase you'd swear had solid-gold lock and buckles, though she was dressed common enough. Seemed mighty anxious to get goin...*

Howard ended the comfortable drone as politely as he could, went to his car, and set out on Highway 77 for Corpus Christi, something under two hundred miles away. He came down into the city in well under three hours.

He knew the town, having walked the grounds of General

Taylor's encampments there, to study the terrain all about. One year, he had presided at the annual meeting of the state historical society in its sessions at the Plaza Hotel. He now went directly there and inquired whether Mrs John Wentworth was registered.

After a brief search, "No, sir."

Of course, he thought, and tried again. "Then, is a Miss Macdonald staying here?"

"She checked out yesterday. —Do you care to register?"

"Yes."

"*Oh* yes. Dr Debler. How long do you plan to be with us?"

"I can't quite say."

Not until I find her, he promised himself.

※

He thought of Corpus Christi as his Hades in his search for her. He went to all the hotels. None claimed her. He sat for hours in various lobbies, watching all the women who came and went. The weather was hot and still and he felt unwell, but his longing pity gave him power to persist against hunger and dread. She must know all by now—the newspapers and the radio newscasts kept the Hassett murder alive if only to announce the victim's funeral, or to repeat that no trace had yet been found of the murderer, who supposedly was last sighted when his rented motor cruiser had passed an outgoing vessel in the ship channel. Sources close to the investigation by the police believed an early break in the case would soon be announced, though for the present the authorities preferred not to comment on speculation. Howard inquired at all the movie houses for the starting times of each show, in case she might seek distraction for a mindless hour; and going a little ahead of time, he watched the crowds coming in or out of the air-cooled theaters; but he never saw her among the throngs who returned to daylight or neon shine in bland stupor from the art of darkness.

He was clouded by doubts about his own cleverness—perhaps he should simply have waited at Boca Chica for her to return there? Do you suppose she read the papers here: would it be acceptable to her if he should place a message in the personal columns of the Corpus Christi *Caller-Times* newspaper? But he could not imagine that she was the sort of person who read such items in newspapers. He pursued his baffled thoughts, walking most of the day without plan. He returned several times to the waterfront to stare at all possibilities, as he put it to himself, by looking out over the expanse of the Gulf. On a particular morning he strolled out on to the T-head municipal pier. The bay was calm, jade-blue in sunlight, wine-purple where cloud shadows floated. Aircraft from the naval station now and then droned overhead. Suddenly he stood still the better to see. Who was that standing alone at the edge of the pier and gazing out across the water toward Mustang Island and the sea-colored sky far beyond? He felt a throb of certainty in his breast. He went forward. Then only did it occur to him that he might be unwelcome; but the power of his resolve made him persist. He came up to her and modestly spoke her name.

"Diana?"

She turned.

A friend.

※

"We can talk here," said Diana.

They were in the place where she had found a cheap refuge—the Vista Bel Court, a row of pale brown stucco rooms a few blocks from the Gulf in the South Beach area. She brought Howard there because one of her hardest tasks was to face the world, as she said; and he had found her only because she believed that she must force herself to walk out once a day to stare at the commonplaces of life and escape from her circular thoughts.

※

The proprietess of the Vista Bel, Mrs Florence Schrottke, enjoyed a full life, managing her apartments, with a double devotion—one, to the strictly professional side of her duties; the other, to a devouring curiosity about all who came under her roof. It was wonderful, she often reflected, how fast you could make friends in her situation, and she believed in keeping herself up. She had a face like that of a glad sheep, with heavy makeup added. She was plump, her hair was bleached to a wiry gold, and during her office hours in the apartment at the street end of the Court, she wore a lacy blouse with gabardine cowgirl slacks embroidered in bright yarns. Diana never saw her without a lighted cigarette. Of all her details, her ratcheted voice and a chronic baritone cough gave the greatest evidence of avidity and experience. Her eyes were prominent and sad, however much her mouth chattered and smiled.

It was her view that women were all pretty much alike. This was confirmed again when after absolute solitude Diana brought a man that day to her room, Number 18. Mrs Schrottke—"Flo"—was therefore much enlivened now to see that pretty little Miss Macdonald, who always looked so tired, go past the office with a tall, good-looking fellow who followed her in a stooping walk. They disappeared into Number 18. Mrs Schrottke was sure that there would at last be something to get out of that girl. But she hadn't much time to think just then, as she was going to the Hassett funeral at the MacQuoddy and Sons Twilight Parlor and she had better get ready: not that she knew any of the bereaved families or even anybody who knew them; but the tragedy belonged to the whole city, as news, and she took her proper share in it.

❧

"Howard," said Diana in the gloomy shelter of her coop-like room, "I did not want to see anybody. But I am glad you are here."

It was, for the moment, all he could hope to be told; but he was reassured.

For a little while there was constraint; but Diana was soon aware of his longing diffidence, and a spark of her dimmed spirit revived. She must put him at ease. The best way must be to avoid nothing of what was in their thoughts.

"The most dreadful of all," she said, "is *not knowing*."

"He will try to reach you as soon as it is safe."

"How can he? He is a fugitive. —How dreadful that nobody here knows him—they would know he could never deliberately harm anyone. I know for certain—I know the death was an accident—how could he know about the poor young man's silver plate in the head? A barroom brawl, yes, childish and vulgar; but killing: for it is killing, and he must always keep running away from it. Yet I have, too, this feeling that even if it is hideously full of risk, he will try to find me. That is why I go out to the seafront where so many different people come and go all day, where nobody knows what he looks like. He always wanted to be near the ocean—and then I think of that boat he rented, and that dash that night past the steamer on his way to the open Gulf and the—"

She could not say it, but the fear in her eyes reached Howard, and he had the same thought of the near-hurricane sweeping down the coast.

[217]

She braced herself to add, "But he is a skillful sailor."

"Yes, yes. Many small craft, people out fishing, even, have ridden out big storms."

"But where could he go?"

"Mexico? Perhaps you will hear from him there."

"Oh! He will write to the General Delivery at Brownsville: Oh, what do I do: stay: go back: I only wish."

He was reminded of Boca Chica. "I went to look for you at the beach. After I saw what I saw, I was glad you were not there."

He told her of what the storm had done to the shack and the dunes; then he jumped to his feet and exclaimed, "The paintings! I have all of Ives's pictures in my car outside. They were protected by the lean-to, which did not blow down. They must be kept safe."

She asked Howard to help her to dispose of the paintings properly: they must be taken to an art store to be crated and shipped collect to Mr Rijkmann of the Murray Hill Gallery in New York— she scribbled the address—who had been planning a show for Ben in the coming season, for which this was the collection. She suggested a figure for insurance.

"I ought to hear from Mr Rijkmann," said Diana, "and yet I don't know where I'll be. Please take them away and arrange matters, but tell them to hold them until I can give a return address for where I'll be."

Instead of distracting her with its mechanical details, the matter of the paintings gave her further pain. Howard saw that she was paler. Her eyes had an unfocused shine in shadows of dark stain. She was weary to death. He must leave her.

He asked, "May I come back later?"

"Yes. I will try to sleep. Come back this evening and take me somewhere for a little supper. Forgive me if I am not very good company."

"Forgive!"

"How will I ever repay you for your kindness and your concern, Howard. But for you—"

"No, please. The minute I heard. How lucky for me that I found you."

"And for me."

Like a ghost, she came to him and turning her face aside to his shoulder, she embraced him with hardly a touch, and let him leave. He went like a famous man justly rewarded for achievement.

Later in the afternoon, Florence Schrottke returned to her property after the funeral, where she had had a perfect view of the Family, and at the end, when she filed past the open casket to pay respects, she saw something so pathetic about the figure of a man, not yet old, forever beyond touch and breath and, yes, well, beyond *you-know*, that she had to suppress a little gasp of remembered desire intruding on general grief. She found control by saying to herself, *Why, Flo Schrottke, at a time like this, to think of . . .*

She was still somewhat shaken when on the doorstep of her office she found the regular bundle of the evening *Times*, from which she always distributed a copy—one of her services—to each room. Her attention shifted sharply.

The Hassett case was once again a front-page sensation. Standing on her doormat, she read about it.

A trainee from the Naval Air Station had been practicing landings and takeoffs in a light plane on the smooth oceanside beach of Mustang Island earlier today, when on one of his approaches he had sighted a sizable pile of wreckage in the surf. He landed and taxied to it. It was the battered hull and a jagged piece of the cabin of a motor cruiser which had the name *Millie P.* painted on its stern. The contents of the cabin—lockers, bunks, engine controls—seemed to have been torn away. A ripped blanket was caught in some splinters. A tin tackle box was awash in the hull. The pilot opened it and found tubes of paint and some brushes, and a chart of the

Gulf coast waters. He immediately took to the air again to report his finding to Corpus Christi police, who went at once to inspect the wreck, which they identified as the boat hired by the missing murderer Benjamin Ives, whose victim, in a brawl at the Tux 'n Tails nightclub, was being buried this afternoon. According to police sources, there now remained no doubt that Ives, in an attempt at escape, had headed out into the unseasonable near-hurricane on the Gulf, and that his boat, rented from the U-Pi-Lot boatyard of this city, was wrecked in the storm. There was no trace of the escapee, who evidently had been trying to flee to Mexico by sea, as indicated by a coastal chart found on the wreck. The port of Tampico, in northeast Mexico, had been circled in red pencil. When queried as to the possibility that Ives may have survived the wreck, Police Chief Harvey LaCrosse expressed doubt that anyone caught in a small boat which had been wrecked on the open Gulf during the recent storm could have remained alive. Chief LaCrosse added, however, that in cases of *corpus delicti*, it was not possible to speak with certainty.

"My good God and Jesus!" exclaimed Mrs Schrottke in general satisfaction mixed with decent pity.

She might as well distribute the paper at each door before going inside. Everyone was out all day except Number 18. At that door Mrs Schrottke leaned and listened, but heard nothing, so there was nobody to talk it all over with just then. Later, while she was taking her regular gin and papaya juice with her evening meal in her back room, she did not see Howard return; but having her cigarette afterward on her narrow stoop from which in her glide rocker she liked to watch the sunset she saw Number 18 and that fellow leave together. She clicked her tongue and said, *Flo, how can you be so many kinds of a fool. There he was, all afternoon, they must have heard me at the door with the evening paper and kept still as mice.* With a deep pull on her smoke which made her cough with a sluicing pleasure in herself, Mrs Schrottke knew that now at last she had something perfectly exact to lead up to next time she had one of her chats with Miss Macdonald, who wouldn't be able to get around the fact that she'd had a man in her room for several hours.

If at their table, where they ate and drank little, Howard understood that Diana did not want to say much, he felt close to her thoughts, and he believed that she was glad of his presence; for her eyes sought his in longing for answers—any answer, really—about what to believe, what to do. They had both seen the evening news story and its implications muted them.

At one point Diana did say, almost inaudibly, "He used to say the sea is the mother of the world."

A tremor filled her for a second when she had the idea that at last it might be where he was at home forever, taken by the contending currents, which would roll him and play with him and absorb him until no part of him remained.

"Will they ever be able to know?" she asked.

"It may be that he will never be found," answered Howard, convinced that there was even now nothing to find. Her face pleaded for certainty. He decided to take a risk. "Don't you think, now, that you should leave here—not stay and be tormented and at the mercy of public news?"

"I don't know. I don't think I should leave until everything is really certain."

"I understand. But it must be so hard. I think you should spare yourself."

She smiled remotely, as though to tell him that she had never done so.

"There is one mercy," she said. "I am so exhausted that I seem only half awake, and I sleep and I sleep."

"I should take you back to the motel."

She nodded, and reached across the table to touch his hand gratefully. "Tomorrow?" she said.

"Of course. Always. Any time. When you need me, call me at the hotel. I'll stay there waiting. —I've brought some work with me."

"I will. And, Howard, thank you for bringing my father's photograph. He was—"

"I know. He meant much to me, too."

Leaving her, he saw that for her, among many needs of the hour, privacy was one of the greatest.

※

Everyone had been thoughtful with attentions to John Wentworth after his divorce of the previous year. But, with the passing months, the gossip about Jack, Diana, and Ben Ives had drifted away until the shocking news story of recent days, and now suddenly the affair was again in every drawing room in Georgetown.

Billy and Cecile Millard were about to leave for the rest of the summer at their place in Canada. They had a small dinner to say goodbye to a few friends. One of these was a socially accepted, widely syndicated columnist who asked Cecile all she knew about Diana. She obliged.

"That's an earful," he said, thanking her with a pat on her hand. "I wish I had a picture of her. —D'you by any chance have one?"

"I have one," said Cecile, "but I put it away for fear of wounding Jack. No matter what he is or is not, he is one of our most devoted friends."

She went to a Louis XV desk which stood between two silken windows, opened a drawer, and brought out a photograph of Diana framed in rosewood inlaid with a crisscross of ivory. It showed Diana full-face, brilliantly lighted from above, against a background of flowers and crinkled silver paper. It was the original of a picture which had appeared in *Mode*.

"I liked this so much," said Cecile, "when I saw it in the magazine that I asked her for it. It used to stand over there on the table next to Franklin. You can have it, if you like."

"Oh, how too marvelous. I'll return the frame."

"Don't bother. She gave it to me."

꙳

The Ives murder case, as national wire service news, was enlivened everywhere with the addition of the picture of smash-hit playwright's estranged wife, the society beauty who had run off with genius-murderer, now a fugitive from justice presumed to be drowned at sea in an escape attempt during a hurricane in the Gulf of Mexico.

꙳

Howard Debler assured himself that he had brought enough notes in his briefcase to keep him occupied for many hours. He remained in his room at the Plaza Hotel all day, in case Diana might telephone. No call came. Several times he was tempted to call her, but he thought perhaps she was sleeping, and he hoped she was. He read and reread his notes, trying to become absorbed beyond other thoughts, but without success. He resolved that if she did not telephone by four o'clock he would call the Vista Bel.

An hour before then, Diana gave in to a need which had been urging her to act on it ever since her arrival in Corpus Christi. Moments of revulsion had restrained her, but her hunger to know everything possible about Benjamin prevailed. She dressed in thin clothes—the heat was extreme—and set out to see where her life had been cut in two.

She called out a greeting to Mrs Schrottke, who was sitting on her stoop. "I'm going for a little walk."

"In this heat!" exclaimed Mrs Schrottke, and began to fan herself with the evening paper, which she had not yet had the energy to read. She was a trifle disappointed to see Diana go out, for she had thought to drift, a little later, to Number 18, and by a few idle, half-laughed-over references to her past, lead up to the long visit yesterday afternoon of that really classy-looking fellow. *Now* who knew when Number 18 might be coming back?

Diana found her way to the Tux 'n Tails. In the hot falling sunlight the club's signals of gaiety looked like a false expression painted over a tired face. The neon sign was moving, the top hat was incessantly tipped, the cane twirled. The door was open, letting a damp exhaust of cooled air out upon the passerby. She went in. No customers were there yet. Someone in the far interior of the dark room looked out through a glass square in a swinging door and then disappeared. The ceiling was lined in striped canvas in pink and white, supported by gilded iron poles. She regarded the battered fittings, the chairs at the tables, made of sticky-looking chromium bars bent into shape to support pink imitation-leather seats and backs.

One of those chairs, she said to herself.

Booths of varnished plywood lined one wall of the room.

Over there, she thought.

Despite the noisy cooler which blew currents of air along with the smell of wet excelsior, old odors of drink and smoke and human ardor in search of the fugitive and the incommunicable still lingered. In honor of the sum of the aspirations brought to that place, as well as what had happened there to her life, she was filled with pity. She returned to the hot day, where everything was paled by the white sun, until to her eyes the long reaches of the heat-wavering streets looked like scenes on overexposed film. She walked without aim, like a vagrant whom no one knew. *I wonder,* she thought, asking herself how long she could keep on her way. She passed an old church made of time-darkened brick with Gothic steeples of weathered green metal. One wing of the main doorway was open, showing cavernous dark within, as though cool depths might be there.

She turned back and entered to rest before going on.

In the last pew she sat at the center aisle. The air was no cooler; but the dimness within was welcome. The distance to the altar seemed like a line to infinity. In the air above the sanctuary a red glass lamp showed a single pinpoint of light. Exhausted in spirit and flesh, she shut her eyes and tried to become nobody.

She had no fixed prayers, but she said to herself, *For him. For me.*

As if she had lost consciousness but retained a strange awareness, she felt she had come to the last deep of her life. She could think of no moment beyond this one.

A dipping flicker of the distant red lamp returned her to reality. Her eyes were adjusted to the near-darkness. She saw a small black figure kneeling in silhouette at the marble altar rail. There was no one else in the church.

Presently, a thin waft of sound came into the air, a reedy thread of song. The kneeling figure, a woman, rose and turned, and began to walk down the center aisle, singing a Mexican hymn.

> *Bendito, bendito,*
> *bendito sea Dios,*
> *los ángeles cantan*
> *y alaban a Dios.*

As she came nearer, she was, Diana saw, old beyond counting. A black shawl hung from her head. The faint daylight from the open door showed her small face, crumpled by a poor lifetime's furrows.

One eye was whitened over by a film of blindness. The other eye held a spark of life. Her hands were folded on her bony breast, holding a string of beads. She walked with a controlled, nodding limp that had a ghost of vigor in it. Leaving her private devotions before the altar of her faith, under its lighted wick aloft in the air, *Blessed be God*, she sang in her childlike voice, out of all the ancient hardships that had marked her tiny, dried, birdlike being. It was a protestation of life—*of still believing in life*, thought Diana, feeling a tumble in her breast.

The doorway daylight grew stronger over the little figure as she came to the end of the aisle. Her single eye narrowed to look at Diana. Seeing more than Diana knew, she paused and took up from the font of blessed water behind the last pew a few drops, and extended her twisted little hand to Diana, who out of politeness reached to touch her clenched fingers. The old woman then with a moth-light touch made a trembling line downward on Diana's brow and crossed it with another. She kissed her thumb three times and nodded urgently to impart her strength. Pouching her lips forward in a grim smile, she said, "*Vaya con Dios*," and, nod-limp, nod-limp, took her way out of the church homeward, wherever, thought Diana, that could be.

Slowly as in a dream, Diana lowered her head to her hands resting on the wooden rise of the seat before her. She shut her eyes. The words *How beautiful* came into her mind, and she was not sure what they meant to describe, but in a moment she knew, and said to herself, *She was giving thought to me, not to herself, as no one has done for me in such a way since I left my father, and he later left me in the war.* Then, *No*, she thought, *Howard is like that.*

Presently she felt able to return to the white day, and her rented room.

When she reached the Vista Bel, she met the result of what Flo Schrottke had meantime discovered in the evening paper. It was Diana's syndicated photograph. The caption described her as playwright John Wentworth's divorced wife, who had left him for artist-murderer Benjamin Ives, now reportedly lost in a Gulf of Mexico hurricane.

Mrs Schrottke's many friends included a reporter on the morning paper who was really only middle-aged. No matter what anybody said, he was really quite a nice-appearing fellow. He could make her laugh the way she needed to, now and then, when he would come over to have one of their nighttimes together; and then what he did with her would make her give little breathy yelps of ecstatic shock.

In answer to her fervid phone call, he was there at the Vista Bel waiting with a staff photographer.

With a whimpering laugh of betrayal, Mrs Schrottke, as Diana came toward the stoop, cried out, "That's her!"

The flashbulbs went off, the photographer called out "This way, honey!" asking for "Just one more," and as Diana, with her handbag before her face, ran for Number 18, the newsmen tracked alongside her and for a few intense and frightening minutes had their way with her in the name of the freedom of the press. When at last she was able to slam and lock her door against them, they knew they had enough for a front-page story in tomorrow morning's paper, in which the reporter had promised to include the name of the Vista Bel Court, with a photograph of its hostess, Mrs Florence Schrottke, standing out in front.

Clarity of mind came to Diana for the first time in days. She telephoned Howard to come for her immediately, telling him why.

She was leaving the apartment. Swiftly she packed her bag. He came straight to her door. His car was at the street. Handing him her purse, she asked him to pay her bill. He dealt with Mrs Schrottke, who now wondered if she might have been hasty, and asked if she could just run out to say goodbye to the little lady. With a menacing scowl which struck her like an interesting blow in the chest, Howard said, "Not acceptable," and left her with her success somehow lessened, as so often seemed to be the aftermath of her works.

Howard was troubled by Diana's harried look. Hoping to lighten her heart, he said, a little nervously, "Good riddance to the Wife of Bath."

For his sake, Diana met his effort, and quoted:

> *Of remedies of love she knew perchance,*
> *For she couth of that art the olde daunce.*

※

"Where?" he asked in the car.

"Anywhere," replied Diana in a ghost of a voice.

"Far, somewhere," said Howard. "The other reporters will be swarming all over there tomorrow. I have to get you way out of all that."

"Oh, please."

"It is time to go, anyway," he said quietly.

"Yes. I finally think so."

With that admission, she put her hands over her face and turned away as though into oblivion.

He drove out of the city. The first gold and silver rays of late day were beginning to show. Ahead lay the open plain. For a long distance they went in silence while Howard worked on his thoughts and hunted for words.

At last, he was able to say, "I think there is only one place to go, where you will be taken care of, and be private, for as long as necessary."

"Where?"

"I want to take you to my home in Grand Plains, near Amarillo. My mother's house is big and comfortable enough—it isn't fancy. My mother is a kind person, though she pretends not to be, and she is wise, in an odd sort of way, and she will help with anything I ask."

"Oh: I don't think I could impose—"

"Where else?"

"I don't know."

"With us, you will not be alone, and you will be safe."

He drove for almost a hundred miles while they said nothing, but he was heading across Texas toward the high plains. He thought she was sleeping, but at last she said, with thanks, that she would stay until she felt stronger, and until the danger of publicity had faded out of the news. He nodded; and then she did fall asleep, lying at an angle toward the car door. He leaned across her and pressed the door lock down.

Under the dashboard was a little light which came on when he adjusted the instrument lights to their maximum full. He kept the under-light on so that from time to time he could glance at her and be sure all was well with her. When a rough spot in the road shook the car, her sleeping inert body was briefly tumbled, and when that happened, he was choked with tenderness to see her subject to the accidental powers of the commonplace.

When he paused for fuel she did not awaken. As he started down the road she moved in sleep to rest against his shoulder.

"Yes. Yes," he said silently.

About seventy miles farther along, he began to smile at a scene in his thought. It showed Clara Vetchison Debler meeting Diana

Macdonald. With the drawing of Diana in mind, upstairs on the windowsill, or on the desk where she preferred to set it, Clara said, *Well. There she is,* and her son said, *Yes.* He pressed his lips to silence an impulse to laugh over Clara's darting gift for connecting the remote with the immediate. He drove on, content with thinking of a future which must be in his power to create.

PART SIX

AT HIS USUAL CORNER TABLE in the Restaurant Amboise in Fifty-sixth Street, Gregory Blaine was taking his first dry martini before lunch when Jack Wentworth arrived from Washington to join him. While still several tables away, Jack was rapidly explaining why he was late. His bright voice caused nearby people to look up as he went by, and several, including strangers, recognized him, which he expected but ignored.

"—vow I'll never enter another tunnel so long as I live. The wretched train sat there for forty minutes in the dark, all I saw was one small blue light outside my drawing-room window—yes, Henri: thank you, the two vermouths, half and half, no ice—and then there were as usual too few cabs. I *am* sorry. How've you been? You look a little heavy, but after all, it's been over a year since I've seen you. We live far too much by the telephone."

"Everything's all right. This is my first. Fine. You look fit."

"I am. I think I should warn you that I am feeling extremely shrewd, too."

They were meeting to discuss terms and plans for a collected edition in two volumes of Jack's plays, which Adam and Blaine would publish in the spring.

"Sorry to hear it. It won't do you any good. Your tax agreement won't allow any increase in your royalty rate."

The two old friends sparred for a few minutes in their convention of devious publisher and greedy author, and then moved comfortably into practical details. Gregory wanted to call the volumes *Collected Plays of John Wentworth*. Jack said that was dull, and proposed his own title: ***Curtain Calls: The Plays of John Wentworth***.

"I suppose you think it catchy," said Gregory.

"Hideous word, but yes, it *is* eye-catching. And besides, it's *theater,* about which I do know something."

Gregory sighed and agreed to try the title out at the autumn sales conference next week.

"You'll see," said Jack confidently. "Let's order. Should you diet?"

After the menus, Jack asked, "How long were you in California? What were you doing there?"

"A week or so."

"Yes, but what were you *doing* there?"

"The usual thing. Talking with an author about a manuscript."

Jack was a connoisseur of evasions, and scented one now. He said, "But do go on: who was it: what was it?"

Gregory inflated his heavy cheeks with a full breath and let it go in a gust of resignation.

"All right. I was only trying to spare you a possibly painful reference."

"That's kind; but it can't have anything to do with the only painful thing I've been trying to submerge for almost two years. —Or does it:"

"I'm afraid it has."

"You cannot mean Ben, or Diana—I've no idea where she might be."

"Berkeley."

"No."

"I went to see my author, Howard Debler, who is at the university there. I went to talk about his book—a very good book, perhaps even more than that. Anyhow. She married him."

In spite of his habit of refusing to show serious feeling, Jack sat back in his chair and stared open-mouthed at Gregory.

"Married him!" he said. "Who on earth is he—Debler?—is he that rangy young man I met, a Naval officer, during the war? She hardly knew him."

"Yes. I'm sorry. I didn't want to get into it with you."

But Jack insisted. Gregory told him the story of how Howard had rescued Diana, had taken her to his mother's home; how she had been ill for weeks; and how recovering she was helped to get well by doing the job of typing Howard's book in final draft. Six months later he was appointed to the history faculty at Berkeley, they were married, and went to live in California.

"You saw them both?"

"I did."

"How was she."

"Happy, well, beautiful. She is expecting a child."

Jack looked away to face emotion and hide it. Gregory felt a beat of sympathy for the distress in his friend. *Yes, in spite of everything, he has suffered in more than his pride.* He remained silent. Jack hated to let anyone observe his feelings. When he was able to face Gregory again, though, his heart was tumbling rapidly,

"Well," he said, in an attempt at indifference, "I hope she can adjust to the cobwebs and acids of certain academic types. Her style will certainly alienate some of them. —Still, of course, there are others, all charm and wit. I know them all. I've lectured often enough on campuses." He made his face expressionless and asked, "Tell me. Did she speak of Ben?"

"Yes."

"What did she say?"

"I don't remember, exactly."

"Yes, you do. You're sparing me."

"No, well, the general thought was that after the dreadful part, she was free, and she owed that to Ben."

"How good that makes me look. —Did she speak of me?"

"Yes, and fondly."

"Only fondly?"

"What else can you expect, in her new life?"

"Are they in love?"

"I would certainly say so."

"Well, that's something, I suppose. One thing, anyhow. I assume their wedding wasn't anything like mine, with the Chief Justice of the New York State Supreme Court doing the mumbo jumbo."

"No," said Gregory, "they had a church wedding."

"Anglican, surely."

"No, R.C."

Jack sat back in disbelief. "But none of their people would marry them, after all the goings on—"

"Yes. She joined up. She said it began for her when she needed it most, in her last day in Corpus Christi, though she didn't know it at the time."

"What on earth could have made her do a thing like that!"

"We didn't talk very much about it. She did say, though—you know the way she has of not sounding serious about serious matters—she said that, with a choice between nothing and possibility, she settled for possibility. But of course there was more to it than that. It was just her way of saying that she didn't want to talk about it."

"And he—the husband—let her?"

"All he said to me about it was, *Well, I take the historico-cultural view of it, on the one hand, and on the other, whatever adds to her happiness is all right with me.*"

"What *does* she see in him."

"I've just told you. What's more, they *like* each other."

Jack sighed a little crossly at how things turned out contrary to his sense of justice. He asked, "How do they *live*?"

"Live?"

"Don't be dense, Gregory. Their house. Their *place* in their little provincial world."

"Ah. Yes, well, Debler is a full professor, well thought of, I gather; and their house is one of those wonderful old California mansions, enormous and fancy. She's done it all up in just the right way, and if you're asking if they're in want, emphatically no. There's a lot of quiet evidence that they're very well off. Along with a nice view of the water."

"Well, it *is* a marvelous bay, at least," said Jack, and he added, "Yes, I suppose it's all her money, her father's estate. I wonder if her husband minds."

"Don't clutch at straws, Jack. I doubt if he ever thinks about it. They're both too content about what really matters."

"I see. Well, losers."

"Who?"

"Who? Myself. Ben. —Did you ever know Ben?"

"No."

"Then you can't possibly know what I feel."

"I suppose not."

"Oh, it's more than you are thinking. —I can't live with reminders. I've sent four drawings of his to be sold here by Rijkmann. They're to be in Ben's retrospective show, which opens tomorrow. All his last paintings are included. I'm going around after I leave you to have a private look, and then never again."

"Should I come with you?"

"Thank you, but I think better not. It will be difficult enough alone."

Henri came to ask if they would have coffee. They were restored by the interruption.

"Yes, well, then, remember," said Jack, "the title is *Curtain Calls*. I love it, and so will the bookstores."

"We'll see," said Gregory with a hearty smile.

Jack went to the Murray Hill Gallery and asked for Mr Rijkmann, who emerged promptly from his office.

"We have your drawings already hung with the rest of the show. It is a beautiful show."

"Do you think I might have a look?"

In a small elevator lined in dove-gray velvet, they ascended to two large galleries on the third floor. Drawings alternating with paintings, all widely spaced, the work of Benjamin Ives was a true retrospective. Jack fixed his face to hide response. Mr Rijkmann was alert to emotion and disliked seeing or showing it. He excused himself on a pretext of business.

Jack was alone with the last world of Ben Ives. It spoke to him so directly of so much that he had felt and must refuse to feel now, if only he could, that he wondered how to escape from the gallery without being noticed.

And yet he did not want to leave. There it was—all the freedom, space, color, the many moods of the Gulf in Ben's last paintings. They were the most powerful works Jack had ever seen of his. They were like hearing him speak; seeing him walk with his lunge of shoulder and thigh; feeling his embrace in greeting, farewell, or— or fighting. They summoned up more than responses to art—they told Jack of betrayals, one of which he dared not admit. When he stood before a painting that showed a hand blackened by corruption reaching out of burial in a sandy beach it was like seeing an appeal from Ben himself to live again. Jack's fixity broke. He searched for the elevator and went downstairs and out to the street with such a look on his face that two or three people, passing him on the crowded sidewalk, turned to see him again, wondering what was the matter.

Gregory Blaine returned to his office in lower Park Avenue with a little time to spare before an editorial meeting. The typescript— over a thousand pages—of Howard Debler's book was on his desk. He had brought it from California, and with it, thoughts of his visit to Berkeley which made him caress his ample front in an unconscious gesture, and sigh for Diana and Howard together. They were never demonstrative before him; but their feeling for each other spoke through their idlest actions. Gregory remembered one small incident that showed what he meant.

On one of his evenings at home with them, they all sat with their drinks before dinner on an upstairs balcony between whose elaborate railings and carved wooden canopy they had a fine view of the San Francisco water. The western sky still held a gold afterglow. Lights were beginning to show across the bay, and on ships that moved slowly in the wide harbor. One ship was an aircraft carrier going to the Mare Island Navy Yard. It reminded Howard of an incident in the Pacific war which he thought would interest Gregory. Howard told his story.

"We were signaled to rendezvous," he said, "with the carrier *Franklin*, which was heading to the States after almost burning to death and sinking under *kamikaze* attacks. But the *Franklin* refused to drown. Instead, they were absolutely tremendous on board, saving her, and taking her home under her own power for repairs. She was escorted by the cruiser *Santa Fe,* and we were ordered to accompany her for a stated distance until she was well out of the war zone. Well. I'll never forget," said Howard, and his voice clouded at the memory, "how we felt when we sighted the *Franklin*. There she was, a black wreck, under a dangerously heavy list, her flight deck torn like paper, with jagged edges, and she was taking the swell with such a slow heave that you'd think every wave would be her last. We exchanged signals, and those little code letters coming from her somehow seemed full of angry pride. We never thought she'd actually make it across the Pacific to the Canal and home to Brooklyn; but on board the *Franklin*, they thought they would, by God, and of course they made it. When we turned back to the west, as ordered, our ship's band assembled on the fantail and played them out of sight. It was something."

The story, as such, wasn't what moved Gregory. What did move him was the fact that as he related it for Gregory, Howard never took his eyes off Diana. It was the look on his face as he spoke, and on hers as she listened, that told Gregory everything.

Thinking of it now, *I might as well not have been there*, Gregory said to himself with a touch of fond envy.